Revolution & Roses

Revolution & Roses

P. H. Newby

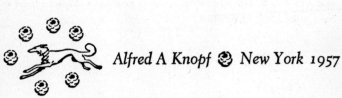

Alfred A Knopf ❧ New York 1957

L. C. catalog card number: 57–8720

© *P. H. Newby, 1957*

THIS IS A BORZOI BOOK,

PUBLISHED BY ALFRED A. KNOPF, INC.

FIRST AMERICAN EDITION

For *Niouta*

Contents

Contents

Revolution & Roses

Chapter 1 No Immediate Danger

For the first time in months Blainey was held up at the dock gates. He sat in his little Italian car, looking into the soldier's face.

He spoke in English. "You know damn well who I am."

Ahead, between the warehouses, the high nose of a Dutch freighter was wrinkling in the heat, but it was still early enough for Blainey to be not properly awake. The clock over the Customs shed was striking seven. He felt heavy with sleep. Perhaps that was why he looked into the Negroid face with such indulgence.

"I've been in and out of these gates for the past three years."

Through the window of the guardroom he could see Osman, still wearing his tarboosh, being shaved by that deaf and dumb barber who wandered through the dock area and found his customers, mainly dock police and tally clerks, where they dozed.

Blainey began to shout. "Osman! I haven't got my pass. I can go through, can't I?"

Osman came to the door, wiping his face with a towel.

"Good morning, Mr. Blainey! Have you heard the news? It is good news. The Cairo radio says there is a government of soldiers. The government of Hilaly is finished. *We* are the governors." He finished buttoning up his tunic and put one foot on the running-board. "No entry without a pass," he said severely. "All is now changed."

Blainey leaned out of the car, still arguing. He was not there on business. He had come to meet his brother off the *Tewfikieh*. Passengers were supposed to disembark at six, so he was an hour late already.

"It is all of no consequence, Mr. Blainey." Osman was proud of his command of English and glad of an opportunity to show it off. He spoke as much to the guard as to Blainey. But the fellow, not understanding a word, closed his eyes in boredom and began picking his nose. He stood with his belly up to the radiator, and Blainey decided against trying to run him down; he needed more room to achieve sufficient acceleration. A line of hooting trucks and cars had formed in his rear, so there was no question of reversing and coming in at the charge.

"You know the regulations, Mr. Blainey."

"Osman, I haven't been asked for my pass for years, and then this morning of all mornings!"

"This morning of all mornings!" Osman was delighted with the phrase. "I am a soldier of Egypt and this is *my* morning! All right, all right! Please to enter and park your car behind the guardroom. You are holding everybody up."

In spite of the five-mile drive along the Corniche Road and this tiresome altercation at the dock gate, Blainey still felt sufficiently drugged by sleep to maintain a certain detachment. And he was technically in the wrong. Obligingly he parked the car where Osman directed and then entered the guardroom to receive the temporary pass which Osman, as a concession, made out and charged him fifty piastres for.

"D'you mean that at long last there's been a revolution?"

Osman was shocked and stood up. "Listen to the aeroplanes of the Egyptian Air Force flying over our city." He had to shout. The jet fighters snarled hysterically, shot out to sea, and whined like flies in the distance. Osman stared into Blainey's eyes with such vehemence he might have been trying to communicate his own sense of rectitude by hypnotism. "The Army is purifying itself. Traitors and weaklings are being purged. That is not a revolution."

"Don't misunderstand me! I wouldn't mind!"

Blainey had walked a good fifty yards before he remembered the car and turned back. The work of the port seemed to be proceeding as usual. A gang of stevedores in loose-fitting pantaloons were feeding the Dutch freighter with bales of raw cotton. A locomotive bunted half a dozen trucks towards the Egyptian Navy Yard. A harbour official in peaked cap and white uniform stood calmly in the well of a launch as it puttered along on its own reflection. Had Blainey been disposed to argue, there would have been little but the officiousness at this particular gate and the Customs clock indicating five past seven to show that this was anything but the beginning of one of his normal working days. But he required no convincing, really, that he was in an exposed position at a moment of crisis. Osman's words had been quite enough. Appearances notwithstanding, the real question was this: when did the rioting begin?

The two jet fighters came in from the sea to buzz the centre of Alexandria; stevedores stopped work, shouted jokes at one another, and squinted into the sun. From the offices of the Port Medical Officer came a burst of clapping. A group of clerks had come out on to the veranda and were applauding the fly-past as solemnly as though it were expected of them. Finding that it was impossible to negotiate the narrow lane between a pile of crated machinery and the warehouses, Blainey parked his car in the shade and set off on foot in the direction of the *Tewfikieh*'s familiar green funnel. If the worst happened and real trouble broke out in the town, he thought, the wisest plan would probably be to camp in the office until some sort of order was established.

There was no sign of Tim in the Customs shed. It was too early in the year for holiday-makers to be returning from Europe. If Blainey's experience was anything to go by, the *Tewfikieh* would have brought no more than a dozen passengers from Marseilles. But where were they? Blainey walked through to the quay, where baggage was coming ashore in a sling. Stevedores shouted, the donkey engine coughed, steam leaked noisily from the ship's siren. Blainey's impression was, however, one of silence. Passengers, ship's officers, Customs officials, travel-agency couriers, and hotel touts stood about in groups, all—so it seemed—caught at the moment when, after a spate of rumour-mongering and speculation, they could think of nothing more to say. The stevedores worked happily enough, but Blainey formed the further impression that the rest of the crowd on the quayside that morning would have needed little encouragement to board the *Tewfikieh*, slip moorings, and sail back to Marseilles.

"Why were we told nothing?" A middle-aged Egyptian turned on Blainey with a lawyer-like vigour. "There was no hint in the French papers, not so much as a hint. *Parole d'honneur!* What is the position of the King in all this?"

Blainey discovered from the Thomas Cook agent that his brother had certainly arrived, was standing on the quay there not five minutes ago, might have taken his seat in the Cairo train, might have walked into town—there were no taxis running—might even have gone aboard the *Tewfikieh* again.

"He was talking to a lady." The agent, a solemn Sudanese who looked smart in his brown cotton suit and peaked cap, was the only man on the quay to be unmoved by the news from Cairo. Blainey's arrival and the Egyptian lawyer's question about the King had broken the charmed silence. A Greek cotton factor whom Blainey knew vaguely by sight harangued the Customs officers on the absurdity of a Customs examination at a time like this. A voice could be heard claiming that the coup was engineered by the British to give them an excuse for occupying Cairo. A passport official in his white police uniform shouted a joke in Arabic to one of the ship's officers up on the bridge. The Thomas Cook agent ignored all this and looked severely into Blainey's eyes. "But, according to my list, he is not going to Cairo. He must have gone back on the ship with the lady."

And, true enough, it was on board that Tim was found. Not that the finding proved difficult. Blainey gave a steward twenty-five piastres to run through the public rooms and round the decks shouting: "Mr. Tim Blainey! Mr. Tim

Blainey, your brother's at the gangway! Mr. Tim Blainey! Will you please go to the gangway?"

Blainey stood watching a young man and woman in earnest conversation. He could not see their faces because they were leaning on a rail, their backs to him, apparently attracted by the sight of baggage being hoisted up through the foredeck well.

"Mr. Tim Blainey!" shouted the steward, his sandals slapping the deck.

The young man lifted his head, turned, and Blainey walked towards him. Yes, it was Tim, all right! The very thin fair hair, golden in this sun, the pursed-up lips, the button nose—Blainey found himself identifying his brother, detail by detail. Only when Tim smiled, held out his hand, and said: "Eric! So there you are! It's wonderful to see you," his features rounded with happiness and his eyes staring like blue-hearted daisies, did Blainey experience the rush of recognition. Tim's charm was at work again. To do him justice, the boy did not calculate his effect. He stood with the sun behind him, glowing a disproportionate but perfectly sincere pleasure; he was like a girl in his innocence, and Blainey (who so far had said not a word) looked hard at him with the old familiar irritation beginning to rustle round the inside of his head.

"Sorry I was late getting here," he said.

Tim turned to the girl. "My brother, Eric. May I introduce you? Eric—Miss Elaine Brent. I say, Eric, what's all this rumpus about? Everyone says there's been a revolution and there's martial law."

"You've certainly chosen the right moment to come to Egypt for a holiday."

"It's not *really* a holiday—"

Blainey found himself trying to guess Miss Brent's

age. She must be at least thirty. In comparison with the
women of Alexandria, she was as fresh as a dairymaid, with
pale, swimming eyes and a scatter of freckles at the temples.
But she had wiry lines at the corners of her mouth and
eyes; and when she shook Blainey's hand her grip was
firm.

She smiled, glanced at Tim, and said: "For brothers,
I must say you don't look a bit alike."

"Father married twice." Blainey nodded at her. "I
suppose you're making for Cairo."

After three years in Alexandria without a break it was
difficult, even for him, to restrain interest in a woman
straight from England. They were of an age, barely into
the thirties. Tim was ten years younger, young enough to
be given a few hundred pounds by his mother just to see
the world. As the three of them stood poised on the edge
of that moment which parts acquaintances at the end of
a sea trip—Tim was even smiling and thrusting his right
hand forward—the other two were brought into sympathy
by his very youthfulness.

"What's going to happen?" she asked.

"D'you have to be in this country for a few weeks?
Why not stay on the boat and go to Cyprus?"

"Oh, Miss Brent isn't landing here," said Tim briskly.

She lifted her head in surprise. "What on earth gave
you that idea?"

Tim dropped his hand. "But, Miss Brent, I understood
you were on a round trip, just for the cruise!"

"What, second class on an Egyptian boat? Oh, now,
come! People only do a thing like that if they mean to get
somewhere." When she smiled at Blainey he detected an
uncertainty in her eyes. The dewy freshness was real, but
it did not go deep. Underneath was a professional toughness

one did not associate with dairymaids. "Of course I'm disembarking here."

Tim was prepared to argue the point. He looked at her in astonishment, saying: "But I distinctly remember you saying—"

"Tim! Damn it all!" Blainey was aware of an oddity in Miss Brent's manner, but he could not allow his brother to contradict her in this way. "It's bad luck, this political trouble breaking out just now, Miss Brent, but if you're travelling to Cairo, Tim and I will be glad to see you to the train."

"But I'm to stay in Alexandria."

"Is anyone meeting you?"

"No."

"Are you going to a hotel?"

"Yes."

"Which one?"

"You see! She doesn't know." Tim was triumphant.

She accepted the cigarette that Blainey was offering. "I shouldn't have thought it was difficult to find a room. You think I ought to have cabled ahead?"

Tim with a pipe in his mouth, his brother and Miss Brent smoking cigarettes, they stood watching a commotion on the quay. A little gang of dock labourers, gay with excitement, had come running barefoot to persuade the *Tewfikieh* baggage party to go on strike. The siren leaked steam, the donkey engine coughed impotently, the labourers in their oddly assorted clothes—cotton pantaloons, old khaki shorts, sugar-sack blouses, and faded satin waistcoats—waved hands at one another, roared with laughter, danced between the cabin trunks, and quite ignored the shouts of the baggage master, who leaned over the rail, shaking like a puppet. Customs officials, passport-inspectors, passengers—including the middle-aged lawyer—even the guard from the Cairo train in his peaked cap, all made off down the quay towards the baggage party. Orders were shouted. The lawyer identified his trunk and tried to drag it in the direction of the train. The jet fighters came back, faces turned upwards, and the *Tewfikieh* siren ceased hissing to shake the morning with its bellow. By this time, Blainey imagined, gangs would be out in the town smashing windows.

"Hope there's nothing of yours down there, Tim."

"No, I've only got a couple of suitcases. They're still in the cabin."

"Better get them, there's a good fellow."

Tim hesitated, looked at Miss Brent, and made off.

"You've quite decided?" said Blainey as soon as he and Miss Brent were alone.

She nodded. Any uncertainty had quite disappeared. She watched the excitement on the quay with a wide-eyed, rural innocence that made Blainey think of buttercups and daisies.

"Your brother was quite right, of course, Mr. Blainey."

"About you being here just for the ride?"

"I haven't even a permit to land. Tim knows this perfectly well."

"He's young, you know," said Blainey, "and you've got to make allowances."

Even the policeman had deserted his post at the gangway to shout at the baggage party. But for Tim, there was no one to question Miss Brent's right to go ashore, and the chance that he would question it gave Blainey, in his own view, only one course of action. He could not afford, right at the beginning of Tim's visit, to agree with him.

"I expect you've got a lot of gear."

"Only a couple of cases, like Tim. I can pack in two minutes."

"That settles it, then," he said. "Mind you, I promise you nothing. Even if we get you out of the dock area, we stand a good chance of being lynched by the mob. If you're not lynched, you'll be thrown into jail for making an illegal entry into Egypt. I'll be thrown into jail for aiding and abetting. All right?"

"All right," she said, looking steadily at a minaret which rose, in bands of burnt umber and white, on the other side of the dock wall.

"Not sure I oughtn't to insist on *your* going to Cyprus," Blainey said to Tim when the boy came back.

"Of course I'm not going to Cyprus. I want some stuff for a book. Well, this revolution will do!"

Blainey stared at his brother for some moments.

"Will it, by God!" he said.

They sheltered from the sun behind a mountain of baled cotton. Eric Blainey put Miss Brent's cases on the ground. "See those dhows? See those buildings beyond? That's where the office is. I expect Tim told you I work in my father-in-law's business. He imports coffee."

On Eric's instructions, they had spoken to no one since leaving the boat. Even when questioned, they had not answered. True, there had been only two people, a police captain in a white jacket and a hotel tout, who accosted them. They looked silently ahead, Eric sweating under the weight of Miss Brent's luggage, Tim trundling his own on castors, and Miss Brent carrying a bottle-green hatbox. Everyone else on the quay was running about and shouting. The police captain did not pursue them. Even the hotel tout gave up. Moving silently and laboriously away from the rumpus (officials, passengers, ship's crew, and porters were clambering over the baggage, making political speeches), the trio came as near to achieving invisibility as was possible in the glare of the Egyptian sun. It was only half past eight, but, looking along the quays, they could see heat. A telegraph pole quivered at the base.

"It's all right for us to speak now?" asked Miss Brent.

At this distance from the *Tewfikieh* the dock was quiet. A row of antique dhows leaned their immensely tall masts one against the other. They were so motionless they might have been resting on mud. Their prows stood up in pale, sun-hammered timber. Eric walked to the very edge of the quay, stood with his back to the old hulks, and examined the neighbourhood attentively. The jet fighters made another mock attack over the town, and he watched them, shading his eyes and turning until they were lost among the rigging of the dhows.

"No immediate danger." He returned to the cotton bales and picked up the suitcases. "I suppose the idea of those planes is to discourage rioting in the town. Show of strength. But I wouldn't like to trust to it. Anyway, we're getting out of here by water."

"By water?"

"You don't mind another sea trip?" He spoke to Miss Brent. "We've got our own launch moored down by the office. I've never been out to sea in it, but it ought to stay afloat. The trip will take about an hour. Or an hour and a half. Is that all right? We'll round the lighthouse you can see out there. Look, follow my finger! Those buildings on the right are Ras el-Tin Palace. Once we're out of the harbour, we'll run along on the north side of Pharos. We ought to make Sidi Bishr—that's where the house is—in a couple of hours."

"Pharos!" said Tim. "A trip round Pharos in a motor boat!"

"If you've any better suggestions—"

"But, Eric, you misunderstand! I wasn't criticizing you."

After the respite in the shade they found the sun all the more passionate. Only Tim was without dark glasses. He had read somewhere that strong light was good for the eyes (it served as a kind of optical massage), and he walked behind Miss Brent, squinting through his lashes at solid buildings which shook like curtains. Eric's office was one of them. Miss Brent tried to help Eric with one of the suitcases, but he swung it away from her and they both laughed. What was *really* happening in Cairo? she wanted to know. Was it a sort of *coup d'état?* Eric was sweating too much to guess. Their voices were pitched above the stony drumming of Tim's luggage castors; the drumming rose a couple of notes as he hurried to overtake them, the voices ceased, and the little party passed with sighs into the relieving shadow of a veranda.

"Now, down into the launch with this baggage, Sa'ad," Eric was saying to a bearded man who had come smiling out of a doorway in felt skull-cap and cotton gown. "There'll be no work today."

"No," said the man. The wiry beard clung very close to the jaw. He was very dark, but a healthy ruddiness seemed to be glowing under the carbon skin. "No work. These Egyptians—" he said with a good accent, looking sideways so that the eyes were enormous in their whiteness—"these Egyptians are without religion."

"Sa'ad comes from Aden," Eric explained. "This is our dock office. The real office is in town. Most of my work is done here. Now, while I'm phoning the house why don't you sit down? There's no hurry. Sa'ad will make some coffee."

"Miss Brent!" Tim spoke softly when his brother had gone, leaving them to watch Sa'ad from their shrieking wicker chairs. "I hope I've not offended you."

"I wish you'd call me Elaine, Tim."

"Then I've not offended you?" I really *had* got it into my head you were staying on the ship."

Because of her dark glasses it was difficult to read the expression on her face. Her mouth was relaxed, but it might have been from boredom. "I might as well confess to you, Tim, that you were perfectly right to think I was supposed to stay on the ship."

"What?"

"I'm a journalist on holiday. As soon as I heard of this revolution, or whatever it is, I just had to get ashore, visa or no visa. I thought your brother might help. Well! Here we are! We're going round Pharos in a motor boat because I probably couldn't get out of the dock area in any other way; not because there might be rioting in the town. You're not as simple as you pretend, Tim."

"Oh, really! Don't you think so?" He clutched at the compliment. Unprotected as they were by any dark glasses, desperation must have shown in his eyes, but Elaine showed no mercy.

"You as good as said you *wanted* me to stay on the ship, Tim."

No answer was possible. Tim stood up and walked into the sun. The vacated chair crackled like a fire, and the heat of it was all around him. Sa'ad's head and shoulders appeared above the edge of the quay, shining like liquorice, for he had stripped to the waist. The bags were stowed, he called out, and now was the time for coffee. Below him, a blistered launch with a wooden box clapped over the engine amidships coughed exhaust along the surface of the water; and Tim, without replying to Sa'ad, went down the steps. He took up position where he imagined Elaine and Eric would not bother him, forward of the suitcases, and said to Sa'ad: "You can bring my coffee here."

She had not apologized, that was where the hurt lay! A journalist! How like a woman to say "Call me Elaine" at the moment she was forced to reveal a duplicity! Tim sat waiting for coffee with the feeling he had only to meditate for a while and something of great importance would be revealed. Clearly, she thought he was a fool; she would never have outfaced him otherwise. His lack of guile was so obvious that she had traded on it in front of his own brother, and now, in confessing, she had not even apologized! What did it all mean?

Distant chanting pulsed down to him over the lip of the quay, and the fighter planes came back. They snored out of the town and bolted skywards over the water. Following them with his eyes, Tim spotted Sa'ad still standing on the quayside with arms folded. His white cotton drawers held him like a calyx, from calves to waist.

"No coffee," Sa'ad said firmly, "in launch." The beard rose, the head turned, the cotton drawers broke into a flurry of blue shadows, and Tim was left to stare at the sky. No coffee! Likewise, no common sense, no mother wit, no *nous*, no worldly wisdom, no guile! He was disappointed with himself to the point of bitterness.

"Tim, do come and have your coffee," he could hear her saying.

So strongly was Tim persuaded that he trembled on the edge of a revelation, and that he had only to sit with his head over the side of the launch staring down into the water for truth to be manifest, Elaine had to speak before he noticed her. She had the cup in her hand. "Or will you have it down there?"

They were to be enemies, Elaine and he! He sat without speaking, shocked by the discovery. She looked so pretty, shading her eyes against the sun, and yet—how clear it was! —she was hostile. Why had he not seen it before?

"Oh, no, I'll come up," he shouted.

He scrambled along the launch, rushed up the steps, took the coffee cup, and thanked her with a great show of gaiety, knowing all the time that he was blushing with rage but hoping, nevertheless, that she would mistake the emotion for gratitude. The coffee was mostly grounds. He crunched them between his teeth.

"Elaine," he said, more anxious than ever to please, "you're quite sure you're doing the right thing? The situation may be dangerous. There's still time to go back to the *Tewfikieh*."

"The same applies to you. Besides, I don't suppose we'd be able to get back on the ship now anyway."

"I want you to know, Elaine, that you can count on me. I mean—anything! Anything I can do for you."

Tim luxuriated in his duplicity.

"So there you are." Eric came out of the office. "I've been talking to Lydia. Everything's quiet at Sidi Bishr, but I rang up a chap in town and he says there are a lot of rumours. The Army has issued some sort of declaration, and Farouk is shut up in Montazah. They're going to put him on trial. Might be all nonsense. This fellow says there's a cinema on fire and everybody's trying to buy tinned meat. Let's get in the launch and make for home."

In spite of Sa'ad's protests, Tim removed the cushions from the basket chairs and with them made a comfortable

seat for Elaine well forward of the motor. He was determined to show her every courtesy. Terrifying, really, how
well he could disguise his feelings. He decided she would
prefer fresh air and *his* company to petrol fumes and Eric;
and so it turned out. While Eric gave instructions to
Sa'ad, Elaine stepped into the place prepared for her and
sat sideways, leaning against the gunwale to look ahead.
Tim made himself busy, dusting round her with his handkerchief and glancing at her to judge the effect he was having. But Elaine's sun-glasses made her inscutable!

"Lie down, both of you," said Eric.

"Eh?"

Sa'ad had cast off, and Eric made a sign with his right
hand to invoke patience. It would have been impossible
to shout above the noise of the motor when he first put it
into gear; inside the wooden kennel a circular saw was apparently discovering a nail in a tree trunk, and when Eric
threw back one of the roof flaps a column of blue smoke
concealed him from view.

"Lie down!" he repeated when they had passed between a rusted hull and its anchor chain, speaking through
a megaphone. The launch vibrated neurotically, but once
under way the engine roared from its kennel with less hysteria. "You'd better lie down, both of you, because there's a
very good chance of being shot at."

They could see him quite clearly now, one hand on the
wheel, the other holding the megaphone, and the water
front—brown warehouses and spider cranes—rocking
smoothly behind. He had removed tie and linen jacket.
They could see the throat, red like a turkey's, above the
black pad of hair on his chest—for the apparently button-
less shirt was open to the waist. The wrinkles were pink

on his dark forehead. "Lie down, dammit! Don't you understand there's a revolution going on?"

By moving the cases they could lie staring upwards with heads almost touching in the bows but with bodies running away port and starboard respectively and the cases wedged between them. They could see nothing but sky. Tim was protected, but the sun was high enough to shine full on Elaine's face. Even after five minutes they had seemingly been lying in the bottom of the launch for hours. Every time they passed close to a ship their engine raised echoes. There were no birds or clouds. So they turned their heads and looked into each other's eyes.

"Who would want to shoot at us?" Elaine asked.

"I quite agree. It's *their* revolution."

"Might be the Customs and Excise, I suppose."

"Or coastguards! They might think we were members of the aristocracy, fleeing to Europe!"

She laughed. "I believe you're angry with me, Tim, aren't you? Well, you're right to be angry. But I was *so* keen to get ashore! And it was *so* important to get help from your brother."

She kissed him—only the smallest movement of her head was necessary—on the forehead. The motion of the launch through the water was changing from a smooth, almost imperceptible roll to an unmistakable pitching. Looking between his feet, Tim could see the water front and its shipping rise to Eric's waist and drop back again.

"Whatever made you think I was angry?" he murmured.

Angry with Elaine? It was absurd. Ignoring Eric's shout, he sat up and saw that they had already cleared the harbour, and the white lighthouse with its mole and gun emplacements was nodding in their wake. On his left hand were the buff walls and tufted greenery of the palace Eric had pointed out to them. The island of Pharos! The sea broke brilliantly on the rocks. In comparison, the palace, the forts and minarets were pale and dead. They were an outline petering out where the entrance to the Eastern Harbour lay; and through the entrance, distantly, Alexandria itself.

"Look," he said to Elaine, and she too sat up.

Eric began yelling through the megaphone again. "Don't blame me if they send a launch out to pick us up."

But no one stirred on Pharos. Holding one of Elaine's hands, Tim gazed towards Egypt. How could it ever have entered his head that *she* was an enemy? The revelation was false. But, then, he was deceived endlessly. This was all the more serious because of his ambitions: the great writer—as Tim understood him—was never caught out so easily. The great writer was too much a man of the world.

"Can't see any sign of that cinema fire," he shouted. "No smoke at all. I said, I—can't—see—any—sign—of—that—cinema—fire!"

Chapter 2   At the Villa Dragoumis

WHEN Mr. Dragoumis heard there was some sort of political trouble in Cairo he was secretly pleased. An excellent excuse had been provided for not going to the office that day. Demonstrations were bound to take place. Certainly it would not be safe to venture out of doors. Instead, he planned to spend all day working in what he called his library. For many years now he had been on the point of publishing a book which set forth an entirely novel philosophy of politics; but time and again he had been held up because some point in his argument was insufficiently supported. When this happened he appealed to a wide circle of correspondents—the President of the United States, for example, and Bertrand Russell, both cordial friends— explaining the problem in all its complexity. His command of English was good. Had he not taught himself? Did he not have an English son-in-law? Even so, he always wrote his letters in Greek because he had views on the dignity of his native language. And when the replies came (as very occasionally they did) Mr. Dragoumis ascribed their brevity and general unsatisfactoriness to the decline of Greek as a learned tongue and the unprecedented nature of the problems he was tackling. Even H. G. Wells was baffled. Shortly before his death he wrote to Mr. Dragoumis, saying: "I have had your letter translated and all I can say is that you are well-intentioned." Mr. Dragoumis was delighted with the compliment. But, to be frank, Wells had not been a help. Repeated disappointments of this kind would naturally postpone the completion of his work.

Mr. Dragoumis was a tall, big-boned man with a lot of grey, woolly hair. He took snuff (an unusual habit for Alexandria), and his moustache was streaked with khaki. Nevertheless, he had dignity. He spoke with deliberation and moved slowly. When not at the office or working in his library, he was frequently to be seen walking the Corniche Road, staring out to sea and rubbing his thin cheeks.

"This information must be kept from Lydia," he said on hearing about the coup for the first time. "Her husband has gone into town, remember. She would immediately think he had been murdered, or severely injured at least. Warn the servants!"

And he would have walked into his own room, locked the door behind him, and spent the rest of the morning with his books if Mrs. Dragoumis had not begun crying. She removed her glasses. The small eyes were set deep in the head, like buttons in upholstery, and they glittered with tears. The puffed-up face was even paler than usual.

"But, my love," she said, "Lydia is not a child. She is

a married woman. She is a British subject. Of course we must tell her. In any case, she would certainly guess what had happened the moment we start moving upstairs."

The Dragoumis villa was a stucco-faced box divided into a kind of semi-basement (here were the kitchen and the servants' quarters), the main apartment occupied by Mr. and Mrs. Dragoumis, and an upper, self-contained flat where their married daughter, Lydia, kept house. A flight of synthetic marble steps gave direct access from the street to the Dragoumis apartment, and when there were signs of serious civil commotion Mrs. Dragoumis liked to think of it as an inundation which could best be countered by going upstairs.

"All right, Ariadne!" said Mr. Dragoumis. "I accept your point. There's no need to cry. I am a reasonable man. I can be appealed to with reason and logic. As for being a British subject, that is irrelevant, if you don't mind my saying so! You know that I work for the time when there will be no nationalities and no passports!"

The sight of his wife's tears had confused him, as she knew it would. The advantage was seized. "O Paulos! Reason and logic! All this reading and writing has gone to your head. Sometimes I wonder whether you're in your right mind. Everybody talks of the way you neglect your business. Really, if it weren't for Eric—" and so on.

Mrs. Dragoumis was jealous of the attention her husband gave to the affairs of mankind. When depressed or anxious, she made attacks on it, and these attacks had become more frequent since Lydia's marriage. Yes, in a way she was jealous of Lydia's marriage too. The two people she loved most, her daughter and her husband, had private worlds she was excluded from. Paulos with his books! Lydia with her Eric! There were times when Mrs. Dragoumis felt so lonely and neglected she wanted to walk into the sea.

Mr. Dragoumis did not care to allow himself to be angry. "I'll tell Lydia we're coming up," he said mildly.

"No, Paulos, excuse me." Mrs. Dragoumis had polished her glasses and replaced them. Her pallor was relieved by the dewy flush round the eyes. "I shall go up and tell Lydia myself."

Until Lydia's marriage the top flat had been occupied by a Lebanese family—they had been ejected only with great difficulty—who had often asked for stairs to be clapped on to the side of the house to give them an independent entry. Every time they came in or went out they had to pass through the Dragoumis apartment. In spite of their complaints, this was much less of a nuisance to them than it was to the Dragoumis family, but Mrs. Dragoumis was glad the extra stairs had never been built. The inconvenience was worth putting up with now that it had resulted in a curbing of Lydia's independence.

"Lydia," she called when she was halfway up the stairs, poised like a bandit on a caravan route. "It's your mother coming to see you. Aren't you awake yet? It's gone nine o'clock. There's been a revolution, and our lives are in danger. What, still asleep, child?"

The door still open behind her, she stood in the centre of Lydia's little sitting-room with her eyes on the bedroom door. The girl was in bed. There was no doubt of that. But she did not answer her mother's call, and even Mrs. Dragoumis felt she could not enter the bedroom without an invitation.

"Lydia," she said with her face to the panel. "Your father and I are coming to sit up here until this trouble is over. We would not bother you, but—who knows?—perhaps we shall be killed."

"Come in," said the low voice. There was no preliminary creak of springs or rustle of bed-clothes. The girl had undoubtedly been awake all the time, lying there and listening. Mrs. Dragoumis opened the door and shuffled into the sunny room. Yes, the curtains were drawn, the drained coffee cup stood on its tray by the side of the bed, and Lydia, with elbows like wings on either side of her head, rested quite naked in the middle of the double bed, gazing at the ceiling with her deep brown eyes. Of course she had not been asleep.

Naked! Halfway towards the bed, Mrs. Dragoumis stopped. She saw and yet she doubted. She averted her eyes and looked back again. There was no deception.

"You've no clothes on, Lydia."

"It's so hot in the night."

"Do you *sleep* like that?"

Lydia turned on one side and eyed her mother thoughtfully. She drew up a knee and allowed her left hand to rest on a belly so delicate it shivered perceptibly at the heart throb. "What was that you said about a revolution?"

Mrs. Dragoumis could stand the sight no longer. She snatched a dressing-gown from behind the door and threw it across Lydia's buttocks. The last time she had seen Lydia fully stripped must have been for bathing as a child, and the sight of her now, a married woman, extended pink and white on the connubial bed, effaced all recollection of the reason that had brought her there. Mrs. Dragoumis sat in a chair abruptly. Her face had stiffened with shock.

"Lydia," she said, "whatever must Eric think of you? He must be *quite* disgusted."

Lydia yawned and stretched. She made great labour of standing up. The legs had to be forced over the side of the bed. The toes went searching for slippers.

"When you were coming up the stairs, what were you saying? We are all in danger?"

"Oh, *that!*" Mrs. Dragoumis shut her eyes fast. "Get your clothes on this very minute, or I shall walk out of this flat! We are not the same to each other. We are not mother and daughter. You have changed. I tell myself that you are only twenty years of age, but I cannot believe it. On the one hand, the day you were born—it seems only yesterday. You are a child to me still, or you ought to be. And then, on the other hand, you seem a complete stranger. You might be any age. Twenty, thirty, forty. Lying on the bed like that, with no clothes on! It's far from healthy."

She opened her eyes to find that Lydia, in slippers and dressing-gown, was seated at her dressing-table and brushing her hair.

"Then you are not coming up into this flat, you and Daddy?"

"Of course we're coming up. Didn't I tell you? Something has happened in Cairo, I don't know what, but your father understands it all, and there will be trouble. Naturally, we are coming up. It is more secure."

"I'm sorry," said Lydia.

"What do you mean, sorry?"

"Eric's brother is coming today and we shall be quite full up. What would he think, to find the flat so crowded? He would think his brother was living in a slum."

"You can't be serious."

Lydia put a waterproof cap on, tucked her hair carefully out of sight, and walked into the bathroom. Listening to the swish of the shower, her mother walked hesitantly about the room for some moments and then sat down at the dressing-table, where she stared at her reflection in the mirror with unnaturally wide eyes. Could she possibly be so old as to have a daughter like Lydia? She touched the sagging cheeks with the tips of her fingers. A stranger walking into the room at that moment would not put her at a day over thirty-five. Surely, she thought, no one would take her for more than thirty-five. Young enough to start life again. Young enough to divorce, remarry, and have a child. But she was not thirty-five. She was forty-five!

"Lydia!" she called outside the bathroom door. "You can't be serious."

"What's that? Did you say something, Mama?"

In order to make oneself heard over the hiss of water, one had to shout, and that would not be dignified. Mrs. Dragoumis could not be still. She turned away from the door, sealing her mouth, dramatically, with the palm of her hand. As a child Lydia had been gay but obedient; as a girl she had been wilful but loving; and as a married woman she had—until this moment—remained a daughter. And now they were on the brink of quarrelling, almost as strangers might quarrel. It was like having the Lebanese back. Waiting for her daughter to come out of the bathroom, Mrs. Dragoumis wondered at the little bubbles of terror which seemed to rise internally and burst at her lips.

The telephone rang.

Before she could touch it, Lydia had flung open the bathroom door, rushed out in her wrap and bath cap, and snatched up the receiver.

"Oh, Mama! I forgot you were here!"

Mrs. Dragoumis opened her hands as though to support an invisible burden.

"It's Eric. He's at the office. Yes, yes, my sweet, of

course I can hear you. No, everything is quiet here. We are all safe and calm."

"Then he is at least still alive." While Lydia spoke to her husband Mrs. Dragoumis went to the window and prayed sincerely but silently for strength. Dear God, she thought, through Jesus our Lord, forgive my presumption in ever thinking I was alone. Why should I need husband or daughter if strengthened by Thy Spirit? We are at the beginning of dangers. Dear God, help us all through Jesus, Amen.

"Lydia," she said, when she became aware that the telephone conversation had ceased, "how could you ever find it in your heart to forbid your poor father and myself the entry to your flat?"

"Mama!" Lydia was excited. She did not hear her mother's words. "Eric's brother has come and there's an Englishwoman with him. Eric is bringing them up here in the launch. Did you ever hear such a thing? Oh, Mama! I wish I were with them. They're coming *all* the way by launch! They're coming out of the harbour and by the sea. Actually by sea. The town is too dangerous, Eric says."

Lydia dressed as she spoke. She clearly had it in mind to run down to the beach and keep a look-out for the launch.

"Listen to me, Lydia, for one minute, I beg you." Mrs. Dragoumis found herself speaking with solemnity. The terror had passed. After the brief prayer she was no longer angry. She would have liked to kiss her daughter.

"What is it, then, Mama?"

"I want you to remember that a woman can never please herself. A man can please himself, but a woman, no! Will you remember that? When she is quite by herself a woman is nothing. A woman needs her husband and her family, I need my daughter, before she can be a woman. Can you remember this?"

Lydia slipped into a white cotton dress and gesticulated wildly. "Oh, yes, Mama. Of course I'll remember."

She was so delighted with the thought of Eric and the young brother and the Englishwoman, all coming up from Alexandria in the launch, that she wanted her mother to be delighted too.

But Mrs. Dragoumis went on talking about the nature of women, saying, in effect, that there was no such thing. Inside a woman everything was vague and meaningless. To give this confusion a personality, other people, particularly men, were necessary. She wanted Lydia never to become so proud that she forgot this.

After this plunge into the depths Mrs. Dragoumis came to the surface and found that she had been talking to herself. Lydia's excited voice, telling of the voyage from Alexandria, rose from the apartment below. Mrs. Dragoumis was about to pray again, but she checked the prayer on her lips. She had passed through a crisis. Yes, she was middle-aged. Frankly she confessed it. For the second time that morning she began to cry.

The Dragoumis house marked the eastern limit of built-up Alexandria (on the side of the sea, anyway), and harsh wastes of sand lapped at the very walls. The sea was fifty yards to the north, on the other side of another row of villas, the Corniche Road, and the bathing-huts. By coming down the marble steps and striking due north-east over the desert one arrived at the Dragoumis bathing-hut in about three minutes of laboured walking. For the desert was not flat. It was gathered up into stony hillocks which smoked like volcanoes when the wind was strong enough. And one walked slowly because of the heat. Even at nine o'clock in the morning it could be a little stupefying. At some distance were wooden shacks full of people on holiday from Cairo. And farther off, blocking the sea horizon, was the wooded promontory of Montazah where, the rumour went, the King was a close prisoner.

"We are ruined," said Mr. Dragoumis as he and Lydia crested one of the hillocks and looked towards the bathing-hut. An old-fashioned armoured car, an iron cistern on wheels camouflaged in brown and flamingo pink, was parked off the Corniche Road just opposite the hut, and the crew of Egyptian soldiers were settling in its shadow, apparently to eat and smoke.

"Eric is due to arrive in a matter of minutes, and those soldiers are bound to ask questions. The officer will know that the launch is licensed for the harbour alone. I must send them about their business at once."

"But, Daddy—"

Nodding his huge straw hat, Mr. Dragoumis crunched his way firmly towards the soldiers. He had already seen the launch. The sea was astonishingly calm. There were long intervals between the oily snufflings which passed for the breaking of waves on the beach; the vast body of the sea itself was colourless, and the launch, well away to the left, was poised on its surface like a fly.

Mr. Dragoumis rushed at the soldiers. He saw now that there were only two of them, a sergeant and an *askari*, who were sitting on their steel helmets eating flaps of bread stuffed with soft cheese.

"Have you not heard? The mob is burning Alexandria, and you sit here eating! I've no doubt that if you looked in the right direction you would see columns of smoke." Mr.

Dragoumis's Arabic was not good, but emotion gave him fluency. "You must be off at once."

"No, sir, that is quite untrue," said a voice from within the armoured car. "It is wrong of you to spread such rumours." And a third soldier, an officer this time with green crescents on his lapels, climbed out of the vehicle to stand smiling in Mr. Dragoumis's face. He was a tall, handsome man of about thirty, with—quite obviously—Turkish blood; the face had unusual width at the cheekbones, making an impression of great strength. The skin was red, not brown. "Everything is under control in Alexandria. Who are you? Allow me to ask you that, sir."

Mr. Dragoumis was so disconcerted by the officer's sudden appearance that he blurted out the very information he was trying to conceal. "There is mob rule, I tell you! See that launch out there? Why would my son-in-law choose to come from Alexandria in a launch if there was no danger in the streets? After all, he is not a coward."

The officer looked at the launch through binoculars. "There's a woman with them."

"She is an Englishwoman. My husband is English. He went down to meet his brother off the *Tewfikieh*, and now they've all come up in the launch because the town is so dangerous."

At Lydia's first words the officer lowered his glasses. "My apologies to you, madame. I did not see you. But I can assure you, on the very best authority, there is no danger. We are in control. Your husband has been very foolish. But no, I can't believe it! I can't believe he's brought a launch all the way up from the docks just to avoid going through the town. Please stay here. Do not move from here, either of you."

"You see," said Mr. Dragoumis to his daughter in Greek—up to that moment everyone had been talking Arabic—"Eric is technically in the wrong. The launch is licensed for the dock only. Really, I'm not sure, but perhaps I ought to dissociate myself from this situation. Come back, Lydia, this moment! You heard what the man said!"

Accompanied by the sergeant, the officer had set off for the beach. They were crossing the road when a shout from the third soldier caused them to turn and see Lydia racing after them. By this time Mr. Dragoumis himself was at full trot. He feared; but he scarcely knew what he feared. Seeing their order disobeyed, it was possible that one of these soldiers might try to shoot the girl down; if that happened, Mr. Dragoumis would want to die too. Lydia was his only child and he loved her. As soon as he saw her stretched on the sand he also would demand assassination. In spite of his fear, though, he did not believe he was about to die. How could he die before his work was finished? His fear was so vague that after some moments he thought he was running after Lydia as he had run after her when she was a child—to catch her before she fell. He shouted. The soldier left behind at the armoured car shouted. The officer and the sergeant turned as though to head her off, and the launch—Mr. Dragoumis saw—was still a hundred yards from the shore.

"Don't you dare touch her," he shouted, his anxiety transformed into rage. The uneven ground made his ankles ache. His legs shook. "Leave her alone, I tell you—"

The beach was broken at this point by ribs of rock. They compressed the small waves into near-fountains— bubblings of water which disappeared with a snore. Running over the rock, Mr. Dragoumis would have fallen if the officer had not caught him. And if the sergeant had not held Lydia by the arm, she would have rushed into the sea.

"What's going on?" It was only Eric bawling through his megaphone; but the cry came booming through the surf with a more than human reverberation. To the ear of Mr. Dragoumis it was a Triton conch call.

"Thank you," he said. "No! Let me go, I mean! Tell that soldier to release my daughter."

Having assured himself that Mr. Dragoumis was in no danger of falling, the officer released him and studied the launch through his binoculars once more. He ignored Mr. Dragoumis's declamations; he ignored the struggle between Lydia and the sergeant; he ignored, even, the holiday-makers (most of them boys in bathing-trunks) who had rushed over from the shacks to see what was going on. He had eyes only for the launch.

"Tell me, sir," he said gently, "who is this beautiful lady? Is she married? Ah, no! This is dreadful! She has fallen in the water!"

Because of the rocks Eric could not drive the launch up the beach. As soon as he felt it grate against the bottom he shut off the engine, warned Tim and Elaine to sit still, and plunged breast-high into the water. He could hear Lydia's sea-bird cries. The sergeant seemed on the point of being thrown off a rock; the monkey-wrench which Eric had snatched before jumping overboard should, he thought, clinch the victory. Finding that he had miscalculated the depth, he began to swim. He had taken no more than a first carving stroke when the sea was struck heavily, water was flung into the air only to fall and smack him with surprising force across the head, and he knew that either Tim or the girl had been caught off balance.

"Elaine!" Tim was shouting. "Where are you? Come up! For God's sake, come up!"

Between the rocks the water was five or six feet deep. One moment Eric swam, the next he crawled, wincing with pain. He was disappointed that it was Elaine and not Tim who had fallen into the sea, and was about to stretch out a hand and drag her on to his rock. She had surfaced like a rubber ball to spit water, laugh out of an open, sun-flooded mouth, and shake the darkened hair out of her eyes. Eric hesitated. Obviously she could swim like a fish. Her hat rocked airily on the tiny waves between them.

The Egyptian officer was standing on Eric's rock with the water swilling over his boots. "The launch!" he was shouting in English, apparently to Elaine. "Mind your head! The launch is swinging round!"

He stepped firmly into the sea as though it were a vat of unpressed grapes, trod quickly to a point where he could take the launch in his back and, by slipping an arm under her shoulders, help her to stand. The small boys had joined them in the water, wrinkling up their faces, whinnying with laughter and excitement. The Egyptian shouted at them, and they fell on their backs in mock terror. They threshed the water into spray so fine it held momentary rainbows. Elaine protested that she was perfectly all right and needed no assistance. But as soon as the Egyptian had helped her on to a rock, he lifted her like a child, saying: "You have lost your shoes, lady. You could not walk on these rocks," and carried her out of the waves to the hot beach, where their clothes began almost at once to steam in the sun.

"I am Lieutenant Mahmoud Yehia," he said, standing to attention.

Mr. Dragoumis was relieved. He had been too exhausted to intervene between Lydia and the Egyptian sergeant. With his hat well down over his eyes he had been forced to squat on the sand and listen to the thumping of his heart. The sweat gathered at his nose and chin, splashed on his knees, and evaporated. He could not speak. For a while he could not breathe. Only a little while previously he had thought death not a serious possibility, and this, now he felt so ill, had become something to regret. But strength returned. He lifted his head and saw Lydia smacking the sergeant's face. He saw the brave Eric struggling shoreward. He saw Lydia rush to meet him, saw their passionate embrace with the broken water flaring all round them, and was reassured. Their ardour made him happy. Provided the children loved each other, what did it matter if the Egyptians did confiscate his launch? Even that seemed unlikely now that the officer was showing so much courtesy.

"And I am Paulos Dragoumis," he said, standing up and placing himself between Elaine and her rescuer. "You must meet my son-in-law."

"I was speaking to this lady." Lieutenant Yehia acknowledged Mr. Dragoumis's apology with a nod and went on with his intent examination of Elaine's face. On his own there was an expression of round-eyed innocence. He looked at her nose, her mouth, her right eyebrow, her left; the details were examined separately as though he scarcely understood the relation they had to one another. Having lost her hat and shoes, and uncomfortable in the soaked dress which clung to her body and gave off vapour like smoke, Elaine felt the confidence ooze out of her. She looked boldly back into Lieutenant Yehia's eyes, but knew that she was blushing.

"I beg your pardon." He blinked and shook his head. "You must think me very rude, staring at you like that." And he walked down to the water's edge, where he stood shouting instructions to the swimming boys. Tim stood over the wheel of the launch, which the boys guided into a channel between rocks. Lieutenant Yehia assisted him ashore and returned to the launch for an examination of the four suitcases.

"You have not been through the Customs," he shouted.

Between them, Tim and the lieutenant dragged the launch until the nose was resting on sand.

"It is as I thought." The lieutenant gave an instruction to his sergeant in Arabic and addressed the group on the beach in his carefully picked English. "This is very illegal, and I shall have to arrest you all.

"No." He had to raise his voice to make himself heard over the protests. "There is no alternative. I have my duty. The luggage has not been through the Customs. I don't suppose your passports have been examined. I appeal to you"—he looked straight at Eric—"what alternative is there to arresting the whole party?"

"None whatsoever," said Eric. Mr. Dragoumis threw his hands towards the sky, and Lydia jerked at her husband's arm. "But, darling, the fellow is quite right. He's only doing his duty. Lieutenant, why don't we go over to the house? Then we can be arrested in comfort. You weren't proposing to take us down to the jail, were you?"

The Egyptian hesitated. "Certainly you may go to the house. But first of all you must give me your names."

As they made their way to the road and across the hillocky desert they bore with them the reek of the sea. On the lieutenant's uniform the salt dried out in white patches. He had insisted on carrying Elaine's cases. Lydia could be heard scolding her husband for being so English and agreeing with the lieutenant that it was his duty to arrest them. Her father, too, had a great deal to say. Mr. Dragoumis had

introduced himself to Tim and was helping him drag the
suitcases through the clogging sand on their castors, asking
as they went whether the boy was interested in political
theory and, if so, whether he had ever considered it the
field of human endeavour where, if anywhere, real progress
was hampered by the defects of Aristotelian logic. The heat
ran like water among the sand dunes. The boys who had
followed from the beach stood squinting in the glare and
ran back shouting into the sea. The sergeant stood guard
over the launch. The *askari* sat in the shade of the armoured
car. If there was tumult in Alexandria, no echo of it reached
as far as Sidi Bishr, where the only sounds were the shouting of boys, the whisper of the sea, the slither of feet, the
voices of Mr. Dragoumis and his daughter.

"Look, Eric," she said. "He's dropped the cases and he's
carrying her again."

Eric could feel the sand burning even through the soles
of his shoes. When he came to the suitcases he picked them
up, saying: "She's been walking barefoot. I ought to have
thought of it before."

Until Mrs. Dragoumis made her speech no one saw
how shocking, even disgusting, had been the behaviour of
Elaine and the Egyptian officer. What with the revolution
and Lydia's refusal to provide sanctuary in the upstairs flat,
Mrs. Dragoumis had doubtlessly been through great nervous stress; and the sight of an Egyptian carrying a shoeless
European woman into the house was the final horror that
brought coherence to her jangled sensibilities. At last she
knew where she stood. Her attitude to the *coup d'état*,
to Lydia's nudity, and to the sight of Elaine in Lieutenant
Yehia's arms was all of a piece. She was so scandalized that
everyone else was scandalized too, even Lieutenant Yehia,

and when Elaine found herself abruptly released into a wickerwork seat around which everyone stood arguing, she had to close her eyes in shame.

She also felt ill. Her feet tingled from the slight burning they had received before the lieutenant had begun carrying her, and the sea water she had swallowed now brought on nausea. But was it the sea water? Surely it was the heat. Crossing the sand, she had been really frightened. The sun roared in her ears, the air went hot into the nostrils, the body wilted a little. Even when the lieutenant had picked her up she felt she must rest. Being carried was an exertion. The walk through the docks, hot though it had been, was no preparation for the furnace of Sidi Bishr; and now that she was in somebody's house, there came, instead of the expected relief, a copious sweating. She was, she gathered, guilty of a gross indiscretion. What it was she had no idea, but a voice was raised in such vehemence she sweated the more, sweated in shame, sweated in full confession. Then she was sick out of the side of her mouth.

Recovering consciousness, she found they were putting her to bed. The room was darkened, a delicious coolness played over her body as though she had been washed but not dried, and at once she plunged into sleep again, smiling.

The second time she awoke, the silence of the house made her listen without moving. She could hear herself breathing, nothing else. From the shuttered window a white glow diffused across the ceiling. Only full daylight could burn so brightly, but because the air was so much cooler she was puzzled to know what time it was. She sat up, waited for the sudden ache to clear from her head, and made for the window, where, lifting the blind, she was able to look down on an Egyptian soldier with a rifle slung from his right shoulder. He stood in shadow at the top of the steps. The silence was so intense she could hear the rasp of his hand across his chin as he struck away a fly. He turned his head, the steel helmet lifted, and the brown face looked up at her, expressionless. Dropping the blind, Elaine turned back into the room. Only when she saw her reflection in a mirror did she realize she was dressed in an old-fashioned cotton nightdress.

"You feel all right now? Good."

The voice came from a chair in the corner. It was a shock to discover that she was not alone, but when she saw that pretty girl come forward, the one who had been on the beach that morning, Elaine said: "Yes, it seems cooler. How dreadful of me to pass out."

"Oh, no!" The girl came so close that Elaine could feel the breath on her face, perfumed as though she had been sucking sweets. "You must not say that! We are glad to welcome you! Nothing happens in Alexandria. I hate it, and I want to go with Eric and live in England. It is exciting to have someone new with us. Everyone is asleep," she said when Elaine made no comment. "In Egypt everyone goes to sleep after lunch. But you have had nothing. Let me get you some cold chicken and salad."

"Are you Mr. Blainey's wife?"

"Eric's? Oh, yes, of course." The girl looked alert, cocking her head like a bird. "Why?"

"Because you seem so young," Elaine was on the point of saying, but restrained herself at the thought the girl might interpret this amiss; it was like saying Eric was too old for her. Instead, she made a joke about there not having been time for introductions on the beach, and they both laughed.

"As a matter of fact," she said, "I'd love some cold

chicken and salad. I'm hungry. I suppose that means I'm better."

"Daddy said it was heat stroke and you ought to stay in bed."

"But that's absurd! I'm sorry. I didn't mean to shout. Look! It's Lydia, that's your name, isn't it? You see, I remember. Lydia, if you get that chicken ready, I'll show you whether I'm fit or not."

The girl shut the door behind her not a moment too soon. Elaine held on to the bed until the dizziness passed, moaning in quiet self-indulgence. Never had there been any time in her life when falling ill could have proved more of a nuisance. She would permit no such thing! Forcing herself to the window, she breathed sea air from beneath the lifted blind, marvelling at its freshness. The heart sent its regular throb of pain behind the eyes. She pressed a thumb violently against the wall, and the pain seemed to flow from her head into the thumb and wrist. Witchcraft! Her father had taught it to her! She released the pressure on her thumb, and even the nausea had gone. Illness was out of the question. When Lydia returned with the tray, she had opened one of her suitcases (they had both been placed, an obvious gesture of hospitality, before the wardrobe) and was slipping into grey slacks.

"At four o'clock," said Lydia, "the soldiers are coming back with some police and we are all going to prison."

"To prison!"

"Of course, it's all right for you and for me and for Eric and for Tim. We're British subjects. But Mama and Daddy have Egyptian passports, although they are Greek. The Egyptians can do just what they like with them. Is it true that you haven't got a visa? Eric said so. He said he was going to phone the British Consul."

"Oh, no!" Elaine lowered her fork. "They'd put me back on the *Tewfikieh*."

"Oh, but I don't think he meant it," said Lydia. "Eric only talked about phoning the Consul in order to please Tim. Tim doesn't understand Egypt. How should he? He's only just arrived. You see, if Eric phoned the Consul, it would show he knew you had no visa, and it is much better to appear ignorant of a matter like that. We shall be in a much stronger position when the Egyptians are actually trying to break into the house. Eric can ring up the Consul and say: 'We are being attacked.' Then who knows what will happen! Perhaps the British Navy will come. There will be so much trouble that no one will think to ask about your visa."

By the time Elaine was breathing normally she found that her mouth had dried. With consternation she found her voice came in a croak. "But why should the Egyptians try to break into the house?"

"Because Mama says she's not going to let them in. She was very upset to see that man carrying you. I think she's a bit hysterical. She's locked all the doors, she's had all the shutters bolted downstairs, and of course Daddy would always let her have her way over something like this. She has too much imagination, really." Lydia looked at the tray. "You're not eating anything. Isn't the chicken nice?" She tasted a morsel and nodded approvingly. "As a matter of fact, the Egyptians would never take an old woman like Mama to prison when she had nothing to do with the launch. She wasn't even on the beach, was she? Mama has nothing to be anxious about, but I'm not going to tell her."

Voices could be heard in the apartment below.

"That's Mama," said Lydia. "Everybody's waking up

now. I'll go and see if Eric is still asleep. He'll be glad to know you're better."

Elaine was roused. Her understanding was sharpened by Lydia's cool remarks about the expected assault on the house by soldiers and police. Time was being wasted. She ought, at that very moment, to be down in Alexandria putting a story together for the *Sun*. It was a wonderful break. The *Sun* relied on the agencies for Middle East news. If she could send a cable to London, there was a chance of becoming an accredited foreign correspondent; no more than a chance, however, because Edwards would probably still think it necessary to fly out somebody in the foreign-news department like Bill Oxford, who had been a Cairo press attaché during the war. Even so, there would be at least twenty-four hours' grace during which she, a mere editorial assistant on the features page, might bring off a scoop. Might? She was confident of it. On her first trip out of Europe, in a country going through a political crisis for reasons she could only guess at, ignorant of the language (and uncertain which one it was), with a head that ached and legs that wobbled, she would nevertheless send Edwards a story to make him grunt with approval. Only two things were needed: escape from the house within the next hour, and happenings in the city which measured up to the story she was already composing about them.

Before opening the door she put on dark glasses and was glad of the concealment when she found Eric and Tim Blainey standing there.

"Oh, Elaine . . ." said Tim.

"You frightened the life out of us, caving in like that." Eric seemed to be angry, but she guessed this was his way of showing concern. "Are you sure you're all right?"

"Well, I've never done anything like *that* before." She smiled at Tim in the hope it would chase the worried expression from his face. "A touch of the sun! But it's so much cooler now, thank God!"

"The breeze is blowing off the sea. It often does in the afternoon. Look here, Elaine, it's all very well, you getting up and walking about like this; but you've had a sort of heat stroke, and I really think you ought to go back to bed. Quite apart from anything else, it will stop Yehia from carting you off to jail. You know he's coming back?"

After a pause she said: "I'd love a cup of tea. D'you think that's possible?"

Tea, now she came to consider it, would be welcome, but the request had been made to gain time. No doubt it was wicked of Tim not to enter Egypt by the usual means and Eric was culpable for making such an entry possible; no doubt, too, he had committed some technical offense in taking the launch out of the dock area. But these transgressions must be of little importance compared with smuggling into Egypt a woman who was not only unvisaed (and therefore unexpected) but also, as a journalist, quite positively unwelcome in a country where the press was probably closely watched at the best of times. She, Elaine Brent, was the person who made the landing at Sidi Bishr a serious crime. Ordinary decency demanded behaviour from her that would involve the Blaineys and the Dragoumises in as little trouble as possible. Climbing out of a window when they were not looking no longer seemed fair.

"The phone isn't working, so I've been unable to find out what's going on in town." Eric seated her in a chair and began lecturing. "All hell may have broken out down there, for all I know. In that case the authorities won't have any time to bother with us. The Cairo radio keeps broadcasting a proclamation. At least we know what's going on. A lot of officers under a chap called Naguib have turned the government out. No mention of the King. So whether it's rebellion or revolution isn't clear yet. As I say, there's a good chance the police will be too busy to come and collect us. So cheer up! Here's your tea."

"But it's *not* the police," said Tim. "It's the soldiers. That lieutenant."

Eric brightened. "That's just the point. What was he doing on the Corniche Road with an armoured car? Must be one of Naguib's men. And my guess is that Yehia and a lot of others like him are converging on Montazah Palace. All the same," he said to Elaine, "I'd still play safe, if I were you, and take to bed. I don't believe you've met my mother-in-law. Miss Brent—Mrs. Dragoumis. Mrs. Dragoumis—Miss Brent."

Eric made the introductions with rapid flicks of the wrist.

But there was no talk at all. Everybody seemed struck silent by the absurdity of the introductions. Eric reflected that he had been facetious. Mrs. Dragoumis—no less!—had been the one to open the front door and let Lieutenant Yehia carry Elaine over the threshold; and even now, six hours afterwards, the cloud of disapproval had not lifted from her face. She refilled Elaine's cup and looked towards the window, sighing deeply. There was some deception in this, because when Elaine felt brave enough to look into the woman's face their eyes met. Mrs. Dragoumis was examining her carefully. The gaze came sideways and, judging by the slight curl of the lip, ironically. Elaine felt she was being invited to understand some ancient feminine mystery.

"The heat," said Mrs. Dragoumis at last. "Thank God you are recovered. I see you well again. Naturally, I was afraid."

"You're being so kind to me." Elaine was fortified by the realization that she spoke better French than Mrs. Dragoumis. "I don't want to be a nuisance."

Mrs. Dragoumis threw her head back and spoke emphatically. "Do not be afraid for yourself. In this house you are safe. The Egyptian will not come near you. Obviously he was attracted. As for taking you to the police station, that is out of the question. That is what he would *say*. He would *say* he was taking you to the police station. But he would take you to another place—"

Mrs. Dragoumis enjoyed talking, especially after the siesta, when she was refreshed and energetic. Now that she had time to grow accustomed to it, she was even a little excited by the thought of an amorous Egyptian, flushed with his sea rescue and with revolution, laying siege to her very own house. Once she had begun to talk, there was no stopping her. She said the first thing that came into her head, contradicting herself, warning of the violence to come, saying there was nothing to fear, admitting for the first time that Yehia might prove irresistible and carry them off to the police station whether they wished it or not.

"We shall not be parted, you and I," she said.

Elaine had become increasingly aware of the seriousness of the position. She cared not so much on her own account as on Eric's. Whereas the Egyptians would probably pack her off on the next boat, Eric was domiciled in the country and had probably exposed himself to a pretty severe punishment. Well, he must lie! He must say he did not know she was without a visa.

Misunderstanding the expression on Elaine's face, Mrs. Dragoumis spoke reassuringly. "Have no fear! All doors are locked. The Egyptians will not enter my house, I promise you!"

Even as she spoke there were footsteps on the stairs.

"Lieutenant Yehia!" announced Mr. Dragoumis from the door, and, wearing a straw-coloured suit of crumpled linen, he presently appeared with Yehia at his side. The Egyptian had changed into what was obviously his best uniform. He carried his cap under his arm, displayed a row of campaign ribbons, and advanced in a pair of squeaking but highly polished brown boots.

Behind him came two other Egyptians in uniform, one in khaki drill and the other in white tunic and black leggings and breeches.

Mrs. Dragoumis stood up. "Egyptians!" she said in Greek. "It is a judgement upon me. How did they get in?"

"Well, I let them in," said her husband. He took out his plain snuffbox and examined his minute reflection in the polished lid. "There was a knock at the door, and I let them in. After all, it was four o'clock. You were all up here talking. At moments of crisis, it is much better to sit round a table and discuss matters calmly. Locking doors and windows indeed! This is folly! Are we not rational creatures? If only the nations of the world would be as sensible as I have just been, there'd be no need for me to write my books." He spoke in English, taking minute pinches of snuff and steadily growing angrier. "And the writing of books is hard work. You have no idea of my labours!"

"We are rational creatures," he said. "We are not brutes."

"No, we are not brutes." Lieutenant Yehia had been frowning impatiently. Now he smiled and looked at Elaine. "It is excellent to see you better again. Naturally, I was worried. You have been ill. Your entry into Egypt was not regular. These are extraordinary days we live in; there is no doubt of that. We soldiers are now the governors of Egypt —" he spoke proudly—"and, although I could not make you well, I could do something else. These two gentlemen are officials. This one is passport officer. This one is from the Customs. I have brought them. Now they will stamp your passport and examine your baggage, yours and the young man's. Then all will be regularized."

Elaine gripped the arms of her chair and tried to avoid Yehia's eyes. Some of her morning fear returned. Then it had been of the roaring heat of the sand dunes. Now it was of the atmosphere of this little room. With the entry of four more men it had become airless. And yet it was not so much lack of air, or the heat, that exhausted her. It was Yehia's absurdity. Surely behaviour like this was unusual, even in Egypt!

The man in khaki drill had produced a notebook from his pocket. The one in leggings and breeches bore an ink-pad in his left hand and a rubber stamp in his right. Equipped in this way, they moved towards her in expectation, it seemed, of examining her baggage and passport. The situation was so crazy she felt herself sliding into a faint.

"I am a journalist," she heard herself saying, "Middle East correspondent for the London *Sun*."

"A journalist!" Yehia came and stood directly in front of her, waving the officials back. Clearly, the bit of information excited him, but, equally clearly, he did not know what to do with it. He lowered his eyebrows and looked fierce. Elaine was not, however, deceived by the expression on his face, and felt the strength come back to her. How the confession (or claim!) had been won from her she did not know. She scarcely felt responsible for it. Perhaps it was a natural consequence of working at such a competitive trade. If someone made a joke, she would have to cap it. And if Yehia, ruddy-faced and solemn as a peasant, decided to make an appearance with passport and Customs officials in tow—obviously aiming at farce!—well, she would cap that situation too!

She was back in her body again, breathing steadily.

"I'm the correspondent for the *Sun*. This is a pretty influential paper, as you know. Now, would you like to tell me what's going on in this country? You say the military have taken over. You're military enough for me. Will you tell me what your plans are? Will you give me an interview?"

Yehia stood thinking. How clean he looks, Elaine thought irrelevantly. His face, which the sun had fired to a smoky red, had a scrubbed delicacy, a fine transparency of the skin, as though it had been steamed. She suddenly realized he had come straight to the house from a hot bath. A Turkish bath! A stiff brush of hair, so stiff that no grease could lay it flat, rose straight from his forehead. Even now, whisps of vapour were trapped in it. Looking again, she saw that they were in fact grey hairs. Yehia was cropped up the neck and over the crown; all his pride was expressed in the frontal brush, which stood like the tuft on an antique helmet. She found herself thinking of him as an old Roman. He looked puzzled and honest; and when he came to his decision, stooping towards her, she realized that the faint smell of jasmine came from him and no one else.

"I will read you the proclamation of General Naguib," he said gruffly. "It is written out in Arabic, so I'll have to translate as I go. Forgive my clumsiness and my mistakes."

He drew a folded sheet of paper from his pocket, held it to the light, and began reading jerkily.

Eric sat on the stairs. He could hear Yehia's voice distantly, and a current of air rose to console him for it. After listening for some minutes he went down to the apartment of his parents-in-law and found that the sentry was sitting in a basket chair just outside the front door. At Eric's approach he stood up. Eric looked into the street. Yehia's driver was asleep at the wheel of the open staff car. Disappointingly, all was quiet. The wind blew straight off the sea. Blue mantled down from the horizon, and the water was transparent only where the dunes appeared to press against it. If this was revolution, then it was a dull business. He had an idea, though, that the real trouble was yet to begin.

"You are not to leave," said the sentry in Arabic. "No one is to leave this house."

Eric could not decide whether this was the same man who had been with Yehia on the beach, but he made his observation nonetheless. "If my launch is pinched or damaged, I shall hold you responsible. Understand? I shall go to Cairo and kick your General Naguib's behind for him."

At the sound of voices the driver woke, yawned, and asked what time it was. He came lethargically up the steps, demanding why his question had been ignored. The time! That was all he wanted to know. He chaffed the sentry noisily, and Eric retired to the hall to consider what effect the revolution might have on his own fortunes. In his speech Naguib had included a conventional piece about respecting the interests of "foreign brothers," holding himself responsible for their welfare, and the like; it was conventional because every leading Egyptian politician had made a similar promise at some stage in his career. But it was hard to believe that a soldier like Naguib could consolidate his revolution without appealing to nationalism and xenophobia. Had not Kemal Ataturk, in a similar position, taxed foreign traders out of Turkey? Technically, the Dragoumis trading company was not a foreign concern. Mr. Dragoumis was an Egyptian citizen, in accordance with the new law all accounts were kept in Arabic, and the company was registered as an Egyptian company; so that, on the face of it, there was no need to fear expropriation or punitive taxation. One could only guess, however. He, as an Englishman, might be discriminated against. There was a pretty good chance of that, he thought.

Upstairs, Yehia was still talking. God, what a bore the man was! Eric climbed the stairs cautiously, re-entered the room at what appeared to be the end of Yehia's speech—an extended commentary on Naguib's proclamation—and found an empty chair between Lydia and her father, from where he smiled at the Egyptian, wondering how long the almost inevitable arrest would be postponed. Everyone watched Yehia fold the sheet of paper and replace it in his pocket. Words like "purge," "trust," "traitors," and "brothers," having been solemnly uttered in that room, had left their resonance behind them. No one spoke, and Yehia supported the silence without embarrassment, with dignity even, possibly with a touch of defiance. It was as though he had been praying in public.

"*Ya' salaam*," said the Customs official fervently, and the examiner of passports murmured his appreciation too.

Yehia looked at Elaine. "Does this answer your questions?"

Judging that the performance was over, the company relaxed. Mrs. Dragoumis blew her nose, Mr. Dragoumis walked to the window and thrust one of the shutters back to admit more light, and Tim could be heard saying: "Well, this really is something. I wouldn't have missed this for worlds." But when Elaine made her reply to Yehia everyone was immediately attentive once more. The Customs official was particularly affected. Closing his mouth firmly, he was forced to breathe through his nose, gently snoring.

"Tell me, please," said Elaine with conscious flattery,

"what about the King? What will you do with King Farouk?"

For the first time since she had met him Yehia smiled. He detected the flattery, and it amused him so much that he could no longer look at her. His face broadened and brightened. He put his head back, laughed at the ceiling, and appeared, in his awkwardness and his amusement, much younger—a boyish twenty-five. He was awkward because, having once planted his feet, he seemed incapable of budging them. He twisted his body about, coughing with laughter. Suddenly he was serious. "You are asking too much. I am only a soldier in the King's Army. Now let these men attend to your passport and your baggage. Then I can wish you a pleasant stay in Egypt and go."

The Customs official produced his notebook once more, the immigration officer began moving forward with his inkpad and rubber stamp—the unmasking had come! Eric wondered whether Elaine had had the wit to lose her passport when she fell into the sea. A missing passport would be easier of explanation than one without an Egyptian visa. But no! Even as the immigration officer stretched out his hand Elaine drew the passport from a hand satchel and, with a smiling assurance Eric could only wonder at, wagged it in Yehia's direction.

"You've been so kind to me, lieutenant. I ought to explain that I decided to come ashore only at the very last moment. How was I to know you were going to have this revolution?"

The immigration officer took the passport and thumbed through the pages. "You mean you have no visa to land?"

"But how could I have possibly got one? There simply wasn't time. Lieutenant, you've been so— I mean, can't you—?"

Even Elaine was checked by the sudden grimness which had fallen on Yehia. He took the passport and studied one of the blank pages as though willing the necessary visa to emerge from invisibility. His failure was obvious from the way he handed the document back to her. A minute before, he had been shy with merriment; now he was angry and could stare at Elaine without inhibition. At first the anger was directed against himself; but because it was his own stupidity that offended him chiefly, he could say nothing, merely nod when the immigration officer whispered in his ear, and reflect on the eagerness with which he, an officer of the revolutionary army, had been prepared to facilitate the entry into Egypt of a woman who might even be an enemy of the state.

"*My* passport's all right," said Tim. He stepped forward with the booklet open at the visa, and after examining it carefully the immigration officer stamped it for him. Tim's name was crossed off a disembarkation list with a reluctance that brought out the irregularity of the procedure. Then the passport was returned to him with a snappiness meant to indicate, no doubt, the efficiency with which difficulties were overcome and even revolutions endured. Tim thanked the immigration officer effusively in the hope it would improve the humour of the meeting. He even directed the Customs official to his suitcases.

"Are you Jewish?" Yehia put the question quietly.

"No," said Elaine. Her eye was caught by the campaign ribbons. She supposed they had been earned in the Palestine war.

"Then why should you enter Egypt illegally?"

"I've told you, lieutenant. I'm a journalist with a living to earn. As soon as I heard—"

"You said you were Middle East correspondent of the *Sun*."

"So I should be, once I got to a cable office. Look, here's my union card. There's nothing to worry about, I can assure you."

"I'm not worried on my own account." Yehia would not so much as look at the card. "You don't seem to understand the seriousness of the situation. Mr. Blainey, you are implicated too. You brought the lady up from Alexandria. There is law, even in Egypt, as you shall see! Did you think Egyptian law was of no account, perhaps? You understand why this angers me? You think of Egypt still as a British colony. You come and go as you wish. Those days are gone! You"—he turned to the immigration officer and continued speaking in English, his voice still low but with an emotional tremor—"you take charge of this situation. You are to do what is right according to the law."

"*Si, si,*" said the immigration officer.

Yehia put his hat on. "We Egyptians must observe the rule of law. We must not favour our friends and be corrupt. Let us, all three of us—you as a passport officer, you as an inspector of customs, and I as a soldier—let us all work for justice. In this way Egypt will become truly strong and independent."

"*Inshallah!*" said the two officials piously.

"You understand? I leave everything in your hands! I accept no further responsibility." Having added some further remarks in Arabic, Yehia gave Mr. Dragoumis, as head of the household, a formal salute and left the room stiffly, with his emotion apparently under firm control. Some moments later his car could be heard starting up; and when Eric looked from the window he saw Yehia sitting with the driver and the sentry lolling in the back seat. Such, then, was the enormity of Elaine's crime that the household was no longer in military custody. The civil authorities, as represented by the immigration officer and the inspector of Customs, were in charge.

And the civil authorities were, it seemed, no less amazed by the sudden turn events had taken than was Elaine herself. They talked quietly in a corner while Elaine, not far from tears, apologized to Mrs. Dragoumis and to Mr. Dragoumis and to Lydia and to Eric for the mess she had landed them in.

"What an unpredictable man!" said Mr. Dragoumis. "One moment he is a gentleman, the next he is very rude."

"I didn't like him really, did you?" Lydia asked Elaine.

"Quite extraordinary!" Tim was naturally interested in dramatic situations and, now that his passport had been franked, felt secure enough to behave like a man of letters. "I've never seen anyone change so quickly."

"Well," said Eric to the immigration officer, who was nervously opening and closing his notebook, "what are you going to do?"

"Do, sir?" It was the inspector of Customs who took it upon himself to answer. He spoke softly and smiled. "You see what a hard decision is put upon us. Which way to turn? In this country today we do not know who our masters are. Perhaps the English will occupy Cairo once more."

The immigration officer grumbled in a mixture of English and Arabic. Never in his life had he seen such irregularities. No immigration officer had stamped passports in a private house before. The Army had taken control of the country. Well and good! What did that mean? Was he to go here and there at the whim of an Army officer, examining passports? Perhaps he was. Speaking for himself, he was ready to obey instructions.

Eric was becoming impatient. "What about this lady's passport?"

The immigration officer picked up his ink-pad, shut the tin lid upon it, and had more words with his companion.

"We are going now," he said when they had come to a decision. "Because we do not know what to do. We do not wish to meddle in politics. Everything is dark before our eyes."

With which confession, and smiling sadly, the representatives of civil administration withdrew to walk, presumably, all the way back to Alexandria, for it was not to be believed that tram-cars ran when the state itself was shaken.

At seven o'clock Lieutenant Yehia drove up in a jeep to ask after Miss Brent's health. As soon as she entered the Dragoumises' hall, where he had been received, Yehia stood to attention and smiled. During his absence he had acquired an ease of manner. "I'm glad to see you all still here. So they didn't arrest you after all, those men?" He threw his head back to laugh. "What did they do? Nothing! Then that is their responsibility. I did my duty. They did not do theirs. That is precisely the kind of inefficiency the new government is determined to sweep away! Now let me make a suggestion. Miss Brent, I am ready to drive you through Alexandria to show you, a distinguished foreign journalist, how excellently the Army has taken control. Do you accept?"

Elaine had to confess that, but for a dull headache, she had recovered from her malaise.

Chapter *3* Our Representative in Alexandria

"*I* MUST explain," said Mr. Dragoumis above the noise of the traffic, "just why I attack the principles of Aristotelian logic."

Mr. Dragoumis sat with Tim in the back of the jeep which Lieutenant Yehia, with Elaine at his side, drove through night-time Alexandria. Shop fronts were boarded up, but there were no signs of riot damage; certainly no evidence of fire. Trams ran as usual. They whined on the corners, spitting fire at the antennæ. Groups of white-jacketed police flickered in the moonlight. Although the sun had set, the air was hot in the narrow streets—not so much as a breath came from the harbours—and the city, which took most of its illumination from the moon, had the unsteadiness of moonlight. Façades shook in the humid air. Or was it an illusion brought on by the vibration of the jeep? It would have been too much to claim that the city was normal; there should have been throngs of walkers taking the night air, lights in all the windows, café music. In contrast, the city seemed empty, abandoned to the moon. But at least there were no disturbances, and Yehia might have shown more pleasure that his claim was borne out so well. He showed neither pleasure nor pride. Indeed, they could scarcely get a word out of him. Mr. Dragoumis alone thought he was meditating on Aristotle. Elaine and Tim knew he was sulking.

Tim, even more than Elaine, knew he was sulking. She merely had intuition to guide her, but Tim had Mrs. Dragoumis. As soon as it became evident that Elaine intended to accept Yehia's invitation Mrs. Dragoumis took Tim aside and, with some incoherence, instructed him in his duty.

What was his duty? To be handsome, gay, and audacious! Mrs. Dragoumis wagged a fleshy finger and whispered away in French. For a young woman, quite new to the country, afflicted with heat stroke and wearing sandals now that she had lost what were apparently her only pair of shoes (Mrs. Dragoumis saw great meaning in this), it was madness to go out alone with an Egyptian. What was this talk about writing for the newspapers? It was not credible. What English newspaper could possibly be interested in the affairs of Egypt? Being intelligent, Miss Brent would know this. But she was on holiday, she was no longer a young woman, she said: "Unless I marry soon it will be too late" and quite calmly agreed to go out in the moonlight with a Moslem. Mrs. Dragoumis said that the fate of any woman who had been her guest was of deep concern to her; and a guest who, like her own daughter, was a British citizen had a special claim. Tim was unattached, yet obviously attractive to women. He was not to think that Miss Brent was too old for him; he must not underestimate his own maturity.

Surely, he must insist on accompanying Miss Brent and the
Egyptian lieutenant; and he must so conduct himself that
the eyes of his countrywoman would be opened to Yehia's
unworthiness. Or, at least, this is what Tim had gathered
from the confused intimacy of five minutes with Mrs. Dragoumis in a cupboard under the stairs.

He had to suppress a smile when reflecting on Mrs.
Dragoumis's flattery—*he* was not to be taken in so easily!—
but he had his career to consider, and the foolish woman
might be showing him a path to explore. For this he was
grateful. Ever since setting out on this trip he had been a
little self-conscious about its purpose: to gather experience.
How did one do it? How did one become unhappy? Truly,
desperately, suicidally unhappy? Unhappiness, surely, lay at
the heart of experience. It was the grain of sand around
which the pearl, et cetera! And there was always the chance
that the necessary degree of misery might be withheld! Oh,
dear! the thought came to him from time to time. How to
break into life and be wounded dreadfully? Not physically,
of course; he did not want to be hurt. But how to sight
Doom, darker and deeper (to quote the poet) than any sea
dingle? Could he possibly—to bring these reflections up to
date—fall in love with Elaine?

A drive round a foreign city, at night, with a revolutionary soldier whose romantic ardour for one of the other
passengers he was attempting to frustrate might well provide the very adventure he was looking for. He had gone
straight from the cupboard to the balcony, where Mr. Dragoumis was speaking to the lieutenant, and broken in clum-
sily because he was so nervous.

"Mind if I come along too?"

The words were an accusation, as Yehia well knew. He
nodded as though indifferent to Tim's absence or presence,

only to be tackled by Mr. Dragoumis, who said there was plenty of room in the jeep for a fourth and he would be glad to occupy it for the opportunity it provided of continuing the present conversation. It rarely happened that the philosopher had opportunity to instruct the man of affairs. The country was undergoing revolution. Lieutenant Yehia was one of the leaders of that revolution. Who, then, could ignore the urgency of further talk in which he, Paulos Dragoumis, having devoted so much thought to the framing of an ideal society, would advise the lieutenant on those principles which could alone save the revolution from dictatorship or the mob?

Tim was as surprised as Yehia, and even more confused. Had Mr. Dragoumis, too, received his instructions for the preservation of Elaine?

The moonlight transformed him, transformed them all. Mr. Dragoumis was a wizard. As he spoke on, untroubled by the speed at which they were travelling and the jolting, his wiry hair displayed itself like a halo in the wind. His eyes glittered. Sometimes the winding of the road brought up a stretch of beach like a pearly wing; and against this background the pallor of Mr. Dragoumis's suit was flickeringly, for the tiniest moment, lost. Only the phosphorescent hair, the fishy glint of an eye kept pace. Behind the hair and the eye lay the sea. The voice came at them from moonlight and salt air.

"My system," it said, "is really an anti-system. From all forms of society, democratic, monarchic, ecclesiastic, communist, fascist, I choose the best points. Yes, we can learn from them all. I am not exclusive. I am, in fact, a Selectivist."

A Selectivist! Tim's interest was caught. He would have liked to ask Yehia to stop so that Mr. Dragoumis would not need to shout and they could all give him their attention,

freed from anxiety about falling out of the jeep when it
took a sharp corner. But the notion was absurd! They were
not driving about Alexandria at fifty miles an hour to give
Mr. Dragoumis an opportunity to talk. Tim had to catch the
words as best he could; and he had also—remembering his
responsibilities—to think of Elaine, to speak to her as often
as possible, to speak so close to her ear that he could smell
the brine dried in her hair.

They paused beside a cemetery wall, opposite a wide
gap in the row of houses which stood between the road and
the sea. Over the wall could be seen the uplifted wings of
stone angels, a truncated pyramid in winking black marble,
and a broken column. On the waste towards the beach,
mounds of seaweed, dumped there to rot, impregnated the
moonlight; the air sweated with corruption.

"We are near the centre of Alexandria," said Yehia.
"As you see, all is quiet! No trouble! Why should there be
trouble? Our movement is of the people."

"Can I cable London?" Elaine asked.

"You want to say that here in Alexandria is calm?"

"I want to ask for some money. Unless they send me
some money I might as well go home tomorrow. Will I find
a cable office open this time of night?"

Lending her the cost of the cable caused Tim a quite
disproportionate pleasure. The purser had given him Egyptian money for one of his traveller's cheques; what was more
natural than the wish to place it all at her disposal? No, he
would not be content with a loan of one pound! See, there
were seven, eight, nine, ten pounds! Ten Egyptian pound
notes, half as big again as English notes. He thrust them
into Elaine's hand under Yehia's very nose. It was a triumph! Not that Yehia made any competitive offer; his severe manner implied that the lending of money was too

petty a service to be expected of a military man; had it been a question of intimidating the clerk into sending Elaine's cable for nothing, he, Yehia, would have acted promptly. This was criticism that Tim could sense without check to his satisfaction. Elaine, too, was elated once the all-important cable had been sent and, to Yehia's consternation, talked of taking the next train to Cairo.

Tim, who was now quite intoxicated by the warm night, the novelty and the strangeness of the city, said Yes! To Cairo! And he would go with her! Even Mr. Dragoumis was checked by the proposal. He broke off his exposition of the new form of logic destined to replace classical logic and began an impatient parenthesis about the absurdity of going to Cairo in July. The heat was insupportable! As for the revolution, that was absurd too! The government spent the summer in Alexandria; everyone knew that! How could there be a revolution in Cairo when the government was not there to be overthrown? Mr. Dragoumis had, in fact, noticed the poor attention given to his remarks on the logic of government and was nettled.

"What do you say to that?" Elaine asked Yehia.

"Who rules Cairo rules Egypt. It is true that the final reckoning will come in Alexandria. No, it would be a mistake to go to Cairo when everybody is coming here."

"To see the King?"

"Everything will be arranged quietly," said Yehia. "There will be no public disorders."

Elaine rested a hand on Yehia's forearm. "General Naguib is coming *here?* Could you get me an interview with him?"

Yehia swung the jeep round and charged westwards as though there the answer lay. They crossed a square with an equestrian statue, and the snarl of the engine echoed among flat-faced buildings. Between pillars there were palm trees and the sea. By his refusal to answer any more questions and by his fierce driving Yehia now silenced everyone, even Mr. Dragoumis. They swung from side to side of a narrow street to avoid tram-cars and donkey carts. Here, in the poorest quarter, there were more people about. Brilliantly lit stalls for the sale of sweetmeats were set up at street corners. The over-spill from a café—men playing tric-trac in the moon-light—extended into the road itself, and Yehia braked nois-ily to avoid them. With the jeep at a standstill the passengers had opportunity to smell the goats; and when it was in mo-tion again the hot air whipped the reek of petroleum into their faces. They were near the docks. This was no place to stop, but even when they were back in the European quar-ters Yehia did not so much as slacken pace except to avoid collision. They drove out to Ras el-Tin and looked at the lights in the harbour. They drove north, beyond the railway station, past tenement houses crumbling like cheese in the moonlight, to higher ground. They were dazed by the pro-longed plunging about in this never ending city. Hours had passed since leaving Sidi Bishr. If Yehia was still seeking to make his point about law and order, his passengers had taken it long ago and Tim, for one, was placing hope in the jeep's fuel consumption. Surely the petrol could not last out much longer! If only he knew more about engines and that sort of thing! Perhaps these military vehicles carried fuel to last them for days!

"No," said Yehia, apparently in answer to a demand made by Elaine. He drove delicately down a rutted track. Palm trees crowded about them; the trunks were crusty silver and the remote fronds gobbets of ink that had been hurled against the moon. "I wish to conceal nothing. We have not seen half of the city. Any moment you may see dangerous men."

"We must be at Nouzha," said Mr. Dragoumis.

Yehia switched off the engine, and they all sat listening to the silence. Through the grove came a glint of water. An oasis in the remotest desert could not have been quieter, and Yehia would have liked to hear them admit it.

"Why do you want to go back so soon to Sidi Bishr? It is impossible for a reply to come so quickly to your cable. I tell you it is your duty to listen to this silence and look at those stars. There is revolution, perhaps the King will be shot. But here we are. Alexandria is all around us. All is calm. But I," he said, "I am not calm."

"I want to go home," said Elaine firmly. To his amazement, Tim realized that she and Yehia were stiff with rage at each other. What had happened? For Tim, a move in the direction of peace-making was as natural as drawing breath; and because Yehia appeared the angrier of the two, because he was so much the more of an unknown quantity, and because it was on his good-will they depended for a safe return, Tim's soothing words were spoken to him.

"I'm quite sure you're right, lieutenant. There won't be a reply to that cable until the morning. We really have plenty of time. What a beautiful spot this is."

Yehia switched on the engine, crashed his gears, and swung the jeep round so violently Tim was nearly thrown out. The words had, to Tim, seemed innocent and emollient; but the way Elaine drew her breath in had convinced him of their enormity.

"It was from this point," Mr. Dragoumis yelled into Tim's ear, "that the canal went to Canopus in antiquity. Such wickedness! Such scenes of debauchery!"

Into Tim's mind had come the wholly ludicrous image of himself as a steak in an infra-red grill where Yehia and Elaine were the two elements discharging energy at each other. He began to get angry on his own account. "I must say, Elaine, I think we might be a bit more appreciative. Damn it all! He doesn't *have* to drive us round Alexandria."

"Shut up, will you, Tim," she flung back as they broke into lighted streets once more and tram-lines writhed under their wheels like snakes.

Only Mrs. Dragoumis, with her absurd notions about Yehia and Elaine, could have been pleased with the warfare that had so unexpectedly broken out. Excess of zeal! That was the worst Yehia could be accused of. If he had made a pass at Elaine, Tim was sure he would have noticed. Over-anxiety to show his country in a good light; resentment, possibly, of the distrust that had caused Tim, not to speak of Mr. Dragoumis, to join the party; the emotional disarray that was natural in a revolutionary when he saw the revolution succeeding—all this could undoubtedly be held to explain Yehia's behaviour. And Tim felt for him. Now that it appeared Yehia had fallen from Elaine's favour, Tim was ready to sympathize.

Nevertheless, Tim was alarmed when Yehia dropped Elaine and Mr. Dragoumis at the house and insisted on his remaining in the jeep. The journey from Nouzha to Sidi Bishr had been accomplished in minutes. Yehia drove savagely. Under the headlights, the road ahead was a perpetually rising, expanding mushroom. A huge building, a sports stadium perhaps, passed like a cloud. The moon picked out an elevation of balcony, stucco garlands and fruit; but it was the winking of an eye. Yehia and Elaine were silent. Tim and Mr. Dragoumis clutched at their seats and complained, quietly at first and to each other but loudly, despairingly, as time went by and the jeep swung round tree-shadowed corners at sixty miles an hour, or faster. Then they had arrived. Mr. Dragoumis flew from his seat as soon as he realized the jeep was motionless. Tim was watching Elaine soberly climb out when he became aware that Yehia had swung round and gripped him by the wrist.

"You must stay." The words were curt, but they conveyed a struggle of feeling. "I will drive on and we must talk."

Overhead the front door must have opened; Tim saw his brother against a vapour of light. He saw, too, Elaine's teeth and the whites of her eyes as she turned towards him. Mr. Dragoumis was near the top of the steps and his forehead was a wink of brilliance. Nobody spoke. This was how a man might observe the witnesses of his unexpected translation; a sinner, for example, importunately claimed and snatched up by Beelzebub. Tim was so constituted that the threat of punishment immediately convinced him that he had deserved it. He did not question the rightness of Yehia's action any more than he would have questioned Beelzebub's. He was alarmed, that's all!

As soon as the jeep was travelling too fast for Tim to jump out Yehia relinquished his hold. They took the sea road and drove east. Very soon they were travelling between an empty sea and a firm scalloping of sand. The road, rising slightly, projected them skywards. In the clarity of night the lowest stars raced with them, breaking like rockets when the horizon fell away and fizzling out behind the dunes. The immense night sky comprised two thirds of what they saw. The jeep tilted straight for Cassiopæa, earth fell away, and Tim (gripping the bar behind Yehia's seat) forgot his worries in the perspective of night sea and night desert that opened beneath them. Yehia had wound the jeep off the road. He brought it to a stop on the crest of a gravel hill, turned to Tim, and began speaking vehemently.

"You must tell me how to please this woman."

He made Tim get out of the jeep, and they walked up and down on the gravel, Yehia talking. Sometimes he shouted at the very top of his voice, but it did not matter. There was no one about. Who was he even to think of her? He was the son of a sergeant-major in the Egyptian Army, and he had only managed to enter the Military Academy by the skin of his teeth. But he had done well in the Palestine war. He had been decorated. Nevertheless, he did not know even how to speak to an Englishwoman. He begged for instruction. Was it possible for him to give a present or would she despise him? He was thirty-three years of age and had never married. His life had been dedicated to the service and to the liberation of Egypt from British oppression.

"This woman," he said, "is almost as important to me as my country. Almost! Not quite! This night I am at the crisis of my life. Revolution and this woman! Now, sir, you are English and she is English. Tell me how the thoughts of an Englishwoman move."

Tim was so flattered he failed to notice Yehia's refusal to take him seriously as a rival.

"Well, an Englishwoman, you see," he said. "It's rather like this. . . ."

The journalist, Elaine believed, was a figure of great consequence in the world. Within the limits defined by professional decorum, newspapers should be free to publish what they wanted; otherwise, she would have gone on to say, the private individual was at the mercy of governments, parliaments, big business, trades unions, and officials of all descriptions. At the same time, news was a commodity to be sold like any other commodity, and much of her annoyance with Yehia had been brought about by the realization that Alexandria was not providing colourful material for a press cable. The more Yehia showed his complacency about the prevailing calm, the more she was irritated. How could a man like that understand her anxiety that the Egyptian revolution would not come up to her expectations? He wanted to be gallant. She could see that and, up to a point, appreciate it. But later on, surely, after the palace had been looted, the King guillotined (or whatever they did in Egypt), and the last rifle shot had been fired—then would be the moment for relaxation. Listen to the silence and look at the stars! She could not hide her impatience with counsel like that! To do him justice, she reflected as Yehia roared off with Tim his unwilling passenger, the fellow had probably never before had dealings with a professional woman. The status of women in Egypt, she had heard, was very low indeed.

"Has it occurred to you," asked Mr. Dragoumis, "that Tim has been taken as a hostage? No doubt there is good precedent. I should say that the taking of hostages was common in times of political disturbance. Such as our own."

"Hostage!" Eric was more angry with Yehia than worried about Tim's safety. Whatever the explanation for this midnight abduction, it was difficult to credit Yehia with any real nastiness. Eric knew Egyptians. Yehia's was just the kind of dramatic behaviour you could expect; he would wish to draw attention to himself. In an hour's time, no doubt, he would turn up with Tim safe and sound, giving absurd explanations. "A hostage? How on earth could Tim be a hostage?"

Mr. Dragoumis argued differently. "Consider this matter with the eye of a historian. When was the last military

revolt in this country? Colonel Arabi in 1881. This Naguib
is just such another as Colonel Arabi, and, believe me, he'll
finish up in just the same way. England will crush him. The
King is of no consequence in this matter. The struggle is
between Egyptian nationalism and England. What could be
wiser than to take an English hostage? No doubt Tim is
already on his way to a place of concealment. We shall hear
of Lieutenant Yehia using your brother as something to bargain with." Having been frightened by Yehia's wild driving,
Mr. Dragoumis now responded with contempt; he was
ashamed, he said, that the thought had ever entered his head
of instructing the Lieutenant in political theory.

But for Elaine, who had been asleep most of the day,
the Dragoumis household was exhausted. They drank coffee
and discussed what had better be done. Mrs. Dragoumis
alone feared that Tim was in any immediate danger; Yehia
was clearly mad with jealousy, and her heart went out to the
young man she had, with the best intentions, guided so
dangerously. Perhaps she had sent him to his death! Mingled
with her alarm was a certain amount of pride. Muzzy with
heat and fatigue, she lay back, fighting for every breath,
while the fat tears ran to the corners of her mouth and left
trails which the two candles (the only illumination she now
took it into her head to permit) picked up, glistening like
the tracks of snails. She was an instrument of destiny. The
Forces of Good and Evil had assigned her to do their bid-
ding. The young man, pink as a bud from England, had
not questioned her authority; as a result he might, at that
very moment, be preparing to die. He would think of her
with great respect. Mrs. Dragoumis did not doubt that Tim,
in his extremity, would reflect that his situation bore witness
to her astuteness; and when no one appeared to notice her
distress it naturally became the harder to bear. She said that

he was such a pretty young man, quite ideal as a son-in-law's step-brother. A loud sob caused Lydia to go to her mother. She kissed her gratefully, for she interpreted the emotion as an indirect tribute to the success of her marriage. Just why she could not have explained, but for once she thought that her mother's tears reflected credit on the family, and the pair of them sat side by side on the settee, clasping each other tightly and staring at the unwavering candle flames.

"Suppose you're sorry you ever smuggled me ashore," Elaine said to Eric soon after one o'clock, when Tim had still not returned.

"Blessed if I can see how you're to blame. Why don't you go to bed?"

"Not only because of Tim. I mean because of everything. It strikes me I've been an almighty nuisance all round; Army officers, Customs officials, passport-examiners, all charging into the house."

"I'm not sorry at all." They were sitting in basket chairs on the balcony. "There has scarcely been a dull moment since you landed. As for Tim, he's almost certainly bound to come to a good end."

"Why are you so jealous of him?"

"Jealous!"

"That's the wrong word. There is *something*!"

Eric threw his cigarette stub into the street. He was irritated by her knowingness. As an illegal immigrant into the country, she ought to realize she was much too insecurely placed to have time for prying into other people's motives. "You've got to remember I've seen practically nothing of the boy. He was only ten or eleven when the war broke out, and I've been away from England ever since. We had some months together in '45. He's been thoroughly spoilt, I'd say. But I'm fond of him. Damn it all, he's my brother. Bit of a wet, but I'm fond of him if only for his mother's sake. As for being *jealous*!"

"You make me feel I ought to apologize."

"Damn it," he burst out, "where the hell can they have got to? This is precisely the sort of situation Tim might be expected to get himself into."

"But it isn't his fault."

"He could have jumped out, couldn't he? I'm going to phone the Consul."

Elaine became aware that she was alone. Even when asleep she had, apparently, been under Lydia's observation; so this was the first time since arriving in Alexandria. She was free! The steps down to the street wore a skin of sand, and it crackled under her feet so that she stopped to listen to the silence of the house and found, after some moments, that what she took to be silence was the perpetual rushing of the sea. A wind blew towards the darkness of the sea, raising a fuzz of moonlight along the ridges of sand between her and the beach huts. As she pressed forward the sand played round her ankles like silk, and she tried to think of the foreign-news room in the *Sun* office as a way of not thinking about Tim.

She turned and looked back at the house. There was no sign that her absence had been noticed. A brush of light lay on the darkest shadow to mark where the candles burned. At that very moment some one, perhaps Williams himself, was in the foreign-news room, having to make a decision about the cable she had sent: "Could cover Egyptian crisis if funds cabled c/o Dragoumis, Rue Segar, Sidi Bishr." It was easier to dwell on the situation if she imagined the cable in Williams's hands; she could evoke his blunt features and the toss of his head as he made a decision. But even Williams faded as she came down to the road and crossed to the beach at the very point, so far as she could judge, where she had landed that morning. She could hear the water funnelling up among the rocks, then running like a thousand fountains as the wave subsided.

"Tim!" she shouted. "Tim! Are you there? Tim! Tim! Tim!"

The voice was tiny, even to herself. Shouting made her gay. She was quite alone. Or was she alone? Anyway, there was no one to be seen so far as sight could penetrate through this milky haze. "Tim!" she cried, holding her hands to her mouth. "Are you there?"

She succeeded in lighting a cigarette. Her eyes still dazzled by the cupped brilliance, she heard rather than saw his approach.

"Is that you, Tim?" she said sharply. Afterwards she marvelled that it did not occur to her the dim figure might be anyone but Tim. "Well, say something, can't you?"

"Elaine!" He rushed forward. One moment he was a form making angles in the moonlight; the next he was a mask with enormous shining eyes. "What on earth are you doing out here at this time of night?"

"Well, I like that! I come out looking—"

"For me?" He struggled for words. "Oh, Elaine, I'm not worth it! Honestly I'm not. Don't touch me. You'll be sorry after, when I tell you. I'm a monster. I shall never forgive myself."

"But are you all *right*, Tim?"

"I want to kill myself."

"What's happened?"

"I can never tell you. Never! Never!"

"Then that's settled. Let's forget all about it and go home. Everybody is very worried. Eric was phoning the Consul when I left."

Elaine held him firmly by the arm, steering steadily past the bubbling rocks and up towards the road; but the moment she disclaimed interest in his adventures Tim broke loose and stood threateningly in her path. The moon had so far declined that it stood over his left shoulder.

"Elaine, how can you say such a thing?" His voice was thick with feeling. "I can't keep it to myself. If I don't tell you, who *am* I to tell?"

Suddenly he was on his knees, kissing her hands.

"You must forgive me, Elaine. I swear I didn't realize what I was saying. Talking to a foreigner about Englishwomen! Elaine, you do like me, don't you?"

"Of course."

"I should feel a lot better, then, if you'd kiss me."

"Well, then."

"No, I mean on the mouth."

"Tim," she said, having successfully disengaged herself from his passionate clutch, "there is just one thing I'd like you to tell me, no matter what else you mean to keep dark. Did Lieutenant Yehia say he loved me?"

"Oh, yes! That's what all this trouble is about. I told him how to make love to Englishwomen. That means you! Elaine," he said gruffly, "how did you know what had happened? Because you did know, didn't you?

"Answer me, Elaine!" he said repeatedly but in vain as they crossed the moon-struck dunes.

At breakfast time the Cairo radio gave instructions not to believe in rumours but to advance in defence of the Army and in defence of Egypt. Tying on his red sash, Ibrahim, the cook-servant, climbed up from his kitchen to listen to the bulletin and, when it was over, stood smoothing the creases out of his white gown. He was a serious youth with fine features, more like a Spaniard than an Egyptian. "I do not tell you a rumour," he said to the company, "because I know the truth of this matter." His eyes were large with virtue, and his nostrils quivered. "Aly Maher is Prime Minister again. A good man, so, if God wills, all will now be content. This General Naguib is a great man. Now that he is Commander-in-Chief of the Army, the war against the Jews is to begin again. This is not a rumour. Everyone in Alexandria is talking this way. I tell you that Egyptian soldiers will march into Jerusalem and Tel Aviv and Haifa."

Ibrahim paused. "No, what I have said about the Jews, perhaps that is rumour. But Aly Maher is Prime Minister, that is the truth."

When Mr. Dragoumis had translated these remarks for Elaine's benefit, she began to wonder whether the revolution would peter out into respectability; for all she knew, the Egyptians might have a habit of changing their governments with a show of violence. A new Prime Minister would, she guessed, have a program of social reform. Candidly, she would have preferred a revolutionary general with a lot of noble but impractical ideals, and she turned to Eric in the hope he would contradict Ibrahim. After all, was it so foolish to look for colour? She did not believe that Egypt's deepest need was a shake-up that foreign observers could write off as a mere constitutional crisis.

"I hate to tell you this," Eric remarked with relish, "but you'll never get a story worth cabling back to London."

"You mean everything's going to blow over?"

"I mean you're a woman."

He had come to the conclusion, apparently, that Elaine

was justification for quiet laughter. When she and Tim appeared together in the early hours of the morning, Tim unable or unwilling to give an account of his adventure with Yehia and she urging that he ought to go to bed immediately, Eric had exhibited the most extravagant joy and relief. She knew it was mockery. The more the Dragoumises questioned Tim, the greater was Eric's delight. "What did he say? . . . What did he do? . . . Are you quite sure he has not inflicted some injury upon you?" Eric had walked up and down, listening to the questions and Tim's increasingly incoherent and evasive replies. When at last he himself began to speak he said it was perfectly wonderful to see his brother safe and sound; and it was all due to Elaine going out at *just* the right time and going to *just* the right spot. Really! Two people on their first day in Egypt having such strange things happen to them! He implied that Elaine had a keener insight into these happenings than she admitted. It was diverting to witness Tim's confusion and know (he implied) that it was all her fault. She saw Eric's eyes water with laughter. No, it could not possibly be as funny as that.

"What's my being a woman got to do with it?"

"I mean that in a Moslem country like this you wouldn't be taken seriously. They don't take women seriously. They're too realistic."

The gaiety even made Elaine wonder whether Eric was fonder of his brother than he had pretended; perhaps he was expressing relief that Tim was safe in bed, fast asleep, after an adventure more dangerous than she had dreamed. She was suddenly depressed by the weirdness of this new country. How could one be sure that behaviour which at home might be merely amusing or eccentric might not, in Egypt, turn out to be grimly threatening? Fancy Yehia asking advice on love and Englishwomen! And fancy asking Tim, of all people! Instead of being so excited that sleep was impossible, she ought in all probability to have asked the Dragoumises whether they had any firearms she could borrow.

"I thought you were going to help me," she said. She meant to imply that she deserved better than teasing.

"Help! Haven't I done enough?"

"No. It's your responsibility that I'm here, and if anything goes wrong, it'll be all your fault. As for my being a woman and they won't take me seriously, well, there are women journalists in Egypt, aren't there?"

"There may be, though I've never met one."

"Anyway, I'm not Egyptian. I'm English. Do you mean to tell me they wouldn't accept me as a journalist and forget I was a woman?" Her feminist principles stirred from slumber. "Damn it all, I do a good job. Do you mean to say—"

"For example," said Eric, "if a woman rang up a man of affairs here and said she wanted to interview him, he might misunderstand."

"But a woman journalist is like fur coats. Beaver cony is rabbit, not beaver. On duty I'm journalist, not woman. Anything less than that is insulting. Don't you think they'll understand that?"

"That," said Eric, "might be one of the finer flowers of the revolution, if it's a revolution they're having. In any case, it's not had much time to take. For all practical purposes, you'd better assume you're a woman, and don't say I didn't warn you."

Before breakfast Mr. Dragoumis had walked down to the beach and found all quiet. The launch was wedged between the rocks. He had walked to the small general store where, as a concession, they stocked the snuff for which he was the sole customer. He had read the newspapers. Yes, all was quiet. The heat, as usual, was intolerable. There was no seaward horizon but a milky flux no farther out than you could toss a pebble. It was the kind of morning, he said, when more than ever he yearned for the retirement that would allow him to go to Greece and never return. He plucked at his knitted tie and talked once more of the terrible ride at the back of Yehia's jeep. "These things must be known to the world. Perhaps you are right, Eric. Perhaps they will not respect the female voice. Of course, I am ready to phone on Miss Brent's behalf. After all, it is only a matter of eliciting information. Who could do this better than myself? I will phone anyone in the country. I will speak to His Majesty! Now! There is the one to approach. For, you know, I don't believe this revolution will succeed. It is Arabi all over again. I will speak to the King this moment!"

"No, Paulos," said Mrs. Dragoumis. "Oh, no."

"He is a reasonable man. And I? I too am a reasonable man. Why should you cry out against me?" Mr. Dragoumis turned to Elaine. "You can be quite sure your newspaper is receiving the Naguib point of view from the agencies. It is from the palace they will want to hear. I shall telephone His Majesty immediately. After all, I am not nobody. I supply his coffee. I mean," he elaborated, "that even to ordinary people I am not nobody. They do not understand my political philosophy, but still they know I am not nobody."

"Could we telephone the King?" Elaine was struck by Mr. Dragoumis's comment on the agencies; it was almost certainly right. Apparently Naguib and Co. were in control. They would inevitably feed the agencies with the kind of propaganda Yehia had retailed the night before, and what the rest of the world wanted more than anything else was a comment from the King himself. But to *telephone* him! The notion was so absurd she felt sure none of the agency men had thought of it.

"If you telephone the palace," said Eric, "and by some accident you get through, I should like you to remember my warning."

"Then perhaps you'd telephone for me." She was angry and excited at the same time. Why had she not thought of it before? Undoubtedly it was the Palace story the *Sun* would expect her to cover. Hadn't the King children and a new wife? The very least they would expect was an interview with a nursemaid.

"D'you remember the Montazah Palace number?" Eric said to his father-in-law.

Mr. Dragoumis produced a stub of pencil and wrote the number down on the back of an envelope; he remembered numbers visually and it was not until he had written them down he could be sure they were right. The palace number was confidential. It did not appear in the directory and was, therefore, precious information indeed. For many years he had supplied the palace with mocha beans and never, he flattered himself, failed to give anything but complete satisfaction. "Though as a person—I mean as distinct from my being a merchant—it is from my writing that His Majesty chiefly knows me. I am not a monarchist. So much is evident from my work. But not once has he allowed this to interfere with his order. This is a good quality, don't you agree with me?"

Mrs. Dragoumis put her hand to her mouth as Eric went to the telephone. He looked at Elaine quizzically, suddenly aware that the news of his audacity had flashed round the house to such good effect that Ibrahim and the rest of the kitchen staff had come to observe him.

7741

"So it's my responsibility, is it, that you're here?"

"Absolutely!" said Elaine. "What's the matter? Don't they answer?"

At least the line had not been cut. Eric listened to the rhythmic drumming from the palace switchboard; and he stared, barely masking his grin, into the blue expectancy of her eyes. Last night she had apologized for being an almighty nuisance, but now she was different; finding Tim in the dark, sleep, the Cairo radio, breakfast—one of these or all had given her enough kick to be truly the female again. If anything went wrong, she had warned, the responsibility would be his. Responsibility! The very word made him want to act outrageously. When the switchboard operator answered, he decided to announce Elaine as the wife of the British Ambassador.

"*Min?*" The thick Egyptian voice broke into his ear, and momentarily Eric was at a loss. Now that he considered it, establishing contact with the palace did not come within the bounds of possibility. He visualized tanks training their guns on the palace windows, white flags on the end of walking-sticks, and troops up the telegraph poles, cutting wire. A telephone conversation with anyone in Montazah Palace in the middle of a revolution now appeared to be so much out of the question that Eric realized why he had dialled the number so impetuously. The voice said "*Min?*" for a second time, and Eric, quite confident he had a wrong number, looked at Elaine with as little expression as he could manage and said: "Put me through to King Farouk, will you?"

"What can I do for you?" said the voice in quite passable English. "This is the King speaking."

"Look," said Eric, "this isn't a game. I want to speak to the King. Is that Montazah Palace?"

"I am the King," said the voice, "and all I know about

you is that you're an Englishman. Now, if you don't tell me who you are, I shall ring off. Is it the Embassy? What is your business?"

"But—" Eric found he could no longer meet Elaine's gaze. This was not, he decided, a situation he could allow to get out of hand. If he put the receiver down now, he would never know whether it was, in fact, the King he had spoken to. On the other hand, he could allow the conversation to continue and so run the risk of a ribbing from some moronic but quick-witted Alexandrian. Could it *possibly* be the King? Had the revolution made so much progress that he sat alone in the palace working his own switchboard? Once more Eric visualized the tanks and the soldiers up the telegraph poles. But there were no white flags this time. He could see lots of rooms, all deserted except one, and there the King sat, speaking into a telephone, saying: "Perhaps you would like to help me?"

"My name is Charles Dickens." There were, Eric realized, not two but three possibilities. It might be the King, it might be a wrong number, but it was much more likely someone in Naguib's intelligence tapping the Montazah line and sitting, in all probability, comfortably in the Mustapha Pasha Barracks. "My name is Charles Dickens and I've just come ashore from a submarine," said Eric. "But how do I know that this is not a trap? I mean, I've only your word to go on that you're King Farouk."

In the Dragoumis villa there was consternation. The reference to Charles Dickens and the submarine was over the heads of Ibrahim and the kitchen staff, but they immediately understood that Eric was speaking to His Majesty himself; they emitted cries of compassion, for it was well known that the King was shortly to be hanged. Mrs. Dragoumis thought that her son-in-law had gone out of his mind, and was stiff with apprehension. Mr. Dragoumis drew pinches of snuff up his splayed nostrils; he would have walked into his study if his wife had not clutched his sleeve. Only Elaine remained calm; indeed, as Eric soon realized, her state was more than calm. She had fallen into a profound stillness, an abyss of righteousness, like some ancient heroine (Hypatia, say) who had decided on silence as the only answer to scurrilous misrepresentation. For Eric understood perfectly well that, if he *was* speaking to the King, he had not prepared the ground for a press interview.

"And how do I know this is not a trap?" the voice asked. "I have been in radio communication with General Slim commanding British troops in Egypt. He has said nothing of a submarine or of any Mr. Dickens."

"Your Majesty," said Eric, for there was still a slight chance that it might be appropriate, "you must remember that General Slim is a soldier and knows nothing about the sea."

He assumed that by this time the Naguib Air Force would have a plane out looking for the Royal Navy submarine which had been detailed to smuggle King Farouk and all his entourage out of Egypt.

"But if you think," he went on, "that you can't trust me, we'd better ring off and say no more about it, Your Majesty."

"Beast!" said Elaine, emerging from the depths. "You beast! You foul beast!" Quite certain that Eric had been addressing the King of Egypt himself, she was pink with rage over the way in which so wonderful an opportunity had been thrown away. She had taken strength in her abyss of righteousness and now emerged to offer violence. Eric took a punch on the shoulder which was delivered with the kind of downward swing used for sticking stamps on envelopes.

Snatching the telephone—Eric considered it prudent to make no firm resistance—Elaine took refuge behind the mother-of-pearl-studded table where the instrument normally rested and spoke firmly, as she hoped, into the mouthpiece.

"Your Majesty, there is a misunderstanding. I am the Egyptian representative of the London *Sun*. I can give the widest publicity to any statement you care to make. What submarine? There is no submarine. I am a journalist. Yes, I know I'm a woman. What? But I don't see what my age has got to do with it. Eh? Of course I'm young. A personal interview. Oh, Your Majesty, at the palace? *Shut up!*" she hissed at Eric, who was trying to warn her she was speaking to a Naguibite. "You're not going to be at the palace? Well, where shall I come to? What's that?"

Eric depressed the telephone cradle and broke the connection. He judged that the conversation had provided the Naguibite with enough sexual excitement for one morning. Elaine would insist on rushing off to whatever address the fellow cared to give, and Eric could only hope that he had been quick enough to prevent her picking up the place of assignation. He held the cradle down until he judged that the line was cleared. "I suppose," he said, "that's what you'd call a wrong number in more senses than one."

"You cut us off." Elaine held the receiver across her breast, and everyone in the room, Mr. and Mrs. Dragoumis, Eric, Ibrahim and the other servants, could hear it purring like a cat. "I was talking to the King and you cut me off." Her face was set with rage; only the mouth trembled. "What was the number? Tell me at once."

"They were tapping the wires. You don't think you could talk to the King of Egypt like that, do you?"

"What was the number?"

"Elaine, for God's sake, I tell you—"

At that moment a youth in a brown cotton suit with yellow badges on the lapels appeared before the open front door. He had a cable for Miss Brent, and when she read it —"Hundred and fifty pounds to your credit at barclays stop cover harem angle love stop edwards sun"—she made them call a cab to take her into town.

Tim emerged from the bathroom dressed in nylon shirt, khaki shorts, and sandals to eat breakfast off a tray and learn from Ibrahim, who waited on him, that the English lady had left the house in a taxi-cab. She had, it seemed, been alone. Taking her two suitcases, she had departed to a hotel in Alexandria. Ibrahim himself had telephoned no less than six hotels before he had been able to book a room for the lady. No, she had gone by herself. Mr. Eric had wanted to accompany her, but she had been hard, and as a result Mr. Eric had set off for the beach with the idea of taking the launch back to the dock. How long ago was this? Oh, one hour, two hour. Who could say? It was soon after Mr. Eric and the English lady spoke to King Farouk on the telephone.

"Did what?" said Tim.

"Mr. Eric is taking the launch to Montazah for King Farouk. But they will kill him," said Ibrahim firmly. "The Egyptian soldiers will kill Mr. Eric."

Had Tim not already eaten his toast and fried egg, he would have missed breakfast that day. Closely followed by Ibrahim, he rushed down to the Dragoumis apartment. Apparently asleep, Mr. Dragoumis lay back with his linen trousers tight as melons over his splayed-out, bony knees. The eyelids were veined and brown like autumnal leaves, and when they flicked back, the eyes seemed to bulge forward moistly in their sockets. They were fixed on a bouquet of roses which stood, with yellow exclamatory faces, four feet high in the middle of the room, beaded with ostentatious dew. It looked as though it had been put there with a stirrup pump. As Tim stood, held in check by a new anxiety, the dew dripped to the carpet and Mrs. Dragoumis —whom Tim noticed for the first time—gave instructions for Ibrahim to fetch a bowl large enough to contain not only the shell-shaped florist's basket but as much of the overhanging foliage as was possible. And he could fetch some sheets of brown paper too. The bouquet must have contained about eighty blooms. It gave out a hesitant reek, a faint lemony sweetness that Mrs. Dragoumis appeared to find peculiarly disagreeable, for she sat, dumpily erect in her wicker chair, puffing her upper lip so high as almost to seal her nostrils. Tim went and read the card, which stood jeeringly out from the mass of roses.

"To Elaine," it read, "with love from Mahmoud."

So great was the shock that even the thought of his brother being shot by Egyptian soldiers faded from Tim's mind. He blushed with shame. "Flowers," he had said to Yehia as they walked up and down in the moonlight. "Send flowers!" How could he have been so irresponsible? Really, there were times when he despaired of ever becoming sceptical and worldly-wise like Mr. Somerset Maugham.

"I am very glad to say," Mrs. Dragoumis remarked, "that *this* did not come before Miss Brent left. It was brought by a soldier. Of course, *he* didn't come himself! He knew very well what I should have said to him."

Mr. Dragoumis drew a large pinch of snuff up his right nostril and said he could not see where the harm lay.

"Paulos! You say there is no harm when a Moslem sends flowers to a Christian lady?" Her feelings overflowed

from French into Greek, and Tim could follow her no
longer. She made angry gestures at the roses, flexing her
plump wrists. Ibrahim had placed the basket on a large
square of brown paper, which now received the falling drops
of water with plucks as steady as the approach of footsteps.
Tim looked up to discover that the sound *was* footsteps.
Lydia had climbed up from the street, crossed the balcony,
and now placed herself, radiant with pleasure, before the
roses. Her face and arms were stained in the reflected colour,
lemon on the high lights and green in the shadow.

"A man is a man and a woman is a woman," said Mr.
Dragoumis. "These things are evident."

"Oh, Mama! How beautiful they are!" Lydia pounced
on the card. "What a shame that she's gone. They could
easily have cost ten pounds. We must send them after her.
She's only at the Hotel Beau-Soleil. You'll take them, won't
you Tim?"

"Well, I—"

"Disgusting!" said Mrs. Dragoumis. "Are you out of
your mind, Lydia?"

"Don't be so silly, Mama. Of course Tim must take
them. Well, if he won't and you won't and Papa won't, I
shall take them myself!"

"Lydia!"

"I forbid you to talk like that to your mother!"

"Certainly I shall take them myself." Lydia took quiet
pleasure in her defiance and insisted the more as they tried
to oppose her. "These flowers belong to Elaine. Keeping
them here is robbery."

How dearly would Tim have liked to say there was no
intention of keeping the roses, that he himself would see
they were returned to Yehia. Satisfactory as this might be
to Mrs. Dragoumis, there was no doubt at all that such a

gesture would make Lydia contemptuous. Contempt when he wanted respect, if not admiration! No doubt Lydia would admire him if he told the truth, that the flowers were *his* idea. And then what would Mr. Dragoumis say? Worse, what would Mrs. Dragoumis say? Worse still, what would he say to himself? He saw that it was easier to preserve one's self-respect when disgraceful actions were known only to oneself.

"What *is* happening?" Tim tried to sound authoritative and pitch his voice low. It was no good. There was a noticeable squeak. "Why has Elaine gone off like that, and without saying good-bye to me, too? Really, everything is like a nightmare. What's all this about Eric rescuing King Farouk and speaking to him on the telephone?"

"All nonsense," said Mr. Dragoumis. "We tried to telephone the palace for Miss Brent, but there was a spy tapping the line and pretending to be His Majesty. Eric is taking the launch back to Alexandria, that's all. There is no cause for alarm. Personally, I have no doubt that Aly Maher will now quietly negotiate with the British. All will be well. Have no anxiety for Eric. My friend Klingopoulos told me over the telephone there is quiet in the town. Do you think I would let Eric go if there were not quiet?"

"I shall have a taxi, then, and take these roses to the Hotel Beau-Soleil," said Lydia.

"Ibrahim," said Mrs. Dragoumis in Arabic, "take these filthy flowers and throw them on the rubbish heap."

"And even if the town were *not* quiet," declared Mr. Dragoumis, waving Ibrahim away from the roses, "the mind has always its resources. History, for example. You are fresh to Alexandria, Tim. You have been here only a few hours. But no doubt you will understand what it means to me, a Greek and an intellectual, to know that I live on the strip of sand between the sea and Lake Mareotis, where Greeks have been for two and a half millennia! You see what I mean? History puts the individual life in perspective. We do not count. Life is what counts, and civilization!" Mr. Dragoumis began prowling round the room. "Near here are some gardens, not five minutes' walk away."

He stood peering at the roses as though examining them for caterpillars. Apparently satisfied, he thrust a hand into the blooms. "I transact business there from time to time. My friend Klingopoulos has arranged to meet me, and he would be so charmed if you came too. Well, Tim?" Having found a handle of sorts, Mr. Dragoumis was able to lift the roses and move with apparent lethargy but real speed towards the front door, scattering petals and water as he went. "Ariadne, I shall show these roses to Klingopoulos. Well, Tim, what are you waiting for?"

Mr. Dragoumis had taken them by surprise. Tim was the first to reach the veranda, but Lydia and Mrs. Dragoumis were close behind. The roses were already twenty yards or so down the street, a pagoda of yellow that nodded in the blistering sun. Mr. Dragoumis moved to the point where the rising heat set walls and pavement trembling. The roses now were a tongue of flame burning with miraculous clarity from Mr. Dragoumis's right hand, casting no shadow and smokeless.

"Come on, Tim," said Mr. Dragoumis, beginning to cross the road.

"There," said Mrs. Dragoumis. "Klingopoulos will tell your father to throw them into the sea."

Lydia caught Tim by the hand. "Listen carefully," she said. "You must go with my father. If you let him throw those roses away, I shall hate you for ever. It would be wicked!" The sunlight was thrown back, it seemed, by the polished white and brown of her widened eyes. Very deliberately she raised a fold of his flesh between thumb and forefinger and pinched it ferociously. "Bring those roses back to me."

Tim did not catch Mr. Dragoumis until they had reached the entrance to the garden. It was a hotel garden, ornate with flowering shrubs and white-trunked Indian palms. Under the striped umbrellas thick-set men in linen jackets, some wearing tarbooshes, were drinking coffee and smoking. Catching sight of Mr. Dragoumis, one or two raised salutary hands and a spry gentleman in brown-and-white shoes made violent signals from a table. Klingopoulos, no doubt! It was a measure of Tim's confusion that he should be surprised the man really existed. He was a heavy-browed man with no cheeks and wet, voluptuous lips. He ignored Tim. He even ignored the roses, stood up from the table, and began whispering to Mr. Dragoumis when they were still some yards apart. Tim became aware that the same kind of anxious but excited confabulation was going on all over the garden. A hot breeze moved the foliage, and the moving shadows slightly mitigated the heat; but wind and leaves were silent under the susurration of many men communicating across the width of tables and between one group and another.

Mr. Dragoumis set the roses carefully on the grass, ordered coffee, and said to Tim in a normal voice—speaking, of course, in English: "The King has disappeared. Gone from Montazah. Might be in Ras el-Tin. Might be in the Moassat Hospital. He has an apartment there. But, anyway, he's gone from Montazah. I knew that couldn't possibly be the King Eric was speaking to this morning."

Everyone looked at Mr. Dragoumis.

"I am well known here," he said to Tim confidentially.

After some business chat in Greek with Klingopoulos the coffee arrived and Mr. Dragoumis became expansive once more. "My friends," he said in English, "we must not be carried away by the excitements of the moment. I was telling Tim about the Historical Perspective. But it is not only Historical. It is also Philosophical. The King has disappeared. Well? He is not in his palace. Well? There is a revolution. Well? Gentlemen," said Mr. Dragoumis, "the English have almost certainly smuggled him out of Egypt, and it is up to us to reflect on the principles involved."

"What are those roses for?" said Klingopoulos.

"So!" Mr. Dragoumis mused. He looked at Tim and beyond him. "The King has disappeared. And you. One day you will disappear. And me. And Klingopoulos. All the earth will go. We must never forget the scale of things. Oh, if you could only understand this, you would know the secret of the Selectivist mind! It sounds such a platitude, but it isn't. Meditate on scale and dimension. The Universe has no positive Yes and no positive No. Everything is equivocation. These roses, Klingopoulos, are for a lady. They are beautiful."

"Yes," said Klingopoulos, "but what will happen? If you are right and the British have smuggled him out of the country, there will be war! They will put him back by force. Are you listening to me, Paulos?"

"Yes."

They drank coffee and said little for some time. Eventually Mr. Dragoumis sighed and asked Tim what they had better do with the roses. Had they been left in the house, his wife and daughter would, he said, have fought over them. Well, there they were, smouldering against a dark shrub. The petals were opening to reveal sulphurous hearts.

"Lydia said I must bring them back."

"I've been considering the principle involved," said Mr. Dragoumis. "In my view, there is no alternative. We must go to the Hotel Beau-Soleil ourselves and deliver the roses to their rightful owner. Do you agree?"

Remembering that Elaine owed him ten pounds, Tim nodded.

Some minutes later Mr. Dragoumis, Tim, and the roses were in a taxi being driven along the Corniche Road towards Alexandria.

"All those men in the garden," said Mr. Dragoumis. "It is strange to think about them. It is strange that they do not know who I am. Even Klingopoulos does not know. Of course, they know who I *am*. They know my name and where I live. But they don't know who I am in any real sense. I am among them, but they are unaware. They don't know what I *stand for*."

Chapter 4   The King Escapes

$\mathcal{B}$ Y THE time Elaine had established herself in the Hotel Beau-Soleil she had heard the rumour in
so many forms she was sure that all of them embodied the
truth: the King had disappeared during the night from
Montazah Palace. The cab-driver said he had been carried
off by the Americans. The hotel receptionist, when pressed
for a theory, said there was little doubt the King was dead
and the Army was preparing public opinion as gently as
possible. The bank clerk who handed over the hundred and
fifty pounds—he was an Englishman himself and gave her
passport the merest glance when she presented it to establish
her identity—announced it as his opinion that the royal
entourage was hiding in the catacombs of Kom-el-Shogofa.
He had never visited them himself, but he understood they
ran for miles. That was where *he* would make for, the bank
clerk said, if he were the King. If trapped, he would take

poison. The bank clerk was a shrunken young man, but at
the mention of the word "poison" he appeared to fill out
and his eyes became kinder.

What did she do now? That Egyptian fellow on the
telephone had certainly not been King Farouk; the strength
of the rumour was so great that even she had to admit the
voice probably belonged to a Naguibite officer with a sense
of humour. She did not mind being spoofed. She did not
even mind losing her temper with Eric and flying out of the
Dragoumis villa when, as she now realized, she had not the
slightest justification for behaving so badly. But she did
mind the sapping of confidence. At nine o'clock in the
morning she had seen the vision: an exclusive interview in
the harem under the revolutionary guns. Now, two hours
later, the King was gone and she was face to face with her
own journalistic inexperience. What did she do now? Edwards would want something better than mere rumour. She
did not put the problem to the bank clerk in as many words,
but she confessed that she was a journalist quite new to the
country and fluttered before him with calculating uncertainty. He said the best place in Alexandria for news was
the bar of the Hotel Cecil. Yes, it was within walking distance. Look, he'd come to the corner and put her on the
right way; and he was as good as his offer, loping out into
the sunshine with his pinched face cast into utter blackness
by his wide-brimmed hat. Elaine was so grateful she did not
even mind the way he went on about the different kinds of
poison you could buy as easily as cheese if you knew where
to go.

"Well, it's nice to be of service to a fellow country-
woman," he said in parting. "They make a very good John
Collins in the Cecil bar. Or you might try a Manhattan."
He established the impression he would have recommended

cocktails or poison with impartial warmth, and turned back towards his bank with a wave and a badly controlled swagger, diminishing abruptly over the blazing pavements.

Even beer out of a can did little to cheer her up. She disliked the Cecil bar on sight. Her eyes took some time to adjust themselves to the subdued light, and then she saw there were only a handful of people scattered about the basketwork chairs. They were all men and either European or American. Large vanes creaked overhead, and smaller fans peered this way and that among the arrested cataract of bottled alcohol on the other side of the bar counter. There were a potted palm, waiters in tails, pile carpet, and a show of marble. The Cecil bar was, as she ought to have realized sooner, a swagger place to come drinking, and when a tall, yellow-haired woman appeared through some pillars wearing a grey sharkskin suit that must have been cut in Paris Elaine's mind moved naturally from politics to perms. Her sandals and grey slacks would pass muster, she hoped, but after that dip in the sea at Sidi Bishr her hair was a frightful mess. She must have it properly washed and set before giving another thought to missing kings, revolutions, or even—yes, even—Egyptian officers with a thick brush of hair rising straight from the forehead.

"Where's your hairdressing saloon?" she said to the bartender, and within minutes—having bribed heavily to make up for the lack of an appointment—she was lying back in the Hotel Cecil's American-style *salon* being treated to an authoritative flow of rumour from an elderly woman in black who held invisible pins in her mouth. Elaine was happy again. The laving, the rinsing, the setting, the brittle French voice going on and on about the King's escape—oh, why had she not seen before what little consequence the

Egyptian revolution held when measured against the bliss of a hair-do?

She tried not to think about men, but the room was air-conditioned and the cool atmosphere induced her brain to function more normally. Since stepping off the *Tewfikieh* into the Egyptian boiler house she had not really been able to take a grip of herself. Night and day the air was hotter than blood, the threat of violence excited her, she was tipsy with novelty. Sitting in cool comfort for the first time since coming ashore, she felt she had been released from a fever. Men, she thought, men—why are they afraid of me back home? Not so much me, perhaps, but any woman of thirty. Why do the unmarried ones look on any gesture of friend-liness as an attempt to seduce them into marriage? She had seen, as a result of her smile, real panic in a bachelor's eyes. Perhaps he had cause. The reason why Englishmen as a whole had such fear of spinsters, she decided, lay in their respectability. Their thoughts turned with heavy in-evitability to marriage. How unlike the Frenchman! And how unlike the Moslem! Elaine, her mind working on men with as much precision as if she were sitting at home in Hampstead, considered with some joy her entry into a society where men were not sexually respectable but un-afraid and courteous.

"Without doubt," said the *coiffeuse*, "the King under-stands human nature."

"Eh?"

"I said the King understands human nature. This woman, I daresay she'll be in comfortable circumstances for the rest of her life. But perhaps they've shot her, the pigs."

Elaine looked at the woman's reflection in the mirror. "I'm sorry, I've not been really taking in what you said."

She did not know how to say wool-gathering in French. "I've only been in Alexandria a matter of hours, and I don't really know what's going on."

"This woman," said the *coiffeuse*, "must be a regular Delilah."

"What woman?"

"This beautiful woman I've been telling you about. It's one way of making a fortune. She'd be an Italian, without doubt. One of our Italian customers. All the highest class come to this establishment."

"Would you mind," said Elaine, "telling me all over again?"

"At least you knew that the King had escaped with all his family and a fortune in jewels during the night?" Madame spoke with a touch of indignation.

Elaine said yes, this was well known.

Ah! But it seemed that the means of escape were *not* well known. To the certain knowledge of the staff of the Hotel Cecil ladies' hairdressing establishment, His Majesty had, with his own hands, driven a red Cadillac out of the gates of Montazah Palace and down the Corniche Road into Alexandria. The Queen, the children, and the children's English nurse were passengers. And how did they escape so easily when this bolshevik army was supposed to be on guard? Well, it was a beautiful woman, of course. This heroine in the royal cause had diverted the captain of the guard while the royal family went by. A sacrifice like this deserved a statue when the revolution was put down.

"You must understand," said the *coiffeuse*, "that I am a Frenchwoman of France. I am not one of these Levantines. And I tell you that if there had been another beautiful woman to help Louis XVI and Marie Antoinette escape in 1791, the history of Europe would have been different and happier. I," said the pinched lips as Elaine was clapped under the dryer, "would have been proud to lay myself on the royal altar."

Elaine could not fail to be struck by this sonorous language, and she wondered how it would sound when translated into English for use in a press cable; possibly a bit too operatic to slide into the *Sun*. Even if the story turned out to be true, Elaine could not see herself using this phrase to describe the unfortunate woman's stratagem because it implied a great deal more than any journalist could conveniently prove. If, as the *coiffeuse* hinted, the woman had been shot, then all was well. If not, the baroque phraseology might give her good grounds for action in the courts. Elaine realized that she was allowing her excitement to run away with her. The rumour was not a scrap more likely than any of the others she had heard. It drew her more than the others, though. She hoped that the captain of the guard really had been seduced by the beautiful woman, and not only for the opportunity it provided for using the *coiffeuse*'s sonorous phrase.

"Covering the harem angle," as Williams had put it, sounded a much more difficult assignment than when she had thought the King himself was speaking to her on the telephone. It might even turn out to be impossible. The rinse and set had given her such a sense of well-being she could say to herself, walking downstairs: "I'm crazy even to think of tackling this one! I ought to jump back on that boat!" without taking the reflection too seriously. She felt so full of life! A revolution in Egypt? Well, so what? She was there, and she would see it, and what she saw she would write about. She hoped to be on the scene if the King *was* shot, but would not complain if she missed it. Even without the big prizes life was good.

"Well, what is it?" said the voice at her elbow. "Or perhaps you don't drink whisky."

For a moment she did not know the man. The legs came out of the chair with the lengthy angularity of a spider's; they were clad, though, in biscuit-colored slacks, and the arachnid hairiness was exposed only at the ankles, above the collapsed socks. The hand gripping the glass was hairy too. The black fuzz thinned rapidly as the eye came up to the crown of the head; but it burst out fiercely over the eyes. They were eyebrows she had last seen in a pub off Fleet Street, but she sensed that Wyvell Speen of the *Sunday Post* would hate any expression of joyful surprise. He was relaxed and he was drinking.

"Gin and French, then." She took the chair at his side. "And I must say you look comfortable."

"I was equally comfortable," said Wyvell Speen in his wind-in-the-chimney voice, "twelve hours ago in Karachi. But in between there has been a period when I was not comfortable. For example, I have been driven here, from Cairo through the desert, during a sandstorm, with the thermometer at a hundred and ten, by an Egyptian chauffeur in a large Bean motor car. Have you ever heard of a Bean motor car? They went out of production when you were born."

"Don't tell me your name," he said when the gin arrived. He assumed that she knew his. "I never forget a face or a name. Yes, you're that Brent girl. Don't tell me you're working! You're not foreign news! Well, God help the *Sun*. Edwards must be mad. That's his affair. Now, you haven't just blown in from Cairo, you're too spruced up, so you know all about this woman. Have they caught her?"

"What woman?"

"The Englishwoman, of course."

"What Englishwoman?"

"Dammit, there's only one Englishwoman, the one who covered Farouk's break from that palace, what d'you call it? Don't tell me this is news to you, my dear!"

"I've heard the rumour, of course."

"Rumour be damned! Collins, d'you know him? He's the press attaché at the Embassy, and they're down here for the summer. British Embassy! No? Well, Brent, you must be having a hell of a time if you don't know Collins. He's an old friend. Spoke to him on the phone not ten minutes ago, and it's no rumour about this Englishwoman. These bloody revolutionary officers have lodged a complaint at the British Embassy. Can you imagine it? These ferocious Robespierres have rung up the Embassy and said: 'We protest! It is very unfair that your women rape our soldiers.' Of course, she was a British agent. I don't believe these stories about her being on the Palace staff. Have another gin."

Elaine took another gin. For all her thoughts of sexual adventure, she would never be able to lay herself on anyone's altar, as the *coiffeuse* had apparently offered to do, and as this unknown British agent had in fact done. No, it was quite horrid. The kind of sexual honesty she had been considering in the hairdressing saloon would certainly not have permitted the abandon of this awful woman, particularly as British security was not directly imperilled. Only a nympho could have weighed the consequences for the Empire of virtuous inactivity and still gone over the wall after an Egyptian soldier. Either that or she was not English at all.

Wyvell Speen's head had collapsed on to his chest, and whisky trickled from his glass over his trousers. Elaine tried to take the glass from him, but he woke up immediately, swallowed what was left of his drink, and said: "You know, Brent, they might be shooting him at this very minute. Now, that saddens me. I'd be sorry to think they'd do the boy in. Know what I think? I think Mr. Gladstone would have made a good king of Egypt, but I ask you now, how many of us are Mr. Gladstones?" He sighed. "Now, my dear, if I can't buy you another drink, do you mind going away and letting me sleep? No room at the inn, so I sleep here. See you at the press conference."

Elaine noticed, for the first time, that his bags were stacked behind his chair, resplendent with hotel labels from Tokyo to Tucson. Men in enormous hats with coloured bands came through the revolving door. They carried grips, brief-cases, and cameras. Waving his hands in despair, the reception clerk said no, it simply was not possible, there wasn't a spare bed in the hotel. More newspaper men, Americans this time. Some took no for an answer and went straight back out through the door to flare up in apparent incandescence when the sun hit them outside. The rest made for the bar. A gentle, almost soporific vibration, which Elaine at first thought might be the air-conditioning plant, set her empty glass tinkling on the table. Then through the glass panels of the door she saw the passing of an enormous military vehicle of some kind, its caterpillar tracks clanking, the body flushing brown and pink.

"What press conference?" she said when she saw that the tank had made Speen open his eyes.

"Christ! Don't tell me you don't know. Five o'clock at Mustapha Pasha Barracks. Naguib himself is giving it. Daresay they'll show us Farouk's body. And that English-woman's, I wouldn't be surprised. Brent," he said indulgently, "if you're here at four o'clock prompt, I'll take you to the show myself. Don't be late, now."

This time he began to snore.

Some minutes before he heard of Farouk's escape Yehia, tipsy with hunger and happiness, was inspecting the platoon detailed for General Naguib's guard of honour. Having cut breakfast to buy yellow roses, he saw in the troops themselves a flowering of a different kind: the ardent youth of Egypt. They held on to their morning shadows with big brown boots. Shirts and shorts crackled like paper. The reddish sand of the parade ground threw pink light into their swart faces, pink even in the shadow of their British-style steel helmets. Present arms! The drill movements were executed with a sparkle that made him nod with satisfaction. The young peasant faces glowed back at him, and Yehia went along the line, touching the obsolete Lee-Enfields on the breech. My Egyptian flowers of the revolution, he thought, my posy at the feet of the General! A corporal marched them in pursuit of their shadows, and Yehia squinted after them for some minutes before turning under the colonnade. Clay water jars stood sweating in the slight breeze. He caught one by the neck, and the cool, earth-tasting water fell cleanly into the back of his mouth. It occurred to him that no man was entitled to expect greater happiness than he was at that moment experiencing.

Lieutenant Khalil gave him the news through the orderly-room window, and Yehia went immediately to his room. He removed helmet and belt, unbuttoned his jacket, and threw himself face downwards on the iron bedstead. Should he, he thought, kill himself immediately or was there some act of reparation to be made?

The heat and the blackness! There was no air! Yehia lifted his face from the pillow where he had buried it. The fiery morning licked his eyes dry and left them cool. No punishment he could think of was harsh enough. What was death by a firing squad even if (as he would insist) the eyes were left unbandaged? A sudden nothing! They must torture him. They must drive him naked through the desert to a pit of scorpions! A long suffering and a miserable death without honour were the least he could demand. A sympathetic friend, Khalil perhaps, would bring poison that worked slowly and agonizingly. Let them cut the liver from his living body and feed it to the dogs! He imagined the operation and protested: No, no, it is not painful enough! I am a soldier of Egypt and I have failed my country in the hour of destiny! And for a woman! Let all women be cursed, particularly Englishwomen with blue eyes. Surely Allah, in his compassion, would devise a special hell for Yehia; specially hellish!

Yehia stood up and put his cap on. He looked in the mirror to straighten his tie, pressed his shoulders back, walked out of his room and along the veranda to the whitewashed cell where his commanding officer, Colonel Emad el-Dine, was to be found most mornings reading the Cairo papers and smoking Burmese cheroots. The colonel was an intellectual. It was known that he had asked Naguib for the job of press censor after the revolution, and Yehia, even in his present distress, found himself hoping the colonel would not ask one of his favourite General Knowledge questions. What, for example, was the date of the opening of the Suez Canal?

"Sir!" said Yehia, after the colonel had lowered his paper and looked at him over the top of his British Army

issue glasses. "I accept full responsibility and ask to be put
under immediate arrest."

The colonel's eyes were small and dead, like a very old
elephant's; his bulbous face had something of the leaden,
wrinkled texture of elephant hide, and when he threw his
head back in a laugh one expected to see the upswinging
trunk and triangular underlip. He did not, however, laugh
on this occasion. He drew on his cheroot and asked Yehia
what he was talking about. As Yehia spoke, the colonel
watched him out of one unwinking eye, the other being
closed because of cheroot smoke. The one eye did not look
trusting. It appeared to ask questions. What is Yehia's *real*
motive? What are his ambitions? What advantage will *this*
particular confession bring to him? Or me?

"Last night," Yehia said stiffly, "I was showing an
Englishwoman around."

"This is foolishness," said Colonel Emad el-Dine. "No
one holds you responsible for the King's escape. You
weren't on duty last night, for one thing."

"Sir, there is no such thing as 'on duty' or 'off duty'
at a time like this—"

The colonel knocked his tarboosh on to the floor with
the back of his hand. "I tell you you were not on duty!
You leave thinking to people who are supposed to do the
thinking. If anybody has to be punished for this business,
I'll do the choosing, not you! D'you understand? Where
did you meet this woman in the first place?"

Yehia remained at attention. He closed his eyes. On
the seaward side of the barracks, squads were firing practice
machine-gun bursts, and the morning echoed like a vault.
To call Miss Brent "this woman" struck him as inadequate.
For Yehia she had represented a new sense, as distinct as

hearing or vision; at her touch the whole world had been shaken, opening treasure grottoes in the rock.

"In the sea," said Yehia. "She came up from under the water. I saw the sun shining into her face, like brightness in a cloud."

"Ah, poetry! This is no time for figurative language, Yehia. Let us keep a grip of the world as it is. This is a time to make men and to break them. Well, at the time Farouk escaped you were in bed with a woman. What concern is this of mine? You were not on duty. I repeat! You were not on duty! Tell me, lieutenant, this experience of yours. Didn't you like it? Frankly, I've no time for saints. I don't want any under my command. Or poets."

"But—"

"Don't contradict me! You may go! Hold yourself in readiness to accompany me to Government Buildings. I may have to arrest the Prime Minister."

Yehia had been aware even before seeing the colonel that he was disgraced beyond hope of redemption, but it had not occurred to him that the elementary justice of having his disgrace recognized would be denied him. It was a rejection so complete that Yehia staggered as he walked. In the shadow of the armoury a corporal was drilling a squad of recruits, and as Yehia's eyes fell upon them he thought of his happiness when, not more than twenty minutes ago, he himself had been on the square with a squad, musing on yellow roses and the revolution. He had been a young man then. Now he was old. The Egyptian people, in their struggle for constitutional liberties, had cast him aside. Having a superstitious regard for the cleanliness of his uniform, he fished a peasant's *gallabieh* out of a suitcase as soon as he reached his room, changed quickly, and felt a lot easier in his mind when there was no longer any danger of the badges of rank and campaign ribbons being spattered with blood as he shot himself through the mouth.

Farouk had escaped! That was the hard fact! No doubt the escape had been well managed, and even if Yehia had been on the watch instead of charging round Alexandria in a jeep he could not deceive himself into thinking the affair would have turned out differently. That was beside the point. It was beside the point that he was not officially on duty. Farouk and his entourage were safe in Ras el-Tin Palace, which gave directly on to the Eastern Harbour; if a British warship lay in the harbour (almost a certainty!), the royal family were as good as out of the country, loaded with treasure and unpunished for their crimes. That he, an Egyptian patriot, had allowed his mind to be occupied with trivialities at the very moment the royal cars had travelled down the Corniche Road to an insolent immunity from justice was too much to be borne. It was all very well for Emad el-Dine to make obscene jokes, but these lapses had meaning; they were remarked by the discerning eye of Allah.

Yehia sat cross-legged on the floor with his service revolver in his right hand so that the moment the colonel's orderly appeared he could give a last message and shoot himself in front of a reliable witness. The orderly was, however, a long time in coming. The machine gun went on firing practice bursts in the distance; the drill squad tramped up and down; a jeep snorted its way into the shadow under the colonel's office. At times Yehia could even hear the sea, for it lay not more than fifty yards away on the other side of the old cavalry stables. Squatting on the floor with one's back to the wall was a more difficult posture to hold than he had thought. Cramp forced him to stretch out his legs, and the sudden movement brought out a wash of sweat.

The heat was so great that it imposed silence. The machine-gun bursts were the first to fade. There were no more jeeps. Perhaps the corporal had found that the shadow had narrowed too much for him to manœuvre a squad under its protection. Anyway, his voice and their boots were heard no more. The sea was the last to be muted, and still the colonel's orderly did not come. Maybe, thought Yehia, the colonel was not going to arrest the Prime Minister after all.

He awoke to find someone standing between him and the light. Jumping to his feet, he caught the revolver in a fold of his garment and it fell to the floor, where the colonel (for that is who it was) put his foot on it. The colonel understood the situation perfectly. The two men looked into each other's eyes from a distance of eighteen inches. They were alone in the room, and there was no sound but a rustle in the rafters which Yehia knew to be caused by a small lizard who lived there.

"General Naguib has arrived," said the colonel. "He is concerned about the King's escape. He says the revolution has been put in jeopardy; naturally I reported our conversation of earlier this morning. You are under arrest."

The clock over the main gate began striking. The two men waited until the sound had died away. It was noon. The colonel removed his shoes, and Yehia, who was barefoot already, took up a position at his side. The two men were facing towards Mecca, ready to perform their noontide prayers.

To Tim's surprise, Mr. Dragoumis—who had kept silent during their run into town—declined to leave the taxi when they arrived at the Hotel Beau-Soleil. He said that in failing to satisfy Klingopoulos's curiosity about the roses he now realized he had been most unwise; if it became known that he had taken these same roses to a hotel—well, there was no knowing what scandal people would talk, and the fact that he was accompanied by a young man would make their remarks only the more cruel.

"Give the roses to the hall-porter, Tim. I'll sit here in concealment. Then we'll go to my town office and I'll show you some of my pamphlets on world government."

Out on the pavement Tim found the heat and glare so numbing he stopped breathing and closed his eyes. The thought even passed through his head that a fault might have developed in the working of the solar system. Surely there had been nothing like this fiery wrath before! He felt cracks open in his body like dried timber, and moved stiffly up the steps of the hotel; if so much as one of the roses came in contact with him, he would, he felt, flare like a torch. Surely it was all a dream! Having advised his rival to send Elaine flowers, he, Tim Blainey, was now delivering the blasted things in person. Hell! Did he think Elaine was going to admire him for being merely useful? If he was not careful, he would become so self-effacing women might think he had no sex at all.

Once out of the sun, he recovered sufficiently to savour something of the nobility of the sacrifice he was in danger of making. He set the roses carefully on a table and was about to approach the reception desk when he heard someone call his name and turned to find Eric sitting in a basket chair, all ankles, elbows, and sweat-lined grin.

"Well, Tim, my boy! Thought you were sound asleep in bed after your night out." He nodded at the roses. "They must have cost you an awful lot of money. As a matter of fact, she's out somewhere. I suppose it *is* Elaine you're looking for?"

"Out?" Tim felt that the unexpected presence of his

brother was too much to be borne. Reasonably cool and certainly comfortable, he sat eying the roses and lengthening his upper lip like a horse; clearly, he had a lot of questions to ask about them. Tim found that the effort needed to anticipate these questions made him very angry. He would have liked to throw the roses in his brother's face. He would have liked to shout: "Mind your own blasted business!" Instead, he dropped into the chair at Eric's side, opened wide his eyes and mouth in an engaging confession of surprise, and said: "You made me jump! Is everything all right down at the docks? You took the launch back. I wish you'd let me come with you."

Eric nodded. "What I'd like to know is how *you* got here, my boy. There are troops out in the town this morning. If you ask me, the trouble's only just beginning. Not a good start to your holiday, I must say. Expect you wish you'd stayed on the boat and gone to Cyprus. Come to think of it, though, the *Tewfikieh* hasn't sailed yet. Well, as soon as I'd dumped the launch I came up here to see what this idiotic girl is doing. You shouldn't have bought all those roses, though."

"I didn't," said Tim. "They're from that Egyptian."

"How very insular you are." Eric levered himself to his feet and sauntered over to the roses; he examined the label and made a longer upper lip than ever. "That Egyptian indeed! Hasn't it struck you yet that we are surrounded by Egyptians? I want to put a serious question to you, Tim. You must answer me with all the frankness of which I know your nature to be capable."

Eric had brought the roses back with him.

"What question?" said Tim.

"Do you really believe a revolution is taking place in this country?"

"I suppose so. That's what everybody says."

"But you don't really believe it, do you, Tim? D'you know why? Because you haven't read about it in *The Times*."

"Was that your question?"

"Yes."

"You're behaving very oddly, I must say. Didn't you want me to come and stay with you?"

Eric looked up in astonishment, caught his breath, and gave a barking laugh which brought eyes upon him from all corners of the lounge-*cum*-entrance-hall. "Oddly? I'm going to be even odder. My suggestion is that we take Yehia's label off those roses and put one of our own on. To be exact, one that says, quite simply: 'Yours in penitence, Eric Blainey.'"

"No, we can't do that."

"Why not?"

"It's dishonest."

"Tim, Tim, Tim! You haven't explained to me yet how you come to be delivering roses for Yehia. I mean to say, why *you*? I can't say that I altogether like this! After all, you are my brother. Have you no pride?"

"Now look here, Eric—"

"Not only is it degrading, it's dangerous. If Yehia is disappointed, he will say it's all your fault and cut your throat. If he's not disappointed, then matters are even worse. Egyptians being Egyptians and Englishwomen being English, the *affaire* is bound to turn out disastrously and then Elaine will blame you. Who else would there be? Tim, in switching those labels, we should be acting for the greatest happiness of the greatest number. I was very rude to Elaine this morning. These roses will make my peace with her. After all, that's what I've come to this place for, isn't it?"

"You must be drunk."

"Well, then," Eric said with a ring of generosity in his voice, "if you don't want me to put my name by itself, let us put both our names: 'Yours in penitence, Eric and Tim Blainey.'"

"But I've nothing to be penitent about."

"Haven't you, Tim? Are you quite sure? Think!"

Tim knew perfectly well that Eric was indulging his rather childish sense of humour, but this last admonition was disturbing. He had already asked Elaine's forgiveness for instructing Yehia in European courtship, and there was no other reason he could think of for further beating of the breast. The sense of guilt began, however, to take possession of him. Eric seemed so very sure. Conceivably he was harking back to that misunderstanding about disembarkation when Elaine had denied being on a round-trip. Tim felt so vulnerable when his intentions were subjected to critical examination that even when he had nothing to regret (he had been right about Elaine's intentions, hadn't he?—as even Eric must have realized when it was shown she hadn't a visa) he could confess to being in the wrong. What a brute he had been to oversleep and miss saying good-bye to Elaine! And what a prig to think there was anything heroic about bringing Yehia's flowers to her! Penitence, though! But for the advice so foolishly given to Yehia, he could think of no further act for which he would need to ask Elaine's forgiveness.

Unless it was bringing these roses!

What if she said: "I was prepared to overlook the way you advised this Egyptian soldier about me, but what I am not prepared to forgive is the effrontery with which you now appear as his messenger"? Tim saw, with such clarity,

Elaine saying all this, her eyes sharpening up and her cheeks colouring, that his rage with Eric began to cool. Elaine was quite capable of it. She might even slap his face for being so presumptuous.

"Do you really think, Eric," he said, "it would be *right* to substitute a label of our own?"

"Look out! Here she comes." Eric stuck his right hand up in the air and clicked his fingers. Turning his head so sharply that he felt a twinge of pain in the back of his neck, Tim saw Elaine walking towards them, smiling and looking more beautiful than he had remembered her. He could see by the tight way her hair sat on her skull that it had been attended to professionally; it no longer partially concealed her ears. Because of shutters and an effect of curtains the light was touched with amber. Seeing the stain upon her face, Tim realized for the first time its eloquence; in the lips there was even sensuality. Yes, he thought, half rising, she's beautiful and I ought to have switched those tickets without any prompting from Eric. The message should have run: "With love from Tim."

"Just the people I wanted to see!" Elaine spoke briskly. "I'm going to General Naguib's press conference at four o'clock this afternoon, but before then I simply must get some first-hand information about the King and his family. My idea is that we go back to Sidi Bishr and use the launch to go to this new place he's supposed to be hiding."

"Ras el-Tin," said Eric.

"That's right. We passed it coming out of the harbour, didn't we? Well, you could put me off at Ras el-Tin. They're bound to have a jetty or something. Now look, Eric, I know you—"

At this moment she caught sight of the roses, looked

momentarily puzzled and then hesitantly pleased. The pinks in her face gathered strength. The change of role, from efficient journalist to flattered woman, had been forced upon her so unexpectedly there was some muddling of effect. By the time she had sunk into a chair before the roses her lips had, however, lost their firmness, and she sighed audibly.

"Oh, Eric," she said. "My dear, *dear* Eric! You really shouldn't have taken my tantrums so seriously. I didn't really think you were talking to King Farouk. I knew it was all a mistake or a joke or something. But these roses! Oh, you *are* a darling!"

Bending down to smell the roses, she could not, surely, miss the label; it was as big as a post-card. Yet when she stood up, raising her eyebrows and smiling, Tim could not see the label anywhere. It must have got itself thrust down between the blooms; and this meant, he thought, that fate was too strong for them. Every passing second made it more difficult to tell Elaine that the roses were not from Eric. He would have liked to speak, if only to rob Eric of his glory. The thought of Elaine's face, though, when she realized her humiliating mistake kept him silent. She must have been terribly, terribly angry with Eric to assume, at the mere sight of the roses, that he had come to make peace. Tim thought he knew enough about women to realize that an assumption of this kind, if it turned out to be false, would wound deeply. Well, he swore that she would never know. Eric would keep his mouth shut even if he had to— well, what, precisely?

"I didn't know you two had had a row," Tim said.

"Huh!" Eric wagged his head with infuriating complacency. "That's all over now, and we'll say no more about it. Entirely my fault. You were quite right to be cross with me, Elaine, and under the circumstances there was nothing for it but a lot of flowers. No smell, you notice. That's the trouble about Egyptian roses. The thought behind them is none the less tender."

"Shut up!" said Tim.

"Eh?"

"I said shut up!"

"But, Tim, dear, Eric was only—"

"No, Elaine. I'm not jealous. I told him to shut up, and he knows why."

"Look, my dear brother." Eric leaned forward and patted Tim on the knee. "Elaine doesn't want to hear us squabbling. She wants us to do something to help her get a good story for her newspaper. And you sit there, obsessed by this personal vendetta. We are brothers, aren't we? We should love one another. You come here of your own free will, accept my hospitality, and tell me to shut up when I'm in the middle of apologizing to a friend of yours. Very well, then. We'll change the subject, since you don't seem to like it." He turned to Elaine, "I'm sorry I can't ferry you over to Ras el-Tin on the launch. I took it back to the dock this morning. And, of course, now that you're out of the dock, there's no way of getting you in again."

"But I *must* get a story. I must get something unusual and exciting. Is it really impossible to get into the docks again?"

"As a matter of fact, there is a way in," said Eric, "but I'm not sure I ought to tell you."

"Hell!" Tim stopped short as they came out of the hotel some minutes later. "Mr. Dragoumis! I'd forgotten all about him!"

Mr. Dragoumis lay in profound slumber at the back

of the cab. His chin was stuck so firmly into his chest that Tim expected to see a sizable indentation there when the heavy head was raised.

"I've got it! I've dreamed it all!" Mr. Dragoumis leaned forward and gave the sleeping driver a sharp poke between the shoulder blades. "Drive to my office at once! Forty-three Sharia Kismet. Oh, Eric!" His face was large with excitement. "I've had a vision. I must set it down on paper at once. I tell you, it's the answer to everything!"

"When we've dropped the old chap at the office," said Eric, "we'll drive on to the Cosmo Club."

The buildings of the Cosmo Yacht Club had been constructed in the Japanese style by a wealthy lacquer merchant, and when Elaine, Tim, and Eric climbed from their taxi they found themselves looking over a low wall and a patch of scrubby grass to bamboo walls and curved roofs the colour of mulberries. Eric said that the club, of which he was a member, gave up dressing its servants in Japanese costume after Pearl Harbor; the club looked silly enough in the first place, but it looked even sillier now the waiters were rigged out as Ancient Egyptians in belted white shifts and striped Pharaonic wigs. There were a club gondola (genuine, brought from Venice) and a sea-shell-studded grotto where a plaster Neptune spouted sea water out of the top of his head. But, to compensate for all these deficiencies, the club gave directly on to the Grand Harbour and there was no reason why any club member should ever need a dock pass or pay Customs duties. He could be taken off a boat with all the contraband his porters could carry, make straight for the Cosmo Club, discharge cargo into a waiting taxi, and be on the road to Ramleh within a matter of minutes. Certain legal members maintained that the practice had continued so long it was now, by virtue of an obscure law, quite legitimate; others, the literary coterie, believed a privilege had been conferred on the club by Mohamed Ali as part of his plan to revive the fortunes of Alexandria. Whatever the reason, the free access to the Grand Harbour was an anomaly. To avoid comment, most members contrived to disembark their contraband at night.

The moment Elaine, Tim, and Eric entered the club a tall man wearing a uræus circlet over a headcloth appeared in a doorway. Eric introduced him as Abbas Effendi, the club secretary, and they paused to have a conversation with him about revolution and alcohol. Eric provoked anxiety by saying there was a tendency for revolutionaries to have austere, abolitionist natures (Cromwell, for example) and he would not be a bit surprised if one of the first acts of the new government were to close down every bar in the country—particularly the bar of the Cosmo Yacht Club, which was an affront to the Department of Customs and Excise anyway.

Abbas Effendi moaned pathetically. "This is *real* revolution, Mr. Blainey! The bar profits pay my wages! If there is no bar, how am I to be paid?"

"Mark my words, Abbas! Next week you will be thrown into the gutter. Well, anyway, what'll you have now?"

They left the secretary drinking Scotch and ginger beer in the bar and walked down a broad, carpeted corridor, which debouched, it appeared, into the harbour. The club house was creaking like a ship. A wind moaned soporifically in the roof. Ancient Egyptian waiters stood up and sat down as they passed. A pleasing marine reek of salt-rotted timber and bilge oil rose through gaps in the floor boards to indicate they were no longer walking on dry land but were supported by piles. The landing-stage, when they emerged on to it, was deserted. The gondola and a dozen or so expensive-looking sloops shivered on the blaze of water, and only Elaine, protected by dark glasses, could be sure the exclamatory radiance would not bemuse her into the harbour. Eric and Tim wrinkled up their faces like monkeys.

"So far so good," said Eric in a whisper. "No one seems to be watching. Now that the gondola has been fitted with an outboard motor, I suspect you will find no more suitable craft for your purpose."

"Isn't there a proper launch?" asked Tim.

"It's the gondola or nothing. There's a pretty stiff breeze blowing. Now, it's a funny thing about a gondola. Very difficult to handle in a stiff breeze, especially with choppy water. It wouldn't surprise me if you got turned over."

"But aren't you coming too?"

"Certainly not. This is a very dangerous mission. On second thoughts, I don't think you ought to take the gondola, even though it has an outboard motor. When the sentries see a gondola approaching, throwing up a great wake, they're bound to think there's something up. Probably they'd open fire. The best thing is to go in some sort of sailing craft. Tell you what, I'll lend you *Jenny*." He led the way on to a jetty where a number of rough-looking sailing dinghies were moored. "She's local-built," he said, pointing to the one that appeared least seaworthy, "and, in a way of speaking, she almost knows her own way about the harbour. We'll have the sail up in a jiffy."

"Sentries," said Elaine. "Do you think there'll be sentries?"

"If you're not coming with us, Eric, I think you ought not to be so damned alarmist."

"Alarmist? This is a revolution, my boy. Now, look,

I'll hold her steady while you get settled. Sit side by side. That's right. Now unlash those straps over the sail. Fine! See that rope? When you pull on that you'll hoist up the sail, but you'd better wait until I get you pointed out into the harbour before you do that. Let Elaine take the rudder."

Tim had found a paddle. Eric procured a boathook and led the dinghy by the nose round the end of the jetty. "You mustn't think I'm afraid to come with you," he said. "But why should I? It isn't my role. I am a spectator. I will watch you and admire you. When it is all over, you shall have my applause. That is as much as you can reasonably demand. And, what is more," he added, setting his boathook squarely behind *Jenny*'s stern, "I'm a family man. Right, now! Off you go!" He thrust with the boathook. "Haul away there! Now, remember! That's a valuable boat you've got there!"

Tim hauled on his rope. A dirty sail opened like a fan and took a fierce buffet from the wind. Elaine screamed. The little boat turned as though caught in a groove, Tim found his right hand trapped in an evertightening knot, and all the shipping in the harbour swung to the masthead. The keel was being kicked vigorously. Tim shouted with pain, mysteriously the chasm of blue water disappeared, and *Jenny* began to scud. They were travelling at what seemed an alarming rate. Tim freed his hand and noticed Elaine was clinging to the rudder, screaming quietly to herself and staring ahead like a frightened figurehead.

"I thought you knew how to sail this boat!" she shouted.

"Never sailed a boat in my life," he said.

Eric, already reduced to a tiny figure indeed, could be seen waving from the jetty. The sail protected them from the sun, the wind cuffed them about the head with sea smells and town smells (predominantly musty, like ancient camel harness), the water boiled under their bows as if in a kettle.

"But I must say it's rather fun. After all," he said reassuringly, "the principle of the thing's clear enough. It's all a matter of angles. You have to control the angle at which the wind strikes the sail. Like this."

He would have taken the rudder, but Elaine came near to spitting. "Leave it alone! Don't touch it!" Her face was white under the freckles. "Oh, God! I wish I hadn't come! Don't touch it, I say!"

"But we've got to change course. We're going straight into that ship."

They were cutting along at a prodigious rate and the moored cargo ship expanded vigorously; a couple of men leaned over the side with pink faces that inflated like balloons. Unless *Jenny* did change course a point or two, Tim calculated they would ram the ship in the third port-hole from the right. He tried to reason with Elaine, but she appeared to be beyond the reach of words. She had clamped on to the rudder with the tenacity of real terror. Absurd, really, he thought. What if they did go overboard? She could swim, couldn't she? He wedged his feet against the side of the boat and set his weight against Elaine's weight to move the rudder round the notch or two that would permit them to clear the hull which now, rusty and stained with the old vomit from its portholes, swayed above them. Then he saw the anchor cable. If *Jenny* missed the ship itself, she was bound to foul the cable.

Tim thought, too late, of the extreme measure of striking sail. He had no better advice to give Elaine than "Close your eyes!" He kept his own open. By this time he was lying back on the rudder, staring skyward with an exhilarating anticipation of the shock. The hull swung like a massive pendulum in the blue air, and the cable, as though attached to some remote counter-balance, cut off in a different plane. It removed the little red flag from the top of the mast, and when Tim saw that go he knew they were safe. They were through. He heard men shouting down from the ship. Momentarily their voices echoed against the hull, but as the sun burst out again the voices broke under the wind.

"Oh, Tim!" Elaine slowly relaxed her grip on the rudder and dared to open her eyes.

"I've got the hang of it now, you see." Tim decided he could be magnanimous. He would never, never make any reference to her loss of nerve. He would be astonishingly calm. "Now, let me see. I'd almost forgotten what we were out here for. That must be Ras el-Tin Palace straight ahead. That big pink building." The wind, he calculated, was striking the sail at just the right angle. He had mastered the boat, and Elaine knew it! If he had ever been so happy before, he could not remember it; and, what was more, being the realist he was, he doubted whether he would ever be so happy again.

Elaine had lost her straw hat in the excitement. She was in sufficient command of herself to ask Tim for a loan of his handkerchief and to make a cap out of it for the protection of her precious hair-do. When she had slipped the dark glasses back up her nose once more she looked as prim as a penguin; but it was all so much show! Tim knew perfectly well she was ashamed of having lost her nerve and grateful for his presence of mind.

"I wish we'd taken the gondola," she said.

"We went *between* the ship and the anchor cable." He began laughing and wished he could make her laugh too. If it had been possible he would have taken one of her hands, but he dared not release the tiller or the boom stay. "It's just wonderful, being with you," he shouted. "It's the first time we've been alone together since—since—"

"Mind that buoy!" Elaine grabbed the tiller, *Jenny* checked like a horse before a doubtful jump and plunged a couple of points in the wind. Tim eased the little craft back on to course. This was not easy, for Elaine had taken a grip on the tiller once more and he did not care to assert himself too vigorously; to be frank, he had not noticed the buoy, and wondered whether it marked the edge of some channel or a sunken wreck. His excitement was in no way damped, however.

"I've never liked being with anyone as much as I like being with you, Elaine," he cried. "If only we could go on like this, sailing for ever. Hot sun, blue sea, and you. Please don't laugh at me." He did not honestly believe there was any danger of Elaine laughing at him, but he thought the plea might be expected of him. It was common courtesy. "Don't laugh at me, but I do admire you so much. Look, Elaine." He bobbed his head and kissed the back of her hand.

"Oh, God, I wish we'd come in the gondola," she said. "I mean, because of the outboard engine. I wish we'd come in a launch."

Tim sang out of happiness. *Jenny* scudded north. The pink battlements, the severe windows stamped in the sugary façades, the Turkish minaret of cinnamon and chalk, the little green cupola, the terraced palms, and the colonnades of Ras el-Tin wavered above them in the full stare of the sun; the palace smudged the intervening waters with the variegated colours of nougat, confused and broken by the wind and waves. In the shelter of a short breakwater the water was as calm and brilliant as mercury. Here a white sentry-box and an obsolete brass cannon were perfectly reflected. The Egyptian flag flared, as stiff as metal, from its staff. *Jenny* was so near to the royal harbour that Elaine could plainly see the guards in their red breeches and yellow epaulettes gazing curiously in their direction.

She felt Tim's joy like a pain. The helplessness which had descended upon her the moment the boat had felt the wind in its sail now turned to numbness. She would never disembark at that miniature quay, she would never interview the royal nurse, she would never be as happy as Tim. The wording of Edwards's cable recurred to her: "Cover harem angle." How vulgar! Whether it was seasickness or Tim's ostentatious happiness she did not know, but a force was repelling her from the toy landfall which now danced, it seemed, within reaching distance.

"Tim, I want to go back."

"Go back!" He looked down on her in astonishment.

"Turn the boat round! Turn her round, Tim! I've changed my mind. I've got another idea."

"But, Elaine—"

"Turn her round, will you?"

She thrust so suddenly at the tiller that Tim was taken by surprise. *Jenny* turned sharply out of the wind, the boom came round like a baseball bat to catch Tim across the chest and knock him overboard before he could even cry out.

"Tim!" she screamed after him, falling across the tiller to lock it down so firmly the dinghy held on its new course without a tremor. It had turned like a snipe. The southeasterly blew from portside. Once again the speed seemed terrifying. So far as Elaine could judge, the sudden tack was sending her back over pretty much the same course they had come by. She had no inclination to think of Tim. The knowledge that she was in sole charge of this temperamental, elemental, unmechanical craft conferred the calm of the suicide, and she remained as she had fallen, still lying across the tiller, and gazing down into the deep gloss of hypnotically spinning, blue-flushed water.

She was reminded of horses, how they ran away with one and how she hated them for it. A pony she was riding as a child bolted and threw her. *Jenny* flew among the shipping, and Elaine relived her childish fear. How she loathed the forces of nature, particularly when they were used as a means of propulsion! Wind, water, and wild animals (all animals were wild) could not be trusted. She yearned for the security of man-made engines. Armoured cars, for example. Or jeeps. Even jeeps driven very fast in the moonlight.

Lifting her head, she saw *Jenny* was bolting into a moored dredger, which appeared to be clanking all its buckets in alarm. She relaxed the tiller and found *Jenny* responding. They cleared the dredger with ease. After some minutes she was handling the boat quite expertly.

"Overboard!"

"I lost my head."

Jenny, with her sail struck, and the gondola were rocking side by side. Eric had stopped the outboard motor to hear what Elaine was saying.

"You mean he's drowned?"

"Oh, no! I'm sure he's not drowned. We were very near the shore."

"But he can't swim."

"Can't swim? Well, the soldiers would get him out."

"Egyptian soldiers?"

"Eric, he *can* swim."

"I wouldn't know. I never saw him swim. Do you

think you can transfer yourself to this thing? We can pick the dinghy up on the way back."

Ten minutes later the gondola was roaring over the spot where Elaine swore Tim had gone overboard; the red-breeched soldiers were shouting and firing a desultory fusillade of warning shots. The bluish fumes leaked away in the wind.

Eric waved a white handkerchief, but the response was another ragged burst. The comb at the cutwater lost one of its teeth. A couple of holes appeared in the sides of the gondola, one where the bullet entered and the other where it left. As these holes were midway between Elaine and himself, and knowing the glorious soldiers were almost certainly bad marksmen, Eric decided they were shooting to kill.

"There he is!" Elaine suddenly called out. "There's Tim. By that sentry-box. See him?"

Eric turned the gondola sharply to present the smallest possible target, but as soon as the soldiers saw he was in retreat the shooting ceased.

"Damn it all," said Eric as they chugged away from the hostile shore, "I said I was a spectator, didn't I?" His indignation grew. "There's going to be no more of this putting my head into the lion's mouth."

The trams were running quite normally that morning. Klingopoulos gave Mrs. Dragoumis this piece of information when he reported her husband's eccentric behaviour with the yellow roses, and it persuaded her to take action.

"We are on the edge of the abyss," said Klingopoulos, "and he goes into Alexandria with yellow roses."

"You just want to make trouble. That's all you came here for. Go away, Klingopoulos. You should have thrown the roses into the sea, and then there would not have been this misery. Go away. I thought you were my friend, but I shall never trust you again."

Mrs. Dragoumis arrayed herself in white. Her large cheeks, purple with rouge, quivered as she spoke to Lydia about the way one became more sensitive as one grew older. "I am more frightened now than ever I was as a child. I get upset more easily. Existence is becoming too much for me. The horribleness of it all. Roses! Yellow roses from an Egyptian! When you are as old as I am, Lydia, you will know what it means, yellow roses from an Egyptian, and you will be sick in your stomach as I am now."

Dramatic as banners, the purple cheeks went out into the sun under an old-fashioned white toque. Lydia had been ready even before her mother. She did not care why they were going into Alexandria. She was glad to be going out, that was all. If there were any buildings on fire, she would see them. As she disagreed with her mother over the yellow roses, there was even the chance of a quarrel in public.

"How many years has your father had the office in Sharia Kismet? All our married life at least. I've never been there. Can you imagine it? Mr. Dragoumis has an office and his wife has never set foot in it. Well, an arrangement like that might have been all right for our parents. Times have changed altogether now."

There was no good reason for going straight to the office in Sharia Kismet. It would have been more logical to make for the Hotel Beau-Soleil. Alexandria, however, was effervescent. The shop fronts were shuttered, and trucks full of somnolent troops were drawn up in the shadow of tall buildings. A gang of urchins burst out of an alley, screaming with laughter. The blue-breeched police officer who followed them fired his revolver ceremoniously at the sun. Before the tram moved on again, Mrs. Dragoumis and Lydia could listen to the silence created by those two cracks of the whip. Heads appeared at a hundred windows. Yes, there was revolution in the air, and Mrs. Dragoumis, who the day before had dwelt on the chances of loot, rapine, and mob rule, now found herself responding to the crisis with an audacity of her own. Going to Sharia Kismet was as revolutionary an act as anything General Naguib had accomplished.

When Mr. Dragoumis looked up and saw his wife and daughter on the other side of his desk, he was much too excited to realize the revolutionary implications of their visit. He was not even surprised. One is not surprised by intruders who frustrate the expression of an important development in political philosophy. One is angry, and Mr. Dragoumis closed his eyes firmly in the scarcely formulated hope that when he opened them again the threatening vision would have gone.

"Here I am after twenty-five years, Paulos," said Mrs. Dragoumis.

"Quickly!" His right hand appeared from a drawer, cloudy with snuff. He drew the snuff up his nostrils, but excitement and rage robbed him of his customary skill. He sneezed violently. "Out of here, in God's name, woman! And you, Lydia! Go into the next room. The boy will make you some coffee."

Mrs. Dragoumis stood her ground even when he came round the desk at her, sneezing unrestrainedly. Tears stood in his eyes, his moustache was khaki, his outstretched hands might have been groping or exploring. But she did not give way. His behavior was in such contrast to the shamefaced reception she had imagined that she was immediately gathered up in her familiar apocalypse: her life had been wasted, she had been too innocent for the beastliness of this world, and womanhood itself seemed a meaningless perversion. Oh, how glad she was that she had not stayed at home brooding! Paulos was like a man drunk. It was caused by guilt. Where were the roses? How could men so easily reconcile themselves to being animals?

"How can you use such words? 'In God's name,'" she said. "It is not in God's name! How can you mention God?"

"Five minutes!" Mr. Dragoumis raised his voice at them. "That's all I ask. Five minutes! No interruptions for five minutes."

"Why did you mention God?"

"It was a manner of speaking." Before answering, Mr. Dragoumis had paused and looked into his wife's face. He was beginning to recognize the oddity of her presence in this, the rue Kismet office of Dragoumis et Cie., and it had the effect of bringing the details of the office—framed certificates on the wall, the brass knob on the door, the cracked flower vase—into sharp focus. All these details aroused his apprehension. He was ashamed of the shabbiness of his office, but before he could face this unexpected truth he was caught up by speculation. Why had his wife and daughter appeared from nowhere to begin a religious discussion?

"Ariadne!" Only rarely did he address her by her Christian name. The accident that he did so now imposed a gentleness upon him. "I must tell you, my dear one, it is only right, that all these years I have not been honest with you on this matter. But these are times for honesty. Let me put it this way, Ariadne. We have been married a quarter of a century. I have not actually been deceiving you. That is too harsh a word, deceiving."

"Lydia," said her mother, "leave the room at once."

"No! She also must see my candour."

"Very well, Lydia. You think you know what men are because you're so shameless. But listen to your father. He has deceived me for a quarter of a century."

Mr. Dragoumis returned to the dignity of his chair, laid his hands on the desk, and surveyed his wife and daughter with the merry compassion of one who is quite sure he is about to utter something very upsetting.

"I do not believe in God," he said, "I blame myself for not telling you before. Perhaps I should have insisted on you, Lydia, being brought up as an atheist like myself, but I don't go so far as some thinkers. I don't think there's anything damaging about religion."

"Well?" said his wife.

"What d'you mean, 'well'?" He was nettled by the calm reception of his courageous words and could only suppose that Ariadne had been too shocked to make a more sensible comment.

"Is that all?" She was still on her feet, although Lydia had long since subsided into a chair, from where she listened to the conversation with eyes closed. "Go on," said Mrs. Dragoumis. "You were going to confess your wickedness."

"But that's it."

"Oh!"

"What did you expect?"

"Women," said Lydia, still with her eyes closed.

"Women!" Mr. Dragoumis once more plunged his hand into the drawer, grappling for snuff, and as the delicious heat mounted his nostrils the old anger and excitement returned. He had made a great confession, yet

Ariadne failed to recognize its greatness. He had always thought her a religious woman, and her present behaviour disappointed.

"Why are you here?" he demanded. "You walk in and start discussing religion. All right, it is proper for you to be here. I admit as much. But why do you bring up God if you are not interested when I say I do not believe in Him? Really, I am beginning to confess that I do not understand women. What a confession for a philosopher to make on the very day he has made a great step forward in his thinking. Ariadne! And you, Lydia! Listen to your father. In time to come you will be able to tell your children and your grandchildren the day I had my revelation you were with me and I spoke to you about it in the not very nice, not very smart office where I conducted my ordinary business of buying and selling. Think of that!" He paused, with effect. "I had a vision in a taxi. I was given a key, a real golden key, and on it was written the Word. It was *Education!*"

"Paulos," said Mrs. Dragoumis, "I must have a talk with you."

"Education," he went on. "All these years I've been working out my system, and until today I did not understand how my system was to be put into effect. I had not dug deep enough. No wonder Lord Russell was not able to follow me whole-heartedly. He had his reservations. He thought I was a dreamer. So I was. But not now. Selectivism will have its system of spiritual exercises, just like the Roman Church. You understand that, Ariadne? You understand that, Lydia? Spiritual exercises."

"Paulos," said Mrs. Dragoumis. "Where are the yellow roses?"

"Spiritual exercises, so that pupils will see there is not

Yes or No but an infinity of possibilities. The latest developments in European philosophy support me in this:
the sky is endless and the sums beyond counting. If one of
them goes out, the heavens shine less brightly. What yellow
roses?"

"Oh, Papa," said Lydia. "There's Eric's voice! He's
coming up the stairs. Now, don't tell him I'm here, either
of you. I'll hide behind this cupboard. What a surprise he'll
have!"

From the Cosmo Club, Eric telephoned the British
Consulate, and the fellow on duty said that Tim was
probably safer in Ras el-Tin than anywhere else in Alexandria; he would, as a matter of routine, get in touch with
the palace authorities to see what news there was of the
young man, but he hoped they would keep him for a bit.
British subjects ought to be lying low at a time like this,
and he was horrified to hear some of them had been career-
ing round the harbour. There was wind of anti-British rioting. The mob were vigorously pro-Naguib and they believed the British were responsible for the King's escape.
The moral was to keep off the streets!

The Cosmo Club waiters said there certainly were
going to be anti-British demonstrations that afternoon.
They planned to take part themselves. Elaine and Eric
found a wandering taxi and travelled up the Corniche
Road towards Ras el-Tin until they were turned back by
Naguibite troops who had trestles and barbed wire across
the road. The rue Kismet office seemed the obvious place
to make for, and as they slowly chugged south again grinning youths ran into the road, shouting insults and threats.
One of them rapped the window with the handle of a knife,
but the driver produced a whip and lashed at his legs. Eric

explained that the whip was carried in case the taxi broke down and had to be dragged home by a mule.

"I shall never be able to look Tim in the face again," said Elaine. "You really do think those soldiers won't do him any harm, don't you, Eric?"

"He seems to have put them in a thoroughly nasty mood, if you ask me. Wouldn't surprise me if he'd whipped them up a bit. Daresay he was livid, getting his nice clothes wet. 'Shoot 'em down!' Can't you imagine him saying it? 'Sink their boat! Five piastres to the man who brings me that woman's head!' Thoroughly dangerous character, I think he is."

"Oh, shut up, Eric. I'm the dangerous character round here. I've been a beast."

"You're hungry, that's your trouble. We ought to have had a bite at the club. On Thursdays they have *Noisettes de Momie à la Chasseur*."

From the shops of rue Kismet they bought tomatoes, a tin of tuna the size of an elephant's foot, half a dozen pancakes of native bread, butter, and a piece of cream cheese so fresh that it trembled like a jelly as they climbed the stairs to the office. The unexpected apparition of Mrs. Dragoumis, shining in the whiteness of toque and gown but dreadful in the purple of her cheeks, stopped them on the threshold. Her husband, in the background, raising his despairing arms, served to emphasize (too heavily perhaps) the dramatic possibilities of the tableau.

"Roses," he was saying. "What's it got to do with roses? Can't anybody stick to the point of an argument anymore? I was talking about spiritual exercises."

"Boo!" Lydia burst out from behind her cupboard and found it was possible to kiss her husband only by standing on one foot, lifting the other to maintain her balance, and reaching over the bread, the butter, and the quivering cheese. "Oh, it's Elaine! How nice. Did you have those wonderful roses? Don't blush, now! He's *wildly* in love with you. And why shouldn't he be, may I ask?"

Mrs. Dragoumis was so incensed with her daughter that she actually raised her hand for what she plainly intended to be a hard slap on the cheek. Eric, with equal obviousness, misunderstood the gesture and placed the cheese on her palm, where it rested secure only by reason of her deep-seated frugality. She uttered vehement Greek.

"But it's perfectly all right, Mrs. Dragoumis, really it is." Elaine put her tuna and tomatoes on Mr. Dragoumis's desk and wished to make it sweetly clear that Lydia was teasing. "We shall be running off together the first chance you give us."

"You will?" Lydia's eyes were enormous.

"One of the great illusions," said Eric, "is that English-women are without feelings. It only needs the sun to develop them. There's a theory that Cleopatra had British blood. And now there's Elaine. As British as you make 'em. And, for the men, well, think of Byron."

For the first time since her arrival Mrs. Dragoumis sat down. "Running off together!"

"And it isn't true either," said Elaine, "that the English have no sense of humour. So you needn't be cross with Lydia. They were lovely roses, and I understand very well the feeling behind them."

"Roses!" Mr. Dragoumis lifted the tuna from the paper on which he had been working and studied the label mournfully. "The irony of it all! The day I conceive the need for spiritual exercises all people can do is talk of roses. Why is Alexandria known to the world? Because of its philosophers. It was here that Euclid drew diagrams on the sand. And think of Eratosthenes. Now, I am realistically aware of my own importance and I know that my name is not worthy to be mentioned in the same sentence with such as these. But I am not contemptible. Men will talk of me. And this is my day. What do revolutions and wars matter to a philosopher? When Syracuse was taken, Archimedes went on with his mathematics, just as I carry on with my work. First of all I have to break off to discuss religion. And now it is roses!"

"The really important subject is Tim," said Eric. "I'm sorry to have to say he's a prisoner on Ras el-Tin. So far as I can judge, it is entirely Elaine's fault. We are both very upset about it, and that is why we have brought this food. We propose to glut ourselves. Perhaps we shall forget our grief that way. Or perhaps we shall be interrupted, as Archimedes was interrupted. You remember that a Roman soldier came in with a sword."

It is remarkable that everyone—even Mrs. Dragoumis, who looked incredulous at the news of Tim's whereabouts —was able to fulfil Eric's expectations about the food. They were all savagely hungry, though it was not until that moment they realized it. The windows, which were wide open, faced directly on to the Eastern Harbour, and the first of the afternoon breezes came saltily over the viscous blue, purged the office of staleness, and belched through a smaller window on the other side, through an open door, through a corridor, and escaped once more into the parent boiling of air which pressed westward over minarets, flat roofs, and steamers' funnels to Lake Mareotis and the desert. Mr. Dragoumis fell heartily on the tuna sandwiches; Elaine, unaccustomed to the strange bread, had to be shown how it could be filled like an envelope with cream cheese and slices of tomato. So great was their appetite that Mrs.

Dragoumis sent the boy downstairs for garlic sausage and more bread. And as they ate they talked about Tim.

Lydia said she was fond of Tim and hoped he was eating too.

"A prisoner! I cannot understand it," said Mrs. Dragoumis, her eyes filling with tears now that her hunger had been appeased. "No, I cannot believe this story. He fell into the water out of your boat. He is drowned, I know he is! Confess to me frankly now! He is drowned."

"Of course he's not drowned."

"Yes, he is drowned. You drowned him. You did it deliberately. He was a good boy. He had virtue. He ought to have been a priest. Can you deny to me now, as you have hopes of salvation, that you didn't push him out of this boat?"

"Oh, really, Mama," said Lydia in exasperation. "That's the last of the butter and you could see that Elaine still had a piece of bread to eat. Now 'Hamed will have to go down and get some more."

"Push him out of the boat!" They were all sitting round Mr. Dragoumis's desk, treating it like a table, with Elaine at one end and Mrs. Dragoumis at the other. Elaine thought the woman must be going off her head.

With a shrug of acceptance and a softening of the eyes Mrs. Dragoumis intimated her withdrawal from the discussion. She ate the last of her garlic sausage and wiped the crumbs from her mouth. She was reposed, as she was reposed during the closing minutes of Divine service in the Orthodox church when bells rang and the priest in his robes gave the parting blessing; the talk of Good and Evil made her think what helpless creatures we all were, so helpless we could scarcely be held accountable for what we did or didn't do. This Englishwoman had said with a laugh

that she and the Egyptian would be running off together
at the very first chance. If this was not being in the grip
of Evil, what was it? Even the accusation of pushing Tim
into the water left her unmoved. The Englishwoman had
not denied it. Poor, innocent young man! The one crea-
ture, apart from herself, who recognized this abnormal passion for what it was had unaccountably disappeared. Mrs.
Dragoumis had a solemn fear that he would never be seen
again. Dear child, Tim! He had stood between Elaine and
Yehia; now only she, a middle-aged and helpless woman—
only she remained to speak for honour.

"I don't know how you could let him touch you," she
suddenly screamed at Elaine. "I'd as soon think of marry-
ing a crocodile."

"Here!" Mrs. Dragoumis was on her way out of the
room, but Elaine overtook her and laid a hand on her
shoulder. "What *do* you mean? How dare you speak to me
like that?"

"I mean what I say! Take your hand off me!"

"You *wicked* woman."

"*You* wicked woman!"

Elaine dropped her hand. In spite of her anger, she
knew that she could not afford to immerse herself in
trivialities like quarrelling with Mrs. Dragoumis. Now that
she knew Tim was safe, she could not even afford to bother
overmuch about *his* welfare. Here she was, with a hundred
pounds in her bag, on the threshold of the main news page
of the *Sun*, and nothing must be allowed to distract her,
not even the presumed occupants of Ras el-Tin Palace. It
was not, in spite of Edwards's cable, the royal nurse or anybody else in Farouk's entourage she should be interviewing.
That would have been to play her cards all wrong. Everyone knew about the King, but nobody in Europe had any

insight into General Naguib and his companions. As a professional woman, she ought to exploit to the uttermost her friendship with Yehia. This was the consideration that had made her withdraw at the very entrance to the palace harbour, and if she had been tough enough to sacrifice somebody like Tim in the early part of her manœuvre, how much easier it should be to sacrifice herself and her own feelings now she clearly saw the making of her story. By "sacrificing her own feelings" she meant ignoring Mrs. Dragoumis's attack on her character.

"Ariadne!" Mr. Dragoumis had his wife in his arms and was kissing her toque. "Miss Brent, you find us a little distraught! Please forgive us, I beg you. You see for yourself what is in my wife's mind. At any moment the city bursts into flames. Ah, you have to live as one of a minority in a country like Egypt to understand the terrible feelings we have at a time like this. Lydia! See to your mother, why don't you?"

Mrs. Dragoumis blew her nose and pushed her husband away.

"Would to God," she said, "that I had never married, but gone into a nunnery like poor Marie."

"Doesn't mean a word of it." Mr. Dragoumis could assure everyone of this with confidence. "Just distraught!"

The boy brought coffee in. After drinking this the company was more composed, and Eric, who had been sitting with Lydia on his knee in the one armchair the room possessed said: "I suppose there's no doubt about it. Farouk really is in Ras el-Tin?"

"I'm not interested in King Farouk." Elaine allowed herself to speak with a disproportionate vigour; it was a way of releasing the pressure which, in spite of her attempt at professional self-discipline, had been building up inside her.

"I shall have to be going. Naguib is giving a press-conference, and I can't miss that."

"Can I come?" asked Lydia unexpectedly.

"You? But why should you want to do that?"

"I should like to. That's all!"

"Oh, no, I'm sorry." Elaine began to make preparations for departure. "Only press correspondents are admitted. I mean, you've got to be accredited."

Lydia went to her side and linked an arm in hers. "Yes, I am coming. You will do this for me."

Elaine looked into the large, pleading eyes and found herself almost persuaded. After all, what harm would it do? The kid probably didn't see much life. No doubt Alexandria was a dull place normally, and it was easy enough to imagine the boring round of petty tea parties which had to serve as Lydia's social life. Quite apart from the thought of pleasing Lydia, however, was the possibility (which had just occurred to Elaine) that Naguib might speak in Arabic. If Lydia would agree to act as interpreter, her presence would be doubly welcome.

To Elaine's horror, the result of allowing Lydia to come along was that everyone else insisted on coming to the press conference as well. Once Lydia had set her mind on any course of action, it was clear that no one, not even her mother, certainly not Eric, could deflect her. As soon as she announced her intention of going to see Naguib they fell into place behind her. Eric—well, as her husband no doubt he had a right to keep an eye on her. But why Mrs. Dragoumis? The woman was plainly more than a little queer; she said that it was impossible for her to let Lydia out of her sight until the city was calm again. As for Mr. Dragoumis— well, he had a responsibility to look after his wife. If he had been a more resolute philosopher, he would, no doubt, have remained behind and worked out some Selectivist spiritual exercises, but instead he slipped a copy of one of his pamphlets into his pocket, *Federate or Perish*, intending to hand it to the General if only he could fight his way near enough.

"But, please!" Elaine was near weeping. "This is quite impossible. You'll ruin my chances, all of you coming like this."

"But why?" Lydia was amused. "There'll be hundreds of people there. Why shouldn't we come? After all, it's our country, not yours. Of course we're coming."

By way of consolation she whispered to Elaine that her mother's strange behaviour had a simple explanation which, as women themselves, they ought to sympathize with.

"I *can't* take you! They won't let in a party like us."

Lydia laughed and pressed her hand.

"You know," said Eric, "I keep thinking about Tim. I suppose there *is* some foundation for this rumour the King's in Ras el-Tin. Well, I suppose I could ring up and find out."

After making great difficulties Mr. Dragoumis produced the telephone number of Ras el-Tin Palace just as, earlier that morning, he had produced the number of Montazah Palace. The firm of Dragoumis et Cie supplied coffee to both.

"Is that Ras el-Tin Palace?" Eric demanded as soon as he had got through. "Could you tell me, is His Majesty the King in residence?"

Once again he heard the same rich, Egyptian voice, speaking in English, that he had heard from Montazah eight hours before.

"This is His Majesty speaking. What do you want and who are you?"

"Oh, no, I'm not getting mixed up in that again," said Eric, and he put the receiver down with a bang.

Chapter  5 *The Press Conference*

𝒯HE press conference in Mustapha bar-
racks had been arranged before the royal family's escape
from Montazah, and in the changed circumstances General
Naguib must have found more pressing problems on his
hands. Obviously there had to be a press conference of sorts
or the foreign journalists would start spreading silly rumours;
but who could be spared from the serious business of revolution to give it? Colonel Emad el-Dine saw his nomination
as a dizzy advance along the path to the office of chief
censor, and so large-minded did he become at the thought
of his own importance that, hearing an altercation at the
barracks entrance, he permitted the Dragoumis party to attend his press conference, much scandalizing Wyvell Speen,
who had only allowed them all to come along in his 1923
open Bean motor car in the expectation they would be
turned away, so exalting his sense of privilege.

Emad el-Dine had red on his peaked cap and red on his lapels. He came out of the guardroom, where he had been observing the check on incoming journalists, and demanded of no one in particular (speaking English) why these people should not come to the press conference. He would never have behaved in this way if honour had not been so intoxicating. Let all the world come, he said, and when Elaine saw him next he was standing on a platform in a large whitewashed room, saying that he and his fellow officers were not Communists or Moslem Brothers; they were simple soldiers with no thought in their heads but patriotism. Reforms would be made, the enemies of the state would be punished, the Army purged, and a new respect for the constitution established.

"Is it true," said Wyvell Speen, "that the King has escaped from Montazah with the help of a woman?"

The conference was plainly intended for foreign journalists. Emad el-Dine spoke in good English and made gross bids for the sympathy of the three American journalists present by cordial references to the United States Ambassador, Mr. Caffery, who (he said) understood very well that current political acts were an internal matter of concern to Egyptians alone; the British, he implied, were being scarcely restrained from marching on Cairo. But General Naguib was a man of resolution and honour (only then did Elaine realize she was not listening to the General himself), and no imperialist coup would succeed. The Egyptian raised both hands and gave a little skip by way of illustrating the vigour of the New Army.

The afternoon sun flared through the open windows and was reflected so dazzlingly by the walls that the timbers of the high pitched roof—the room had no ceiling—looked floodlit. There was nothing to sit on. The dozen or so jour-

nalists, Mr. Dragoumis, wife, daughter, son-in-law, and
Elaine stood on cobbles which, well scrubbed as they might
have been, gave off an ancient, not displeasing smell which
told that the place had once been a stable. They looked
up at Emad el-Dine's lead-coloured countenance, smelling
the tenuous phantom of horse stale and fodder. Eileen
was still angry she had not managed to come to the conference alone. To have Lydia standing at her side and whispering made her feel unprofessional.

She had a notebook contributed by Eric which was
half filled with jottings and figures to do with coffee-importing. The pen, filled with green ink, came from Mr.
Dragoumis's breast pocket. Lydia divined Elaine's third re-
quirement and offered her left shoulder as writing-desk.
Only Mrs. Dragoumis, standing close and wiping perspira-
tion (or could it be tears?) from her face had no direct
offer of assistance to make. But there was no doubting her
interest. She looked over Elaine's shoulder and read the
words out as Elaine set them down in the large scrawl that
was imposed by the quivering of Lydia's shoulder and the
copious flooding of Mr. Dragoumis's pen.

"Pompous," Mrs. Dragoumis read aloud, weighing
the two syllables heavily.

"Sh!" Elaine covered the writing with one hand and
hissed fiercely.

"Is there any statement about the King?" asked one
of the Americans.

"It will be for His Majesty to make statements about
himself." Emad el-Dine removed his cap and beckoned to
one of the soldiers on duty, who brought him a glass of
water. "His Majesty consults Aly Maher, the new Prime
Minister. This is very satisfactory from the point of view
of the Army. What more can you expect me to say?"

Wyvell Speen returned to his original question. "Did the King escape from Montazah with the help of a woman?"

"Escape?" Emad el-Dine returned the empty glass to the soldier and thanked him ostentatiously. "How should the King wish to escape in his own country?"

"Then the revolution is not directed against King Farouk?"

"It is directed against corruption in the Army and the government."

Wyvell Speen, clearly irritated by this evasiveness, lengthened his neck like a cockerel; without moving an inch he appeared to have advanced on the platform.

"Is it not true," he moaned, struggling as though to force the words past some plug in his throat, "that an officer called Mahmoud Yehia is to be court-martialled?"

"Who?" Elaine's cry was quickly followed by one from Lydia, who had received a jab in the neck and an injection of green ink.

"Shut up, for God's sake, Brent," Wyvell Speen hooted.

Mrs. Dragoumis read steadily from Elaine's notebook: "Heat—liar—"

"Sh!"

For all her numbness, Elaine found that she could move. She made towards Wyvell Speen. "Who did you say?"

"Mahmoud Yehia, if it's all the same to you."

"I know him!"

But that Wyvell Speen should know of Yehia's existence was incredible; since arriving in town that morning he had, to her certain knowledge, spent most of his time soundly sleeping in the entrance hall to the Cecil. He could not have learned about Yehia as a result of special investigation. The implication was obvious: Yehia was being gossiped about. He was in trouble, and every journalist in Alexandria but she knew all about it. Court-martial! Was he a royalist in disguise? Up on the platform Emad el-Dine looked surprised too at the mention of Yehia's name, but there was no comfort to be gained from that. No doubt he was surprised the news had got out. Elaine felt a mantle of heat and knew she was colouring heavily.

"How nice for you," Speen muttered, keeping his eyes fixed on Emad el-Dine but admitting an interest in Elaine's confession by moving his head sideways in her direction, raising an eyebrow, and almost palpably twitching an ear.

Yehia's name, once mentioned, had transferred interest from the platform to the floor. Everyone looked at Elaine —everyone, that is, except the members of her party, who were caught up in speculations of their own. Mrs. Dragoumis gave shuddering sighs and asked for a chair. They were raised to prominence, Elaine particularly, as unmistakably as if the floor had been jacked up beneath their feet. One of the Americans called to Elaine and, when she looked in his direction, set off a flash-bulb that froze everyone bloodless. Elaine clapped on her dark glasses and said to Eric: "Oh, God, I wish I wasn't a journalist," but she gazed at Emad el-Dine with as much fixity as Wyvell Speen himself. The cameras were flashing off like an electric storm. This angered Emad el-Dine, who said they were in military precincts, the country was under martial law, and he would be well within his rights in confiscating the films; he was giving the press conference, and if photographs had to be taken, they ought to be taken of him.

"I was asked a question," he said when he had succeeded in regaining attention, "and the answer to it is yes, Lieutenant Mahmoud Yehia is under arrest. He had a traitorous association with an Englishwoman."

"I deny that absolutely," said Elaine in a loud voice,

to everyone's stupefaction. "I happen to know this officer, and I also happen to know I'm the only Englishwoman he's ever met."

"Did I say English? I'm sorry, I meant Italian." Emad el-Dine was determined that Elaine should not steal the show. For the first time in his life he was giving a press conference, and it was not at all what he had imagined. Anger was giving way to alarm. He really had no authority to be talking about Yehia at all; he had been surprised into discussing the wretched fellow, and if he was not careful these journalists would go off with the wrong story. He smiled at Elaine, signalling his readiness to assign whatever nationality to Yehia's mistress she cared to name provided she would only drop the subject and let him turn to more important matters; but Elaine did not understand the signal.

Italian! That was what the woman in the hairdressing place had said! One of her customers! The full misery of the situation was being revealed. The traitorous association mentioned by this colonel on the platform must have been the one that made possible the King's escape. Her first thought was of timing. What opportunity had there been for the Italian woman to get at Yehia?

"They're polygamists at heart, these Egyptians," Lydia whispered to her, "but of course some women don't mind. It's what you're used to."

"Has the Army any proposals for the reform of the laws affecting land tenure?" asked a serious-minded Swiss journalist who was plainly concerned that the press conference had taken such a frivolous turn.

Emad el-Dine's face, bulbous with pleasure at the introduction of so congenial a topic, produced a confession of the highest social ideals. Speen was disgusted, thrust his notebook back into his pocket, muttered that if there was one subject he could not stand it was the law affecting land tenure, and grabbed Elaine's arm.

"What d'you know about this wog officer, Brent?"

"How dare you call him a wog!"

"It is quite impossible," said Emad el-Dine, "to speak on such important matters when there are interruptions." He looked at Elaine, whose voice had rung out so passionately. "The press conference is over."

He turned heavily, descended some steps, and left the hall by a whining door, working his torso as he went as though he had a delicious itch between the shoulder blades. The journalists did not wait even for the door to close behind him. They gathered round Elaine and the rest of her party, most of them ready to ask questions but some, particularly the Swiss journalist, to make angry remarks: "Why do you behave like a cow kicking over a bucket?" for example, or "Anybody would think you were paid to bitch the job up!"

"Do you mind saying who you are and just what's going on?" said an American with the kind of avuncular geniality that implied he knew the answer already but was hoping public confession would do her a power of good.

Elaine was aware that she was making a fool of herself, but was helpless. No detail would be wasted, trust Wyvell Speen for that! Fleet Street would know of her humiliation; and, through Fleet Street, England. Disgust came to her in waves. First of all, she was disgusted with Mahmoud Yehia for falling victim to that Italian woman (she was sure it was an Italian); then she was disgusted to find herself capable of so much disappointed jealousy; finally, she was disgusted with the profession of journalism. And, of all her disgusts, it was this one alone she could express to the sweat-creased faces that surrounded her.

"Anybody would think you were gossip-writers, not foreign correspondents! All you're interested in is scandal and —and—indecency!"

"Not at all," said the Swiss journalist, still very angry.

"It's your fault," she said to Wyvell Speen, "with your silly questions."

"For the second time, Brent, where did you—?"

"You silly little man," she cried, "if it hadn't been for you, we should have had all that stuff about peasants. That's news!"

"Isn't Yehia news?"

"No, he's of no importance whatsoever. He's a horrible beast."

The anger of the Swiss journalist was a real nuisance to her because she had resolved to cultivate his acquaintance in the hope that, as time passed, her mind would grow like his and allow her to ask questions about peasantry and land reform. Wyvell Speen represented everything in journalism that she despised; it was he, with his childish striving for some personal angle on the news, who had raised Yehia's name in the first place; and for that alone he deserved contempt. The main consideration, though, was to be serious-minded. The Egyptian revolution had to be understood and presented to the world with the right kind of emphasis: the standard of living, the exploited poor, economics—problems like that would require full treatment. In comparison, Yehia and his fate were not of the slightest importance.

Turning to the Swiss journalist, whose stony features had set in an expression of rage, she said: "There are a number of vital statistics I should like to ask you sometime, if you don't mind; expectation of life, cost of bread, that sort of thing."

"Pah!" he said, walking out into the sun. His mouth

was as rectangular as a letter-box, full of teeth. "Pah! Pah!" he said, swinging his head as he went.

Eric had been enjoying the press conference very much so far, and he changed his mind about fetching the Swiss back to apologize; he realized that his prompting had been on behalf of a fellow countrywoman and not a recognizable justice; nationalism, he thought, could be pressed too far.

"Well, I wonder what this chap wants. Come to turn us out, no doubt. Time we went, anyway."

A young Egyptian—he could have been scarcely more than eighteen—dressed in a vaguely military uniform and wearing the insignia of a lieutenant, walked through the loose cluster of journalists, came to halt in front of Elaine, saluted, and said in muffled English: "Please to come with me, lady. Colonel Emad el-Dine will speak with you alone."

"Oh, no," said Mrs. Dragoumis when her husband had translated these words for her benefit. "Alone is not possible. Not possible. How disgusting! I must come too, as chaperone."

As Emad el-Dine sat in his office awaiting Elaine's arrival he spoke to himself gruffly but so quietly that it would have been impossible for anyone else to pick out what he was saying. He was giving himself the verbal congratulation he deserved. The press conference had not been abandoned because of the interruptions; that would have been to act on an obvious cause, and Emad el-Dine distrusted the obvious in all things. As he had picked out the face of that extraordinary Englishwoman in the hall, he had been aware of the beginnings of an idea. An Englishwoman! The mere fact of her being English had been enough to set his brain working. She said she knew Yehia. And Yehia was under arrest for allowing himself to be seduced from duty by an Englishwoman. Or was it an Italian? Without being *quite* sure of his ground, Emad el-Dine thought he was on the verge of a good piece of counter-intelligence.

He was aware that, but for his own intervention at the gate, the Englishwoman and her party might never have been admitted; clearly, a less perceptive man would have turned them away—perhaps this was just what she wanted. Intelligence agents, he knew, disguised their intentions; they told clever lies and, of course, they pleaded for what they did not want. Emad el-Dine was proud to have frustrated her by insisting that they enter the military compound when they were on the point of making off with plans, photographs, and notes of the military preparedness of Mustapha Barracks. He had seen through them at once.

"What is your name, please?" he asked as soon as Elaine and Mrs. Dragoumis were seated and coffee had been served.

"Brent. Elaine Brent. I'm representing the *Sun*." She might well have refused to answer any of his questions if it had not been for the coffee. The unexpected hospitality pleased her.

"How did you come to know Lieutenant Mahmoud Yehia?"

"I knew him very slightly."

"Aaah!" said Mrs. Dragoumis, turning up her eyes. She understood enough English to be shocked by Elaine's duplicity, and handed her emptied cup back to the waiting orderly with breathy sighs that were intended to convey mourning for womanhood. Elaine tried to ignore the rebuke, but felt herself blushing.

"How could I possibly know him? I've only been in the country a few hours. I don't care if I never see him again."

"Worse and worse," said Mrs. Dragoumis in French, and had to be given more coffee.

Emad el-Dine had accepted her presence as normal chaperonage. He had scarcely looked at her until she began sighing, and then he ascribed her behaviour to a very proper fear. The Englishwoman was not afraid of him; he could see that. This Greek woman, though (he knew she was a Greek immediately; there was no need for her even to open her mouth), was frightened.

"And who are you?" he said in Arabic. "Eh?" He would attack where defence was weakest. "What did you say, lady? Don't lie to me, now! I won't have it! You understand that the country is under martial law? You understand what that is, martial law?"

"Don't bully her," said Elaine.

"I do as I please!" Emad el-Dine stood up and shouted. "Answer my question and don't lie. *You* are the Englishwoman who corrupted an Egyptian soldier. Don't you dare lie." He came round the desk, trumpeting, throwing his head back, and glaring at her over his upthrust chin. "You were an agent of Egypt's enemies. Nothing can save you. You are English, but that will not save you. Answer my question! You are the Englishwoman who caught Yehia. He told me. He said your name. And then you come back, seeing what you could see of our military preparations. If Farouk escapes from Egypt, we shall hang you in front of the British Embassy. Do you understand that?"

"You said the woman was Italian." Elaine felt stronger and calmer already.

"It was a way of saying beautiful. Italian women are

more beautiful than Englishwomen; but you are beautiful too."

"Thank you."

"You confess you are the woman? No?" During the interval between uttering the compliment and understanding what he had said, Emad el-Dine was aware that the Englishwoman's manner had softened. He decided to be quick-witted and follow up what was obviously a very clever line. "Certainly you are beautiful." He even stopped shouting. "You, madam," he appealed to Mrs. Dragoumis, "you would say that she was beautiful? Only a lady such as that could —could"—he was at a loss for the word—"succeed with a patriotic officer of the new Egyptian Army. He will be brought in at once."

Orders were given to the coffee orderly, who made off and returned with a corporal. Watching Elaine's face carefully, Emad el-Dine gave further orders in Arabic, a lieutenant appeared at the window wearing a steel helmet, doors opened and were slammed, and Mrs. Dragoumis could be heard saying in her counterfeit French how wrong it was to ask one woman about another woman's beauty.

"*Ce n'est pas naturel,*" she said with horror.

"It is as natural to hang a woman as it is to hang a man." The future censor allowed himself a little humanity. "Do not be afraid. Farouk will not escape. He is surrounded by our tanks. Instead of hanging, we shall give you a long time in prison."

Elaine was sure he was right. The moment Wyvell Speen had mentioned Yehia's name she had known in her heart that if there was a woman in the case, that woman must be she. The beautiful Italian who, in the words of the *coiffeuse*, had laid herself on the royal altar, and Wyvell Speen's mysterious Englishwoman who had covered the

King's break from Montazah, were fantasies based on herself. There *could* be no other woman. Poor Tim could have vouched for that. To Emad el-Dine's surprise, she began laughing and, to her own, she could not stop. She blew her nose, and that did no good. Still giggling, she rummaged through her bag, but there was not another handkerchief to be found and she had to demand one of Mrs. Dragoumis —it was a man-size handkerchief with lace borders—to wipe the tears from her eyes.

She stood up. Happiness made her restless, and she took a few steps towards the window, still laughing and wiping the tears from her eyes. "This is all so silly. Don't take any notice of me, please."

Yehia was the last person she wanted to see while in such a state, but, short of fainting, she could think of no way of avoiding the meeting. She was driven before her emotions as *Jenny* had been driven before the wind. Indeed, it was rather like being out in the harbour once more; or, when a child, riding that horse. The horse, the boat, and the near-hysterical mingling of fear and gaiety rushed her along helplessly—or nearly helplessly. She saw that the Egyptian colonel was standing between her and the window, and was able to restrain the assault upon him that her feelings suddenly dictated. No, she said, stopped laughing, and was serious in a moment.

She promised herself that no journalist would secure an interview with the woman who raised the siege of Montazah; not even Elaine Brent, Egyptian correspondent of the *Sun*. She was living a story she could never write. Yes, her scruples were unprofessional, and she would be thirty-two next birthday!

When she looked up, Yehia was standing in front of her.

Momentarily she did not recognize him. He was wearing a wide-sleeved white gown gathered at the waist by a leather belt; the low neck revealed the coppery chest hair, very thick and shiny. He was barefoot. She was aware of the nakedness of his feet, once she noticed it, to the exclusion of everything else. For the first time she understood that Yehia was in disgrace. She thought they had stripped him of his uniform and made him dress like a peasant. He stood, without speaking, watching her; but she could not have said whether he was pleased or angry. She looked unhappily at his feet and only lifted her gaze when she realized, from the self-conscious wrinkling of the toes, that she was embarrassing him.

He was very calm, she thought, and more like a Roman than ever; a pulse ticked in the muscular neck, the eyes gazed straight ahead, and he carried his upbrushed hair like a helmet. But for the wrinkling of the toes, she might have thought him quite unmoved to see her once more.

"This lady," said Emad el-Dine, "she says that she knows you, Mr. Yehia."

"Why is she here?"

"She says she knows you. Do you know her?"

"I know Miss Brent."

"She is an agent. You know that? You were with her last night when the King and his family escaped?"

"Ah?"

"Don't you understand me? I suggest this is the woman Farouk used to decoy you."

"No," said Yehia. "It was another woman."

He moved towards the colonel, but the two soldiers who had been dozing on their feet two paces in the rear seized him gently by each arm and tethered him to the spot. Yehia made no attempt to fight free. He planted one foot rhetorically forward and addressed Emad el-Dine in a sonorous flow of Arabic which he permitted no one to interrupt; Emad el-Dine opened his mouth, but Yehia spoke the louder. The head and shoulders of the steel-helmeted lieutenant appeared once more at the window. Mrs. Dragoumis, quite unexpectedly, began humming, and the tune was so gay there was no doubt she was calculating an effect.

"See these Egyptians, how they talk," she seemed to be saying. "What beasts they are! Monsters to devour us!" And this was done with no more than a high-pitched, melodious whining.

Yehia shook off his two guards and paused as though to see whether they fell to the ground or not. "I am a ruined man," he said in English. "No one else shall share my ruin. The responsibility is mine."

Elaine was bathed in thankfulness. After so many encounters with the foreignness of Egypt, here she was at last in a situation where a man behaved in a way she understood and admired: Yehia was trying to shield her. It did not matter that, in her own judgement, she stood in no need of protection; Yehia was behaving with nobility. There was little enough nobility in the world, and heroes were out of fashion. All the more important, then, to show Yehia she could measure up to his nobility by refusing to permit him the entire responsibility for the escape of the royal family.

"It's as much my fault as yours, Mahmoud. Don't be silly, now. If you hadn't been showing me round Alexandria—"

"You are *not* the woman."

"I don't believe that for a minute, now. There is no other woman, is there?"

Mahmoud Yehia was silent.

"You know very well there isn't. It's all very well being magnanimous and keeping me out of it, but I'm not a bit afraid of the colonel, and if you ask me, anyway, it's quite absurd to pin the responsibility on to one man. They're making you a scapegoat, that's my opinion."

The expected glow of satisfaction made no appearance on Yehia's face. On the contrary, Elaine's words seemed to outrage him even more than Emad el-Dine's direct insults. He shot a few words of sharp Arabic in the colonel's direction; Emad el-Dine took no notice, though. He had taken refuge behind his desk when Yehia had offered his assault, and he stood there, vaguely of the circus, with head thrown back, triangular lip pendulous, invisible trunk aloft, and eyes bright with self-congratulation. Yehia had silently confessed this was the woman who had seduced him!

"I tell you," said Yehia, "that they are right to arrest me and they will be right to punish me." The words were quiet, but they sounded ferocious; his jaw was set and his eyes glazed with patriotism. He looked at no one. "When the King escaped I was not there to stop him. My place was in the path of his car. Perhaps he would have escaped just the same. Perhaps, if I'd been out with my patrol, he might not have come our way. I might have known nothing. But at least I'd have been there, on duty, watching and waiting. And where was I? I don't know where I was! Walking about in the desert. Perhaps that is what I was doing. Not thinking of my country and the revolution! I will not say what I was thinking of, but I was not thinking of my country and the revolution! Any soldier who doesn't think about the revolution all the time is a traitor."

Elaine knew very well what Yehia had been thinking about instead of his blessed revolution, and she did not allow his present excited manner to confuse the issue.

"Well, you're being very silly, if you ask me, Mahmoud. You're taking too much on yourself. It seems to me you no more failed in your duty than anybody else last night. If you're not careful, you'll be developing into a proper megalomaniac. Anyway, you're certainly no more responsible than I am—"

"You're not a soldier."

"Don't be silly. This is just a matter of finding scapegoats. If you're one, then I'm one too, that's all I've got to say."

She addressed these last remarks to Emad el-Dine, who seemed so pleased she guessed he did not know what scapegoat meant.

"And, what's more," said Elaine, "I'm really very glad indeed that the King and the Queen and the children managed to get away safely. Why shouldn't they? They've got a right to life. If they'd been murdered, I should never have had anything to do with you again!"

Because of her ignorance of English, Mrs. Dragoumis had an incomplete knowledge of what was going on; but clearly Yehia was in disgrace, clearly it was because of his passion for the Englishwoman, and clearly she could not let the occasion pass without telling him what she thought of men who fell prey to sexual passion. She stood up (much to everyone's surprise, for they had forgotten her presence) and addressed Yehia with all the contempt she would naturally have for the fallen. She accused him of carrying the *mademoiselle* into her house—*her* house!—as though she were his bride. At this time of the year, what with the great heat and the boredom, young men and women ought to be separated from one another; boredom was the cause of lust. Of course, there was this revolution going on, and that ought to be enough to take people's minds off their bodies.

But did it? Not at all! In the hottest part of the year sensible people were resting and church-going.

"Oh, really!" said Elaine when the flow of Levantine French had ceased.

But Yehia spoke to Mrs. Dragoumis with courtesy. His French lacked the fluency of his English; indeed, he paused unconscionably, searching for key words, and Elaine would have liked to break in with suggestions; but his gravity deterred her. "Madame, you are—right! This is not—a time for—men—and for—women! It is a time for—people! For —the people! All other thoughts are—wicked—treacherous! May—God—punish me—for my—ignorance."

"This is really beside the point," said Emad el-Dine in a satisfied way. "What interests me is this: a certain officer fails in his duty because of a woman. Now, who is this woman? I say"—he pointed at Elaine—"she is you. I accuse you of being this woman. I also accuse you of being an agent of King Farouk. What is more, I accuse you of being a British spy. Now, what do you say to these charges?"

Elaine walked across and slapped his face, hard. She was thoroughly upset by Yehia's politeness to Mrs. Dragoumis.

Telephoning the Consul again was a disagreeable course of action, but Eric could see nothing for it; in the first place, reporting one's difficulties to an official seemed a tame way of rescuing Elaine. And, what was more, it was undignified. Having confessed to the loss of a brother to King Farouk, Eric did not care to ring up and confess he had lost a woman journalist to the revolutionaries. The official mind, reflecting that all this had happened within a matter of hours, would think him careless. Eric did not wish to be reproved by an official who might subsequently try to cheer him up by making some fatuous remark about Elaine being safer with the Naguibites than wandering the streets of Alexandria. Wasn't something like that said about Tim?

Eric had wanted Lydia and her father to leave the barracks with the journalists. Lydia said no, she was not leaving without him, and Mr. Dragoumis, who had gazed on Emad el-Dine under the impression that he was General Naguib, now understood the truth and refused to move either. He said that the absence of Naguib probably meant he had been overthrown by his fellow conspirators. This was a development that any student of politics would expect. It meant that the situation was more dangerous than ever and he could not possibly leave Mustapha Pasha Barracks unless Ariadne was at his side.

"Then wait here and don't let any strange men engage you in conversation."

The door through which Elaine and his mother-in-law had disappeared was, however, locked, and when Eric went out of the main door to inspect from the outside the part of the building to which he had been denied access, he discovered that it appeared to consist (on the ground floor, anyway) of whitewashed cells in which half-naked soldiers were cleaning officers' kit. The women must be in a room on the other side of the block, and unless Eric went through the locked door, he could not see how he was going to get at them. He returned and hammered on the panels. He shouted. There was no response. Now that the journalists had left, he, Lydia, Mr. Dragoumis, and the batmen seemed to have the barracks to themselves. The door looked flimsy, and in any case Eric did not believe there was a lock in Egypt that would withstand kicking. The correct procedure, experiment revealed, was to drive the foot squarely through the three-ply panel, insert a hand, and turn the key which was to be found in the lock on the other side.

The young officer who had led Elaine and Mrs. Dragoumis away rushed forward, saying: "I saw you break that door, sir. Is that civilized?"

"Where are the two ladies?"

"Sir, they have left. I was on my way to tell you. They left by the colonel's private door and would wait at the tram stop."

"They've left?"

"Yes, it's quicker through the colonel's private door. This damage is very shocking. The door was excellent. If I did not love English thought and literature so much, I should have to arrest you. I am a graduate of the Faculty of Arts. Because of that, I shall explain it away and have some ordinary soldier punished. Go, sir, you and the lady and the old gentleman. I tell you, the other ladies have left the barracks."

"You know, I'm very sorry about that door."

"It's quite all right, sir."

"You're sure you can get some soldier blamed for it?"

"Oh, yes, sir, that will be very easy."

"You won't have to take the blame yourself?"

"No, no, no."

"Then I think," said Eric, "we can leave with a clear conscience."

The Anglophile officer accompanied them to the guard-room. Once outside the gates, they had a clear view of the tramway halt, but Elaine and Mrs. Dragoumis were nowhere to be seen. Eric turned to tackle the Egyptian, but found that he had disappeared. A fat-faced sergeant, black and sweating, stood with a revolver in his fist, and three soldiers with rifles were drawn up behind them. It was the

full guard, and Eric supposed he ought to have been hon-
oured by such a send-off. He was beginning to think how
disgraceful it was that a man with an English education
should have turned out such a liar.

At this moment Wyvell Speen emerged from the profound shadow of the flame trees. "What goes on?" he said.
"Where's Brent?"

"You've not seen her, then?"

"Not since the press conference, if you can call it that.
What goes on? I want to see that girl. D'you mean to say
she's still in there?"

"And my mother-in-law," said Eric. "I expect the pro-
prieties are being observed."

Mr. Dragoumis moved to the single-handed assault of
the guardroom, but the sergeant lifted his revolver and
shouted. Eric took his father-in-law by the arm and led him,
spitting bad Arabic and trembling, over to Speen's open
1923-style yellow automobile.

"And you," he said to Lydia.

"But what goes on?" Speen demanded.

"In return for an exclusive story—'Bewitching English
Woman Journalist Held by Naguib,' we'll tell you as we
go along—you're going to take us to the British Consulate."

"I don't think she's bewitching," said Speen.

The sun was full in their faces. They settled themselves
cautiously on the hot leather upholstery, and the driver—
the same, presumably, who had brought Speen up from
Cairo—pulled his yachting cap over his eyes and drove at
forty miles an hour with no more than ten yards' visibility.

"This must be put on an official basis," said Eric, re-
ferring to the way everyone was being detained one after
another: first Tim and now Elaine and Mrs. Dragoumis.

It was probably only a matter of time before they all found themselves in the clutches of one or other of the several parties to an Egyptian civil war. A war in which there were two sides only was too much to hope for: being Egyptian, the affair would necessarily be complicated. How could the British, for example, keep out of it? There was some likelihood that the Consul, once he had heard their story, would detain them in what he called the safety of the Consulate. Sooner or later a mob would invest the place and the only way of communicating with either Elaine or Tim would be through some neutral power—Switzerland, very likely.

Further ahead than that it was difficult to see. Assuming that Elaine and Tim were not shot out of hand by their respective captors, their fortunes probably depended on the outcome of the struggle for power. In the course of the drive to the Consulate Eric had come round to Wyvell Speen's theory that Elaine was the mysterious Englishwoman being blamed for Farouk's escape. She was, then, in the running for a gold medal and a pension if the revolution was put down; public opinion would demand nothing less. And if Naguib came out on top, the young Englishman discovered in the dungeons of Ras el-Tin might well find himself transformed into a political sympathizer, paraded before journalists for propaganda purposes, and offered a job as adviser to the Ministry of Culture. If the revolution succeeded, Eric felt sure there would be a Ministry of Culture.

Of course, it was more difficult to envisage Elaine's fate if Naguib triumphed; and Tim's if the King rode the storm.

All these reflections made the coming interview with

the Consul seem a trivial preliminary to events promising real interest and entertainment; trivial yet necessary. But so trivial that, after they had forced their way through the mob of British nationals (Maltese and Cypriots mainly) demonstrating for a battleship that would carry them all to safety, Eric felt he had been thwarted over an exasperating detail when he was told by one of the clerks that the Consul himself was on holiday in England.

"But I was speaking to him on the phone this morning."

"Must have been the Acting Vice-Consul, sir." The clerk spoke warily. He was a mild-faced young Greek, whom Mr. Dragoumis at once bombarded in his own language while Lydia translated for her husband's and Wyvell Speen's benefit. Yes, the Consul was away, the Vice-Consul was ill, and the Acting Vice-Consul would probably not be able to help either; he was Mr. Waldo Grimbley, who had been Professor of English at Cairo University until last year when all British officials in government pay (and that included university teachers) had been summarily dismissed as a reprisal for the various British attempts to defend themselves against terrorist attacks in the Canal Zone. Eric had heard of Grimbley, but thought he had left the country with the other dismissed officials. Presumably the fellow had hung on in the hope of winning the job back; and here he was, Acting Vice-Consul in Alexandria, filled with delight, no doubt, at the confusion of the country that had injured him.

"Well, we must see somebody," said Eric. "Grimbley will do."

On the whole, he was glad he had changed his mind about telephoning and decided to come in person. A formality though this reporting to the Consulate might be, nevertheless he was gratified with the greater opportunities for losing his temper that a personal interview would provide.

"This is a complete waste of time." A sullen expression had been developing on Speen's face during the exchanges of mixed Greek and English. "We ought to see the Ambassador. Why don't we go and see the Ambassador? Hell, that's just where I'm off to. That Brent in the hands of the wogs, I can't stand the thought of it. Can you imagine it? I always said the *Sun* was a thoroughly immoral paper, sending a woman on a job like this! I can't stand it, I tell you." And, with head down, he bore through the ranks of Maltese and Cypriots, still talking, plainly upset and not above making a single-handed attack on Mustapha Barracks if the British Ambassador proved as uncooperative as Eric guessed he would have to be. Eric was surprised by Speen. He had not thought him capable of so much emotion.

As they were shown into the office of the Acting Vice-Consul, Eric wondered what significance he ought to read into the clerk's disparaging comment about Grimbley's ability to help them. He decided it was merely an expression of the professional's attitude towards the amateur. For the immediate purpose, Grimbley's amateurishness was invaluable; it might inhibit any contempt he might feel for a man in Eric's unheroic position. "A woman, is it, now you've lost?" he might say. "First it was your brother, now it's a woman. Well, what d'you expect me to do about it, eh?" No, an amateur Acting Vice-Counsul would surely be more sympathetic.

Grimbley was remorselessly beating a bluebottle to death with a fly-whisk which had apparently been the tail of a henna-coloured horse. He had to reverse the whisk and use the wooden handle for the *coup de grace*. Flicking the fly on to the floor, he looked up, saying: "Blainey, which of

you is Blainey? I've heard of you. Now, which branch
of the family is it? There was an Irish branch. I knew the
Gloucester Blaineys. Old Sir Edward."

"I was born in Stoke-on-Trent," said Eric.

"Oh, my God!" He snorted down his big, bony nose.
Shutting his right eye, he turned his head so that his left eye
could peep at the three of them from behind the protection
of this enormous beak. He was clearly confident that he was
observing without being observed. "Well, what d'you want?
Sit down, ma'am. Sit down, all of you. Forgive me for not
getting up. Hope you're not after passages to England. No
time for yellow-bellies."

"Yellow-bellies?" said Mr. Dragoumis.

"Cowards." Grimbley eyed him suspiciously. "You
British? Well, I can't imagine what you're doing here, then!
I can't help you. If it's a dispute with Blainey here, I can't
help you. This country's done away with the capitulations.
Your son-in-law? Why didn't you say so?"

"Cut it out!" said Eric.

"Eh?"

"Cut it out! I don't want to have a row with you about
your manners. I'd much prefer to quarrel with you over
the incompetence with which you will handle the information I am about to place in your hands."

Waldo turned his head abruptly to the right and
brought his rested eye to bear on Eric's face. He seemed
not ill-pleased by the manly tone the conversation had
adopted, and began to fill a pipe with golden, frothing
tobacco which lit up like hay when he put a match to it.
His eyes flashed in the sudden brilliance. "Didn't I speak
to you on the telephone this morning about your brother?"

"This is another matter altogether," said Eric and,
while Waldo emitted more thick smoke than so light a

tobacco appeared capable of, explained how Miss Elaine Brent, a British journalist, an illegal entrant into the country, was in the hands of the Naguibites and probably charged with spying. He thought it best to mention Elaine's lack of a visa. All information that would harass and alarm the unspeakable Grimbley was plainly desirable. But all he did was smoke his pipe and shut his eyes.

"Look, Grimbley, are you taking this in?"

"Eh?"

"D'you understand what I've been telling you?"

"Of course I understand, you fool. Can't you see I'm trying to fit it all in? You won't see it the way I do. You haven't got the official angle on it. But, by God, Blainey," he said, putting his pipe down and spilling hot ash on to his blotting-pad, "I think this is just about the turning of the tide."

Eric thought of the Greek clerk's warning and wondered whether he was justified in wasting any more time.

The blotting-paper began to smoulder. Smoke from the spilled tobacco rose like fumes of incense. A cunning look came into Grimbley's face. "This lady is your wife. This gentleman is your father-in-law. He is Greek. Therefore he admires England. Yes? Good. Then we are all British in sympathy. The news about this English girl is what we have been waiting for. At last we can take vigorous action." He pressed a button, and the Greek clerk appeared. "Get me the British Embassy at once, Georgiou, and tell them it is a matter of national importance. Well, the Consul will be sorry he's in England when he hears about this."

Grimbley was a changed man. His aggressive bad temper had been replaced by geniality. He snuffed out the blotting-paper with the ball of a large thumb and smiled, blushing slightly at the way he was giving way to emotion.

"You see," he said, "we now have an admirable pretext for taking this bloody country over again. Folks back home won't stand for it. English girl a prisoner of the Egyptians. Handled in the right way, this ought to see General Slim back in the Citadel within forty-eight hours."

The clerk returned to say that the Ambassador was not available but one of the secretaries could take a message. Grimbley snorted his impatience. Yes, he would speak to the secretary if no one of any seniority was available; and the clerk was on the point of leaving when Grimbley held up his hairy-backed hand and clicked finger and thumb like castanets. Receiving silence and attention, he spoke slowly. His eyebrows were tremulous with excitement. Burning shreds of tobacco, undetected among the confusion of the desk top, set fire to a piece of newspaper, but Grimbley let it flare. He was speculating with an audacity for which fire seemed a natural concomitant. "Georgiou," he said quietly, and not daring to look his clerk in the face, "we can still get through to the Canal Zone by phone, can't we?"

"I wouldn't if I were you," said Eric.

"What's that?" Grimbley's purpose was not to be shaken so easily. He was grinning like a drunk.

"I wouldn't phone up the British Army, that's all. They wouldn't take any notice of you, and you'd lose your job."

"You think they wouldn't take any notice of me?"

"Why should they? How are they to know you are even what you say you are?"

"Quite right," said Grimbley, dropping some of the hysteria. "We must leave details like that to the Ambassador. All right, Georgiou, I'll speak to the secretary now. Put him through, the silly ass." And as Grimbley spoke to the

Embassy about the Egyptian Army's detention of Elaine
Brent, he extinguished the burning papers on his desk with
judicious splashes of water from a carafe. In addition to
the remote reek of rotting seaweed from the shore, the
electric fan was now stirring a soup of tobacco smoke, the
stink of burnt paper, and the steamy tang of water and
fire in opposition.

"Of course," said Grimbley with a hand over the mouthpiece, "the Embassy is bound to be stupid about this
woman not having a visa."

"Sorry I mentioned it, I'm sure," said Eric.

"It would have been better if you hadn't."

He restored his attention to the Embassy.

Wearing nothing but his still wet underpants, Tim sat
looking at the sheets of ruled paper on which he had been
invited to write his confession while the rest of his clothes,
hanging from an improvised clothes-line tied at one end to
a nail in the wall and at the other to the back of his chair,
dripped salt water on to the stone floor of his cell.

Perhaps "confession" was not quite the right word.

Since watching Elaine and Eric driven off by gunfire
Tim had experienced the most surprisingly varied treatment. To begin with, the guards, having saved him from
drowning, jabbed him vigorously about the torso with their
rifle butts and gave promise of knocking his brains out
when they had worked up to a sufficient pitch of excitement. The arrival of an officer in putty-coloured breeches,
with golden cord and tassels on his green jacket, changed
all that; he beat the soldiers with clenched fists, apologized
to Tim, and took him through an ascending tunnel to a
little courtyard where a fountain played, and another of-

ficer in tassels, sitting at a table, gave him a cigarette and asked if he was correct in assuming their visitor was English and an emissary to His Majesty.

Their expectations disappointed, they stalked away from him, stiff-legged and leisurely like giant birds, and their cigarette smoke hung in the air. The plump man in a pearl-grey suit who now appeared with a soldier in attendance was less polite than the officers, but his English was better. He said that he disbelieved the story about accompanying a journalist, had no confidence in the story that Tim had newly arrived from England, and, as for the claim to being a writer (for in the shock Tim had confessed as much)—well, that was an obvious lie because writers were old men. He made Tim strip to his underpants. The soldier placed the contents of his pockets on the table, and the plump man (who never smiled, but drew his lips into a seam) examined the fountain-pen, the handkerchief, the few coins, the wallet of English and Egyptian banknotes gummed together by sea water, and the little blue diary which contained no entry but Tim's name and home address. The blankness of these pages transformed the seam of lips into a fleshy pout.

"I never write in diaries," Tim explained. "People give them to me, but I never write in them."

"I said you were not a writer."

"I quite see we were wrong to try and land in the palace. But you've really no justification for keeping me prisoner."

"There is no *alternative*." The face lengthened as though over a suppressed yawn. "We are besieged. Anyone going through the gate would be shot. Pick up your clothes."

He slipped the diary into his pocket, clearly intending

to have it tested for invisible ink. "You say you are a writer. Very well. Write something."

Tim saw for the first time the sadness of his interrogator. The tie was slackly knotted, whereas (one felt) it was normally neat as a knuckle. The man even sighed as he waited for Tim's next move. The thick eyelids drooped.

"Do you mean—write something?"

"We'll give you pen and ink and paper. Write me the story of your life. I should be interested in that. There is no hurry."

"Do you really mean—?"

The man in the pearl-grey suit began to look angry.

"You said you were a writer. Well, write!"

Once Tim was convinced the fellow meant what he said and was not enjoying an obscure sneer, it was natural to think of confessions. He was, presumably, a political prisoner of sorts. He was ordered to write. Everyone knew that the only literature composed by political prisoners under duress was a confession. But what, in Tim's case, was there to confess? In spite of the unusual circumstances, he was still capable of a desire to please. Not that he would have written a false confession to cheer up this unhappy man; that would have been dishonourable. But something, surely, could be done to meet a request which, the more he thought of it, seemed only reasonable. Having landed at the palace without authority and made a number of unsupported claims about himself, he was under some obligation to make good those claims. If he were a painter, he could have painted; if a singer, he could have sung; but as a writer the only possible course was the writing of confessions, and Tim was genuinely perplexed that there was nothing to confess. Perhaps he could say he was an anti-monarchist. It was approximately true. Tim felt the stirrings of his incipient republicanism.

With these thoughts passing through his head, Tim found himself in a clean cell, with an improvised clothes-line at his back and a brilliant play of rippling light on the ceiling—harbour water reflected through the one high, barred window.

He had ruled paper, a bottle of ink, a gnawed wooden penholder, and a new steel nib which the man in grey had thoughtfully sucked before withdrawing and locking the door. What more could the artist require? He had the implements of his trade, he had table and chair, freedom from interference, good light, bodily well-being, and an assured reader for whatever he composed. Would that all authors had been able to say as much! All the possibilities of literature rose before him. How best could he, as an artist, confess himself?

He began to make notes. The person he liked least to recall was Mahmoud Yehia. A true confession ought to include an account of his stupid behaviour with Yehia: advising the fellow how to pay court to Elaine and actually delivering the monstrous bouquet of roses on his behalf. The recollection caused Tim so much pain that he realized all thought of a candid confession would have to be abandoned. It made him really miserable. How could one compose and be miserable?

Instead of people, he thought of places. He saw the sea dip and the stars swing down when Yehia took his jeep over a sand dune. Alexandria itself began to glow in his mind. Here he was, sitting on the island of Pharos itself, and the antique city was spread opposite on the African shore.

Tim wrote and saw. He wandered among the stone angels, the cherubs and artificial flowers of the many-walled burial grounds of the city. As he looked, he wrote. Somewhere near here, he thought, Cleopatra had a palace. Over there Alexander himself lay in a coffin of crystal. But where, exactly? And how many metres down? And which mosque or department store sat on the bones of Euclid?

It was, he found, easier to write when he was describing a city he had not actually seen but only guessed at. He had not walked the streets leisurely after dark. But, walking there in imagination, he heard families talking on the balconies. He looked up, yet nobody could be seen. The voices floated down, the warm night brought out the scent of the jasmine, the constellations wheeled and shone.

The High-Ranking Revolutionary Officer said to the Lesser-Ranking Revolutionary Officer: "It is a detail but an important one. You're quite sure we've got the right woman?"

L.R.R.O.: "Yehia is clearly infatuated. He now admits he knew the woman was an illegal immigrant."

H.R.R.O.: "I mean about her being British. First of all, everyone said she was Italian."

L.R.R.O.: "Oh, no, I've seen the passport."

H.R.R.O.: "Well, what do we do? Emad el-Dine is obviously a fool, thinking up a complication like this."

L.R.R.O.: "Yes, sir."

H.R.R.O.: "Slapped his face, did she? I don't like that. I wouldn't say I trusted an officer who had his face slapped by a woman."

L.R.R.O.: "Sir."

H.R.R.O.: "Yes, what is it?"

L.R.R.O.: "I don't quite understand, sir, what you mean by a complication."

H.R.R.O.: "This woman, of course."

L.R.R.O.: "I see, sir."

H.R.R.O.: "Do you know if Emad el-Dine often has his face slapped by a woman?"

L.R.R.O.: "I'm sure this must be the first time."

H.R.R.O.: "Well, what do we do? That's the point."

L.R.R.O.: "Shoot her?"

H.R.R.O.: "I'm not going to have a bloodless revolution spoiled by a woman. Of course, if we decide to kill the King, it's different."

L.R.R.O.: "We must hold our hands, sir."

H.R.R.O.: "Good officer, Yehia. Sorry it had to be Yehia of all people. Not exactly young, either."

L.R.R.O.: "Never trusted him, sir."

H.R.R.O.: "Aha! Jealous? I'll have no quarrelling over women, you understand?"

L.R.R.O.: "But I am not jealous. I would kill this woman with my own hands."

H.R.R.O.: "And Yehia?"

L.R.R.O.: "Certainly."

H.R.R.O.: "I despair of the revolution. Perhaps we ought to pack her off to Cairo." After some thought: "No, I have a better idea. If you don't want your face slapped, listen, and listen carefully."

*W*HEN an official account of the revolution came to be written it was learned that the Liberation Movement made no decision about the King's execution until the early hours of July 26. This was the night Eric Blainey, Lydia, Mr. Dragoumis, and Waldo Grimbley slept on the British Ambassador's veranda. As no one—not even the Second Secretary, who had obligingly fed them with the rumour and speculation which passed for news on that extraordinary evening—could remain awake after two a.m., mattresses were brought on to the veranda and the not particularly welcome guests stretched out in their day clothes and listened to the guards rustling about the dim garden below. Even Waldo Grimbley would have been asleep when, at five a.m., the last of the Naguibite tanks and armoured cars arrived from Cairo and formed up before the royal palaces of Montazah and Ras el-Tin.

Breakfast time brought the news that the two palaces had fallen. At Montazah, it seemed, the Royal Guards had surrendered after firing a few token volleys into the air, but at Ras el-Tin there had been shooting in earnest. Later General Naguib blamed it on an over-zealous officer; instead of doing what he was told, this officer had, it was said, raced ahead of the armoured car that was to have provided him with cover and so frightened the Royal Guards that they opened fire with a machine gun. The Naguibites replied. After six men had been wounded, including the officer, the Royal Guards decided to surrender. This was the end of the Battle of Ras el-Tin. King Farouk was at the mercy of the revolution.

But, from the British point of view, the most surprising aspect of this final stage of the *coup d'état* was not so much the ease with which it was carried out or the forbearance of the revolutionaries when presented with such an opportunity for loot and massacre; the really notable revelation concerned an English woman journalist called Elaine Brent and her chaperone, Ariadne Dragoumis. These two women, one a British subject and the other the mother of a British subject, were reported safe in the *haramlik* of Ras el-Tin Palace when it had been supposed they were prisoners of the Naguibites. No, even this was not the full extraordinary truth. The two women were known to be in the *haramlik* before the Naguibite troops had even formed up for their final assault on the palace. In some mysterious way they had passed from the revolutionary side to the royal precincts *before* the shooting began. It was even said they had played some part in bringing about the capitulation.

"Very clever," Grimbley was heard to say. "Just what I should have expected."

He failed, of course, in his attempt to persuade the Embassy that Elaine Brent's detention was an excellent pretext for General Slim to march on Cairo. When he, Eric, Lydia, and Mr. Dragoumis arrived at the summer residence of the British Ambassador on the eve of the dethronement, they found that His Excellency was in England on leave and that the staff were having a party in the garden because it was the birthday of the Oriental Secretary's secretary.

"I'm sorry about this," said the Second Secretary after he had tried and failed to telephone Mustapha Barracks. "But I don't suppose they'll come to much harm. Women, you know. Courteous to women, and all that sort of thing." He was about thirty, smiling and neat in his linen suit. "I don't think you ought to be out in the streets tonight. Why not join our party? Harriet says there are going to be charades."

"What about my brother?" said Eric. "He's in Ras el-Tin."

"Quite impossible to telephone either of the royal palaces. The lines have been switched—to Mustapha Barracks, I suppose. Anyway, there's a chap there who says he's King Farouk if you ring up. All a trap, of course. Very clever."

"D'you mean to say you're not going to do anything?" demanded Grimbley.

"What is there to do?"

"Don't you understand? This English girl, those bastards have actually got their clutches on her. Now don't tell me—"

"There is nothing at all we can do," said the Second Secretary firmly. "All I hope is that King Farouk doesn't present himself at the Embassy gates and ask for sanctuary.

Then I *should* be cross. That would mean real trouble. We couldn't possibly hand him over to Naguib. For Naguib the situation would be equally intolerable. We should have to fight it out. Let's hope it doesn't come to that. No, on the whole, I should say this revolution is just what Egypt needs. Naguib's a decent chap, from what one hears. Let's go down into the garden, shall we? We could all do with a drink. I know I could. Those must be Martinis on that tray."

A high wall surrounded the garden of the summer Embassy, so high that the top was masked by trees. When darkness came the wall disappeared. It was merely an opacity beyond the tree trunks, and as servants went round lighting lanterns, many of them scattered along the wall itself, the opacity was broken by sparks just as the sky was being broken by stars. Beyond the trees the lanterned wall might have been continuous with the sky—might have *been* the sky—and the garden huge as a forest. A high-shouldered tent, gay as a fortune-teller's booth, stood under a palm tree. The guests, about a score of them, were sitting at tables or standing in groups, cherishing glasses, laughing.

"I don't feel dressed for an occasion like this," said Eric.

"My dear fellow, we're a fairly unconventional lot. Let me introduce you. This is Harriet. Oh, yes, and Tom Waters. It's his birthday. His party. Oh, now, dammit! What did you say your name was? Mr. and Mrs. Blainey, who've dropped in. You don't mind?"

The Second Secretary pursued Mr. Dragoumis and Grimbley, apparently to ask what their names were too, but they had run into Wyvell Speen, who was standing with one foot on a chair, his trouser leg up, scratching his calf and fulminating against the British Ambassador for being in England when an Englishwoman was in the hands of these foreigners here in Alexandria.

"I agree," said Grimbley, though not very cordially because it irritated him that a journalist should show more zeal than he did himself. "Though I daresay he's heard of it by now. He'll be on his way back."

A heavy explosion from the direction of Alexandria blunted the conversation only momentarily. Mr. Dragoumis said he was reminded of Lord Lytton's novel *The Last Days of Pompeii*, and the Second Secretary, quick to agree, said yes, the heat was intolerable but they were in the best place, out in the garden, taking the evening air. A portable gramophone coughed a wiry tango into the pool of voices. A couple danced, and Eric, who had taken two Martinis in the hope of forming a better opinion of himself, noticed that the woman was Lydia.

He put his glass down and stared. One moment she had been at his side, and the next she was out there dancing with the Oriental Secretary's secretary! What was his name? Waters. Tom Waters. A handsome young man with fair hair that looked pink in the lantern light. They were enjoying themselves. Lydia's face was bright with happiness.

"We are living through history," said Mr. Dragoumis. "Make no mistake, this evening the fate of a nation is being decided. And yet we are concerned with personal matters. Even I am thinking of my wife. Oh, yes, reason tells me she will come to no harm, but I am human, after all. Even philosophers are human. I expect you would like to know," he said to the Second Secretary, "that I am a political philosopher."

Eric took another Martini from a passing tray and carried it out of the range of his father-in-law's voice but to a point where he could watch Lydia dancing. He liked to see her happy, he told himself. The more happiness in the world, the better. A girl like Lydia ought to be dancing and laughing all the time.

He sat on the steps before the Ambassadorial study, sipping his Martini and watching. When the dance came to an end he could see Lydia looking round for him as she clapped. Young Waters turned the record over and they were away into duskiness again, dancing with the gaiety of children. Eric tried to think of them as children. He tried to think of his brother and he tried to think of Elaine. But he had no success. Other couples were dancing now, and a woman in some sort of fancy dress had come out of the tent and was making a speech, trying to persuade everyone to join in a game. Eric did not know how long he sat on the steps—long enough, though, to see the woman in fancy dress (it must have been Harriet) begin her charades. All the dancers did not join in. Lydia and young Waters went on dancing. It was a strain watching them because, although the lanterns brightened as the glow faded from the sky, the shadows became all the darker.

Well, at least she's not worrying about her mother, he thought.

A telephone began ringing in the room behind him. No one came to answer it, and the persistent throb began to irritate. Eric knew it was the Ambassador's office because the Second Secretary had said so. The call, then, ought to be of some importance; but still no one came, and Eric, having lost sight of Lydia and Waters, peered about for them with a sense that he would find them the quicker if only that damned ringing would stop. Where had they disappeared to? Her father was still talking to the Second Secretary, Grimbley and Speen were tramping up and down making speeches to each other, but Lydia was hidden by the tent, presumably, or away in the extensive forest the garden now seemed to have become.

It's his birthday, thought Eric, and soon he'll be as old as me.

Putting his empty glass carefully on the step, he made his way to the Ambassadorial window. It was wide open. All the study lights were burning. The enormous desk bore nothing but two empty trays, a green blotter, and this throbbing telephone. He would count ten, he thought, and if no one came or the ringing did not stop he would have to silence it himself. After the darkness of the garden the brilliance of this mock-Regency room was a little stupefying; he could see the blue walls and a dance of plaster swags lit up like a stage set.

"Nine, ten." He spoke the words aloud. Once he had stepped over the sill, he must, from the garden, have appeared as conspicuous as a shopwalker in a window display. At any moment he expected to hear the pad of the Second Secretary's feet.

"Yes," he said angrily, picking up the receiver and easing himself into the Ambassador's chair. "Who is it?"

"To speak to the Ambassador personally," said a switchboard operator. "Will you take it, Mr. Thomas? He says it's an official communication from General Naguib."

"You've been ringing a long time." If Thomas was the Second Secretary, he was not flattered that their voices had been confused.

"The man says it's important."

"But doesn't he understand we're having a birthday party? Has he no sense of proportion? O.K. Put him on."

So this is what it feels like, Eric thought, to be British

Ambassador to Egypt. He stretched his legs out comfortably and gazed through the open window at the lozenges of light moving up and down a palm frond. As he waited for the call to come through he wondered who Lydia's young man, Tom Waters, reminded him of. That pale hair! Those almost chubby cheeks!

"No, this is not the British Ambassador," he said to the familiar voice that now buzzed in his right ear. "And if you claim to be King Farouk, I shan't believe you."

It was the same deep, throaty Egyptian voice that had greeted him from the palaces of Ras el-Tin and Montazah, and he would have replaced the receiver immediately had he not thought his presence in the Ambassadorial chair demanded courtesy, or at least a polite curiosity. For the first time in their exchanges the Egyptian was at a disadvantage; there was no limit to the identity Eric could lay claim to, from Officer in Command, British Troops in Egypt, downwards, if he so pleased.

"Is that Sir Ralph Stevenson?"

"Don't be absurd," said Eric. "Who are you, anyway? I mean, who are you this time?"

"I have a communication for the British Ambassador from General Naguib and must be assured that you are authorized to accept it." Without waiting for this assurance, the voice went on to say that the Liberation Movement accepted full responsibility for the safety and welfare of all British residents in Egypt. They were not to fear for their property. Any rumours to the contrary were unjustified.

"Is that all you telephoned for?"

"It is most important. All British residents need have no fear."

"Is the King still alive?"

"There is no more to be said."

"That stuff about British nationals, that was your communication from General Naguib?"

"That is all the message."

"Now I've got one for you and the General. Are you ready to take it? Right! You have in your custody an Englishwoman called Elaine Brent and a Greek woman called Mrs. Dragoumis. Got those names? Brent and Dragoumis. Well, here is an ultimatum! If they are not released by midnight, we shall—" Eric paused to consider an appropriate menace; it had to sound convincingly official. "Are you listening? We shall take vigorous action!"

The Egyptian brooded for such a length of time that Eric would have thought he had rung off had his breathing not been audible.

"What vigorous action?" he asked eventually.

"Never you mind, blast you."

What sounded like a powerful steam locomotive began to pull out of a station, and by the time Eric had followed it in his mind's eye to the end of the platform he realized the Egyptian was laughing. Eric continued to think of him as a locomotive gathering speed and, when he was well out in open country, began whistling to himself. The laughter ceased abruptly.

"Vigorous action!" said the Egyptian derisively.

"In other words, we'll come and get them!"

The receiver began to emit locomotive noises once more, and Eric dropped it neatly on to its cradle. Looking towards the window, he saw the long-jawed visage of an anxious Second Secretary gazing in on him. So distraught was the expression on his face, he might have been hanging by the neck.

"What are you doing in there, Blainey? Quite out of order. Whom were you talking to? Whom are you going to get? Good heavens, you must have actually climbed in through the window! I can see your footmarks. Well, what is your explanation?"

"Is your name Thomas?"

"Yes."

"Well, Thomas, to hell with all liberal ideas, I say."

"If you don't come out of that room—"

"Down with self-determination! No votes for women! Three cheers for the British Empire! You'll join me in three cheers for the Empire, Thomas? *Them*, if you want to know, Thomas, was a friend of mine and my mother-in-law. Remember?"

He climbed over the sill to join Thomas on the veranda.

"I disagree with selflessness. I don't believe that the other man is as good as I am. My conscience has been overvalued. I have discovered all too late in life that I am temperamentally a reactionary, and from now on my conduct will be governed by greed and naked self-interest." He patted Thomas on the shoulder. "Don't look so worried. It was only that fellow who claims to be King Farouk when you ring up the palace.

"Well, nobody else would answer the confounded telephone, would they?" he flung back, making his way down into the garden and collecting another Martini as he went. It was the only helpful remark he could think of. Thomas had mistakenly come to the conclusion that he was drunk and rushed into the house, probably to question the switchboard operator.

Eric's earlier gloom had lifted. He was not drunk; the evening was so hot he had the feeling that the alcohol leaked harmlessly away through the pores. But he was elated by his exchange with the Naguibite spokesman, and when he failed to see Lydia in the garden, he did not, as he might have done ten minutes before, sit and wait for her to reappear; he went to look for her.

As expected, she and Tom Waters were sitting in deck-chairs right up against the wall. Lydia's laughter gave them away. A lantern suspended from a wall-bracket threw enough pink light to reveal the pallor of Waters's shirt front and the nylon gleam of Lydia's calves. Eric stood in one spot long enough to assure himself of the decorousness of the scene; it had the propriety of an Edwardian court-ship. Waters had caught both Lydia's hands in his and was pressing them to his chest. He was talking quietly, and Eric, whose eyes had now grown accustomed to the obscurity, saw his teeth gleam as he put a hand suddenly behind Lydia's shoulder and try to draw her even closer. It seemed quite respectable. He was merely trying to kiss her. They were both enjoying themselves. If Lydia were ten years older, Eric would, even now, be tempted to leave them to it; but she was little more than a child. And it had struck him whom Waters, with his fair hair and pink cheeks, re-minded him of: it was Tim.

"So there you are!"

At the sound of his voice they both tried to jump to their feet, but Eric had come so close without being ob-served that he was able to push Waters back again. Waters sat with his mouth open. It is difficult to rise from a deck-chair with a man standing over you.

"Go on up to your father, I should, Lydia."

"But, Eric, darling—"

"I shan't hurt him."

Lydia lifted her head and appeared, as she paced off through the trees, several inches taller. Eric became aware that he was smiling. He was proud of her grace and beauty. That Waters should have tried to kiss her seemed only natural and even commendable. Eric was not angry.

"I'll be with you directly, darling," he called after her.

He had to check his laughter.

"Keep away from my wife, Waters."

Waters might have been expected to make some sort of rejoinder, but he sat in his chair with a contorted stiffness, one knee slightly raised over the other, his right arm thrown up, making no sound but a catarrhal breathing. Eric stepped back and Waters immediately jumped to his feet. He would have run off through the trees if Eric had not caught him by one arm.

"Did you hear what I said?"

"I—I'm not afraid of you."

"I know you're not. Why should you be? Remember she's my wife, that's all."

Together they walked back towards the lights and the chatter. More to provide food for conversation than out of any sense of official correctness, Eric began to tell Waters about his telephoning from the Ambassadorial study. Waters repeatedly broke in with a "Yes, yes," obviously scarcely understanding the import of what was being said. He could have been very little older than Lydia—twenty-two or -three, perhaps—and Eric felt a pang of pity for him until he recollected his new role of imperial ruthlessness.

"Probably it was a bit out of order, him thinking I was Thomas, but I'd decided the only thing to prevent me going completely off my rocker was a spell of bloody-mindedness. So I gave 'em an ultimatum. Are you listening?"

"No," said Waters frankly.

Eric gripped him by the arm and explained in detail the enormity of the offence he had committed; so far as

General Naguib was concerned, the British had begun to rattle the sabre. At that very moment troops on fast camels were taking up defensive positions before the Cairo Citadel; tanks were being diverted from the assault on Ras el-Tin; four men had gone up in a balloon to spot submarines; tank traps, broken glass, and tintacks had been scattered on all the approaches to Mustapha Barracks. Waters was so obviously fresh from England it was quite legitimate to work on his credulity in this way.

"Well, I don't know what to say about this. You're joking, I suppose."

"There's Thomas come out on to the balcony. Never seen anybody in such a flap. Go and ask him if I'm joking. Tell him it would be a great mistake to issue a denial."

Once released, young Waters hurried off in the direction of the house, but Eric shouted after him. Looking back, he slackened his pace. This was not good enough for Eric, who began to shout at the top of his voice.

"Come back when I tell you!"

To his surprise, Waters obeyed. Eric marvelled over this for a moment; possibly the fellow wished to placate him; possibly he was still worried about being caught with Lydia.

"That's all right," said Eric in a normal tone when Waters was near enough to touch. "I quite forgot to wish you many happy returns of the day."

The jangling expectancy of that hot July evening! The secretaries and clerks dancing on the short grass, the motionless figures of Thomas and some other senior Embassy official who stood looking out from the Ambassador's study, the occasional flashes like summer lightning which reduced the trees to black silhouettes, the reedy whine of the gramophone, drink, the clink of ice in glasses, the reek of hot candle-wax from the lanterns—from all this it had now become impossible to escape. Thomas simply would not let them go. The Embassy gates were secured. The guards had been given instructions to permit no one to leave. There were, he said, anything up to ten thousand Egyptian troops coming into the city. Who could say how much shooting and incendiarism there would be? Anyway, it was absurd for British subjects needlessly to be exposed to danger, and all present were welcome to spend the night at the Embassy. No further reference was made to Eric's telephone conversation, though when he approached the scene of his crime he was abruptly ordered away by a big man in Turkish breeches and an embroidered waistcoat.

Even Wyvell Speen was unable to escape.

Lydia's fortune was told by an Armenian stenographer, in spite of her father's remonstrances; he said it was surprising that people still believed in such foolishness and he would have pulled Lydia away by the arm, but Eric disengaged her and said: "Go on, if it amuses you."

"You! An educated man!" said Mr. Dragoumis.

"No, I am not really educated." They were eating sausage rolls close to a bed of geraniums, and the bruised odour of leaf and petal stirred like memory. The aromatic dryness tickled in the nose. It was a good smell, Eric decided, a peppery smell, an extreme smell. From that moment onwards geranium would be his favourite perfume; because he was an extreme man, scarcely awake to the fact of being extreme. "And I don't believe in education."

"Eric, this is the affectation of the educated man."

"No, Father. I don't believe in education, and I don't believe in Selectivism either."

'You don't understand it. When I have finished my book—"

Eric told himself that he ought to tolerate his father-in-law's political philosophizing as he tolerated Lydia's fortune-telling. But the head of steam which for most of the evening he had controlled with difficulty now burst forth.

"Don't insult my intelligence!" he cried. "Your ideas are all rubbish! I understand perfectly well, but they're all rubbish! Shut up, Lydia, for God's sake! I can speak my mind, can't I?"

Elaine and Mrs. Dragoumis had no idea where the armoured car was taking them. The heat, the reek of petrol, and the blindness of their journey—they sat on a metal seat in a windowless compartment—brought on such sickness and faintness that the release, when it came, into cool moonlight was enough to bring tears of gratitude into Elaine's eyes. She breathed the sweet air and listened to the silence. The moonlight threw their sharp shadows, and those of the armoured car and the soldiers, forward into a wide expanse of metalled roadway bound on the right and the left by iron railings; ahead lay ceremonial gates like black lace, a mass of buildings, towers, a flag-staff neat as a pin against the sky. The silence was only comparative. They could hear, perfectly well now, the sea breathing all round them.

The officer spoke for the first time. He gave Elaine a long envelope and said that she and Mrs. Dragoumis were not to be afraid. They were to walk up the road to the gates. The distance, as they saw, was a mere fifty yards.

"Yes," he said. "You begin walking. Now!"

He ejected the last word violently. "Now!" Unmistakably it was an order. Questions were not permitted. He gave Elaine and Mrs. Dragoumis a slight push, and the two women started up the moon-washed road, following their shadows and saying nothing, but feeling defenceless. The road broadened. It sparkled like salt as something crystalline in its quality caught the moonlight.

"My dear," said Mrs. Dragoumis in French, "I must ask you to forgive me for all uncharitableness." Her voice was toneless. She might have been talking in her sleep. "Do you know where we are, my dear?"

The woman's composure frightened Elaine more than any hysterical outburst would have done.

"This is Ras el-Tin Palace." Mrs. Dragoumis began whispering like the sea itself, and Elaine felt the beginnings of a scream in her throat. She did not dare turn her head to right or left. They were like two flies traversing a Siberia of snow. "Let me take your hand, *mademoiselle*, as a sign you forgive me my uncharitableness."

"I don't know what you're talking about," Elaine whispered.

"I have been wicked to you. Do you forgive me? I would beg you on my knees!"

"Yes, I forgive you." If she had not spoken quickly, Elaine thought, the weird woman would have knelt in the roadway. The breeze, warm and dry, blew from behind; it blew out of the moon, pressing them onwards. Elaine knew she was not responding adequately to all this strangeness. Simple fear was not enough. Incredulity was not enough. If only she were fully awake and not dreaming—certainly she was dreaming!—she would have told Mrs. Dragoumis not to be a fool. But they were vulnerable as insects on a table-cloth.

"They are going to kill us now." Mrs. Dragoumis's step did not falter. She was calm as the moonlight itself. "If they had dared to do it, they would have killed us in the barracks. But that would not do, even though you are a spy and you helped the King to escape. You are English, and they are cunning men, evil men, and they would not want to give the English an excuse for—"

Elaine wanted to protest, but she was too frightened. They were about halfway between the armoured car and the palace gates, and it had seemingly taken them hours to get there. She could not understand why Mrs. Dragoumis, who might have been expected to act hysterically, was in fact behaving so calmly.

They moved forward, hand in hand.

Mrs. Dragoumis explained the stratagem. She saw it all so clearly. In a moment the soldiers who had brought them would fire a shot in the air, or throw a bomb; the King's soldiers would think they were being attacked. Then they would fire. Mrs. Dragoumis said that the revolutionaries would then shoot her and Elaine and blame it on the other side. How else could you execute a British spy? It did not matter that no one would believe the women had been killed by the palace guard. There would be uncertainty and confusion; that was all the revolutionaries asked.

"I beg you," said Mrs. Dragoumis, "to confess your sins and come to God with a clean heart."

Suddenly a tremendous voice broke the night. So uncertain was Elaine's grip on reality she even wondered whether this was God Himself reinforcing Mrs. Dragoumis's plea. But the voice spoke Arabic. It roared at the palace. The armoured car or some other Naguibite vehicle carried a public-address amplifier, and it was being used to communicate with the Royal Guards. The bellowing was echoless. It filled the night until, ending abruptly as it began, there was a loud pop like a cork coming out of a bottle, a whistle, and finally silence.

"Confess yourself," said Mrs. Dragoumis, "and be a martyr as I shall be a martyr. I am proud to be martyred by the Moslems. You are a Christian, aren't you, *mademoiselle?*"

"What did he say?"

"Lies, lies, lies!"

Elaine believed Mrs. Dragoumis; she knew the customs of the country and Elaine did not. Never had she known such fear, not even in the air raids during the war. The landward breeze carried an animal mustiness from the city behind. The ground was foreign, the air was foreign, she was about to be murdered by foreigners! The foreignness of her death appalled her. Since she had smacked that silly man's face she had been a prey to this foreignness. At once she had been separated from Mrs. Dragoumis—needless to say, she did not see Yehia again—shut up in a small room and offered a bowl of some dreadful-looking food. If only they had given her a cup of tea! She wished she had stayed on board the *Tewfikieh*. She wished she had never seen Yehia. She wished she had gone in for silver-fox farming with her cousin Millicent when the opportunity had arisen, instead of becoming a journalist.

"You *are* a Christian?" Mrs. Dragoumis had halted their snail-like progress.

Over the palace Elaine suddenly became aware of the familiar pattern of stars. She began counting them. The Great Bear! Automatically she allowed her eye to follow the line of the Pointers to where the North Star should have been; but the palace itself shut out that portion of the sky. The North Star hung too low to be seen and the realization came to intensify the foreignness of her situation; Elaine had never before been so far south.

"Are you?" Mrs. Dragoumis repeated.

"No, no, no, no." The irrelevancy of such a question! Elaine was beginning to think how they might run either to right or to left when the firing began. There were deep shadows where they might hide. She wanted so desperately to live.

"But, my dear one!" They were motionless, about twenty yards from the gates, and Elaine could even see through the gates to the patterned shadow they threw on a court beyond. "All English are Christians. This is the hour for us. Confess that you believe."

Mrs. Dragoumis swung Elaine round to face her; her hair, fluffed out round the clown-like mask of her imploring countenance, shone metallically. She appeared to be as passionate for martyrdom as Elaine was passionate for life; the added joy of snatching a soul from the Evil One conferred a moral and spiritual stature which quite genuinely filled Elaine with awe. As Mrs. Dragoumis fought for Christ she was happy as she had never been happy before. It was self-evident. This was her moment of fulfilment. Marriage, childbirth were as achievements insignificant in comparison. She stepped out of the boredom of Alexandria into triumph. "So little is asked," she said, "and the reward is so great."

"No, I'm not a Christian," said Elaine, turning mulish.

In a hoarse whisper which must have been heard by the Royal Guards and the Naguibites alike, Mrs. Dragoumis began to pray for Elaine, watching her all the time out of the recessed black, unreflecting buttons that were her eyes.

"Stop it!" Elaine shouted at her, a tremendous noise which seemed to throw Mrs. Dragoumis back on her heels. "I'm not a Christian. I don't want to be shot. Help! Help!" The rising cadence became a scream.

"If you are not a Christian, you cannot absolve me,"

said Mrs. Dragoumis fiercely. "I die with my sins. If you do not believe for your own salvation, believe at least for mine. Confess Christ and listen to my sins. There are Moslems all around us. I must have absolution from a Christian soul."

Elaine tried to break away, but Mrs. Dragoumis hung on to her wrists. "Don't you understand, *mademoiselle*," she said solemnly, "that you and I have the greatest need of one another, to help each other sweetly, as best we may, out of this world and into the next world?"

"Oh, let me go, you beast!" Elaine spoke in English, and at that moment they heard the beat of metal-studded boots and looked towards the palace. A magnificent officer, seemingly eight feet tall, had appeared in the moonlight and was striding towards them. Two! Three! Four! Five steps! And he was there, boots gleaming to the knees, breeches with red stripes (red even in the moonlight) distended to the uttermost, tassels at the epaulettes, and a far-off tarboosh that pressed against the stars. And still no one fired.

"Come with me," he said in English. Without waiting to observe whether these instructions were likely to be carried out, he turned smartly and made off in the direction from which he had come. For the first time, now that she had some indication she was not to be shot after all, Elaine felt disposed to pray, and if Mrs. Dragoumis had renewed her proselytizing pressure there is no knowing whether Elaine might not have succumbed.

Instead, she found herself in the light and choking heat of a room full of Egyptian soldiers. Presumably they had passed through the huge gates; manifestly there had been none of the shooting Mrs. Dragoumis had prophesied; and undoubtedly they were still alive, although on what terms remained to be determined. All the soldiers stood up, and the two women were ushered into a farther room where a sergeant sat at a trestle table and in one corner could be seen a made-up bed.

"Which of you is the Englishwoman?" asked the magnificent officer, who, in the electric light, now appeared in full colour: ivory breeches with their scarlet stripes, olive-green jacket, gold tassels, and deep-red, almost mulberry tarboosh. Elaine had forgotten she still carried the envelope until the officer, receiving no answer to his question, took it from her right hand. He held it, frowning, to the light, spoke in Arabic to the sergeant, and left the room hurriedly, wagging the envelope like a fan.

Mrs. Dragoumis thumped down on to her knees and then pitched forward on to her face.

The sergeant did not move his round brown head, but allowed his eyes to switch from Mrs. Dragoumis to Elaine and back again. Plainly, he was suspicious. However, when Elaine attempted to turn Mrs. Dragoumis on to her back the sergeant came round his table and insisted on helping to carry her to the bed. She had either fainted or was in a fit of some kind. Her eyes were wide open, her throat swallowed endlessly, and her lips trilled under the force of her exhalations. It required the collapse of Mrs. Dragoumis to restore Elaine to her senses, to convince her they had survived the walk to the palace gates and there was no longer need to talk about religion. The sergeant fetched a glass of water, but it was impossible to force the liquid through Mrs. Dragoumis's clenched teeth. While Elaine dabbed her forehead and cheeks the sergeant disappeared once more— to call a doctor, she hoped, because by this time Mrs. Dragoumis's face had taken on a marble stiffness and pallor.

"Come at once." The magnificent officer had returned with a vertical furrow between his eyebrows.

"She's ill. I can't leave her."

"It is urgent. We shall send a doctor."

Elaine went on dabbing the white face, and the officer came and stood behind her. "An Important Person has sent for you. Don't you understand? You can do nothing for this woman. Is she your mother? If you don't come at once, I shall order in some soldiers and they will carry you.

"Did you know what was in that envelope?" he asked curiously when Elaine ignored his threat. His new tone revealed that he had never had any intention of carrying it out.

It was a quarter of an hour before Mrs. Dragoumis had sufficiently recovered to tell Elaine that they were both happily dead, and by that time a doctor had arrived to turn her on her stomach and cut her old-fashioned stays with an open razor borrowed from the sergeant. Later she lay in relaxed dignity, smiling at the ceiling. Elaine saw with horror that she really did consider herself dead, and yearned to warm her back to normality; how dreadful she should be struck down in this way, just when she was being so brave.

A couple of yawning soldiers tramped in from the guardroom. They took up position at Elaine's elbows and marched earnestly towards the door at a word from the officer. Without a hand being laid on her, Elaine was bustled into the night. With the officer at their head, the party walked down a flagged cloister, into pools of moonlight. They stepped between white pillars into another courtyard where flowers were growing on a trellis—jasmine apparently, because Elaine thought of Yehia just before she arrived at the realization she was passing through a cloud of sweetness. They halted at a flight of wide stone stairs.

"His Excellency will see you now," said the officer.

As they climbed the stairs a brilliant panel of red and gold opened in the darkness ahead. A uniformed figure moved into position before the tapestry so that no sooner had Elaine stepped over the threshold than she found two men at her elbows again, the officer who had accompanied her from the gates and this new figure, straddling, beribboned, and creaking in British Sam Browne. They climbed carpeted steps, walked along a corridor, and entered a handsomely furnished chamber where a grey-headed man sat at a desk topped with green leather and bearing a great many small objects—enamel boxes, coins, glass flowers, a silver bell, framed photographs, and a tiny bronze hand which Elaine found herself gazing at to the exclusion of all else. She had no special feeling for the hand, but she did not wish to look at the grey-headed man; it lay on a piece of blank notepaper, and Elaine looked at it so hard it began to dissolve before her eyes.

"How does an Englishwoman come to be mixed up with revolutionaries?" he asked in a deep, ringing voice like syrup being poured into an enormous can.

"They would have shot me if they dared."

She saw now, lifting her gaze from the bronze hand, that he was angry. He was swinging his big head rapidly from side to side like a bear, tightening and budding his lips. "A woman! They send a woman at a time like this! Very well! We send you back! We send you back at once! And do you know what you will say to them? No, you will say. We do *not* surrender the palace to a man who is power-drunk, mad, not a patriot! Go back and say that to him, woman! We shall not even write it down. Go and speak these words with your lips. Naguib thinks he will insult His Majesty with a woman messenger, but we send the woman messenger back, saying, No, His Majesty does not surrender the palace to criminals!"

"Excuse me, you're not the King, are you?"

"I?"

As soon as she asked the question she saw its absurdity.

"Don't you know what His Majesty looks like?" His Excellency shot quick glances at the officers and eased himself back into his chair.

"Of course, he's much younger. I'm sorry. After all, I'm not much interested in foreign monarchs."

"*You thought I might be the King?*"

"Yes, what the hell's so funny about that? You can't always tell what people look like from photographs. What's it matter, anyway? I'm not interested in King Farouk. I'm not interested in Egypt. I've only been here a couple of days, and all I want is to get out of it. I don't *like* this country." She was every bit as angry as His Excellency by this time.

"Sit down," he said.

"I'd rather stand, thank you."

"Cigarette?"

She said nothing and shook her head.

"You can't say that about Egypt," he sounded forth, "especially as you've been here such a short time. If what you say is true—two days. How can you say you like or dislike Egypt? Have you seen the temples and tombs? No, it's impossible in the time. There are the Colossi of Memnon, for example; if you saw those, you would never forget them. And what about the Temple of Queen Hatshepset?"

Elaine crossed to a gold plush chair and sat down abruptly. She was, in part of her consciousness, still on the moonlit road with Mrs. Dragoumis, talking about Christianity and waiting to be shot. What had gone wrong? she wondered. Why had they not been as good as their word and shot them down as they approached the palace gates? Then she realized that it had been no one's word but Mrs. Dragoumis's, and she marvelled at the woman's shrewdness. To apprehend in the hour of death the complexity of the cunning that had brought them there! No doubt this quickness came of living in Egypt. For the first time Elaine really understood the plot. The Naguibites would pretend to attack, the Royal Guards would fire, more firing would break out, and two women would be found dead in the morning.

"Don't you understand," she said to His Excellency, "that I'm the Englishwoman who helped get the King away from Montazah?"

"Of course," His Excellency was saying, "this is not the time of year for viewing the antiquities of Egypt."

But Elaine's words caused him to break off and stop swinging his head. "*You* helped the King get away from Montazah?"

"I thought everybody knew about that," she said.

"But—"

"You ask what I've done to be mixed up with revolutionaries. Can you think of any better reason than that— laying myself on the royal altar," she said, "or don't you know anything at all? If this officer here hadn't come marching out of the gates at the crucial moment I'd have been shot down, and Mrs. Dragoumis. How dare you ask me how I came to be mixed up with revolutionaries! I demand to be let out of Egypt at once!"

"Who would have shot you?" His Excellency had quietened remarkably. Plainly, young women did not usually raise their voices in his presence. To be shouted at, to be accused of ignorance (for that is what her words amounted to!), to be scolded in the presence of two junior officers—this was unthinkable! No woman, not even an Englishwoman, would presume to behave in this way without extreme provocation. No doubt everything was just as she had said. How like the Chief of Police not to tell him!

"The Naguibites," she said. "They would have shot us. Do you deny that, then?"

"Very unlikely, I should say." He paused lengthily with eyes closed in aristocratic disdain. "An Englishwoman on their hands—yes, they would release her quickly to avoid provoking the British. I'm sorry they released you. Well, take this lady and examine her story." He opened his eyes and addressed the man in the Sam Browne. "Why was I not told of this woman? Is it that Hafek does not wish me to know? Am I not to be trusted?" The Arabic clanged out of him. When he stood up he revealed himself to be dressed in black trousers which set off handsomely the pearl-grey jacket. He spoke to the two officers as if there were five hundred of them. The anger which Elaine had first felt directed upon herself now sprayed over the magnificent officer, his green jacket, his tassels, his scarlet stripes, and the immaculate cut of his ivory breeches; it sprayed over the Sam Browne, who remained quite still with head slightly bowed. His Excellency gesticulated. Elaine could even envisage the moment when he would apologize to her.

"Go now with these officers," he said, "and make a statement in writing."

He fingered some of the objects on his desk, waiting for Elaine to move, but she remained on her gold plush chair, thinking of the Machiavellian plot of the Naguibites, and hardening with anger at the thought of all she had suffered in the royal cause only to be spoken to by this big-voiced man as though she were a criminal. For all he knew, she might indeed have had some part in the King's escape. Judging by the way he had quickly fallen into suspicion of his colleagues, His Excellency did not seem the man to find it an easy task to keep himself well informed.

"Please go with these officers," he said sharply.

Elaine hesitated. If His Excellency was important enough to deal with ultimatums from General Naguib, he must be a figure of the highest authority. He might not know what went on in the world outside, but presumably he was aware of happenings within the palace itself.

"I'd like to know how Mr. Tim Blainey is," she said.

"Who?"

"Tim Blainey. You remember, he came ashore this morning."

His Excellency's shoulders were rising, his nose narrowing at the nostrils as he breathed in. Here were further developments of which he had been kept in ignorance. "What is this—Tim Blainey?" The words fell from his lips in the wake of a sighing exhalation.

"Mr. Blainey swam ashore. We were in a boat and there was an accident. Your soldiers fired shots at us."

"He is here in the palace? English? He *swam* here from a boat?"

"I saw him with your soldiers. And that's another thing," she said, accumulating grievances. "They deliberately fired at us in the gondola."

His Excellency was checked only momentarily by the mention of the gondola. "This also must appear in your written statement. You claim you are of service to His Majesty during the night; then you are in a boat, a gondola. I must have all this in writing. Why was I not told about this young man?"

He stood with a glass paperweight in one hand, contemplating events that were beginning to get out of control. It was as if he saw them lifting from his very desk, eddying, spinning vaster, and beginning to roar, gathering papers, the desk itself, betasselled officers in Sam Brownes and well-cut breeches, Excellencies in London-tailored jackets, the palace, the crown and star of Egypt, all humming heavenwards.

"All must be in writing," he said again.

Hearing the key in the lock, Yehia sat up and looked at the illuminated dial of his wrist watch. The time was just past 4.30, and he assumed the scuffling of feet and the whispering were caused by the firing party. His firing party! He found it impossible not to take pride in his calmness. For at least four hours he had slept with the unregarding relaxation of an animal, and now he was alert and ready. As the door opened he stood up. Suddenly he was wet with sweat; it burst out of him as his movements stirred the hot, humid air, and he wondered whether, as a last privilege, he would be allowed to take a shower. And how would he dress? Would they permit him decorations and badges of rank?

"Mahmoud," said a voice gently.

"Who is it?"

"Gamal."

The light snapped on and he saw Gamal Attalah wrinkling his face and opening his mouth in preparation for a stuttering sentence. Gamal had been his commanding officer during the Palestine campaign; they were old friends, but had not met for months. Yehia was bewildered to see him at a time like this. So senior an officer did not appear with firing parties. Then it occurred to Yehia that Gamal had come to bear his last messages to the few relations he still possessed; he was on the point of saying there were no messages to give but he would, if it could be permitted, be grateful for a shower, when Gamal patted his naked shoulder and said: "Mahmoud, I've just flown down from Cairo with Salem. It's been decided to let Farouk go."

But for the one guard out on the balcony, Yehia saw that he and Gamal were alone.

"This does not excuse me. He escaped from Montazah, and I insist on taking the responsibility."

"I was coming to that," said Gamal, and he gave the door a kick so that it slammed shut and the electric light bulb danced on the end of its flex. He offered Yehia a cigarette. The two men stood in the middle of the room, smoking and looking into each other's eyes, Yehia quite naked with glistening belly and beads of sweat running down his thighs, Gamal in a buff cotton tunic that hung awkwardly on his thin body.

"I've just heard about it from Emad el-Dine. It's all nonsense. You must have lost your senses."

"It is quite wrong to let Farouk go." Yehia refused to talk about himself. "I'm in favour of putting him on trial. You know as well as I do that he should be put on trial."

"I mean," said Gamal, "you must have lost your head with this Englishwoman. You have suddenly become stupid. Isn't it enough to make anybody curious about you? And now she's in Ras el-Tin."

"She's where?"

"Didn't you know? She went to Ras el-Tin with our demands that the palace should be surrendered. Rejected, of course. So the attack is timed for seven."

"Attack?"

"There's just a chance Farouk may have slipped back to Montazah by boat. By five we shall have sealed off both palaces, and at seven we shall attack. There's no doubt, really, that Farouk is in Ras el-Tin."

"I must be there."

"That's what I was thinking," said Lieutenant-Colonel Gamal Attallah, stuttering and turning his head away in embarrassment now that his main point was made.

Yehia said he would like to wash. Gamal said it was a good idea, they would wash together, and the two men walked over to the ablution shed. Yehia picked up a towel before leaving his room and draped it round his thighs. The guard shuffled in the darkness of the veranda, and Gamal said he was to permit no one to enter the room in their absence. Over the eastern wing of the barracks milky veils hung across the sky, and the stretches of sand between the blocks of building seemed to shift like mist. Yehia waited while Gamal slipped out of his clothes, dropping them anyhow on the boarded floor of the changing-room; and then the two men stepped into neighboring showers and shouted above the hiss of cool water. Gamal said there had been disagreement over the treatment to be given to Farouk. Here in Alexandria, Naguib wanted to send him into exile, but Gamal Salem was in favour of trying the King for his crimes. That was why he, Gamal Attallah, and Salem had flown to Cairo: to seek the opinion of Abd el-Nasser. Twenty minutes ago they had returned with Nasser's recommendation that Farouk should be exiled.

"You are wrong," said Yehia.

They dabbed at their bodies with the single towel, panting with pleasure at the coolness.

"Remember the men who died in Palestine because their arms were defective. They were martyrs. They should be avenged."

"No," said Gamal, "you carry out orders in this matter.

You take charge of the operation at Ras el-Tin. At five thirty you must be there. When you are ready to go, report to me in Emad el-Dine's room. There are other instructions."

Yehia had been prepared for death. The prospect of leading the attack on Ras el-Tin brought a hard excitement and a hunger for life. The thought of the firing squad suddenly became dreadful, so dreadful that momentarily he forgot he was under orders to report to Gamal Attallah and wanted to run away. Surely it was his right, this seizing of Ras el-Tin and the person of the King! If he was responsible for allowing the King to escape from Montazah, then he had an incontestable claim to make amends.

"Gamal," he said, "I must do this thing. God knows, I've earned it, haven't I?"

"Everybody says you'd insist on being shot."

"Not without a fair trial. I am always too impatient. They cannot shoot me out of hand, like a dog. I owe it to myself that there should be a court-martial. And you will speak for me, Gamal. Why was the Englishwoman sent to Ras el-Tin?"

"What is she to you?"

"Nothing! She is nothing to me. But at Ras el-Tin I may meet her. I must know why she was sent there."

By this time Gamal was dressed. He said there was no time for further conversation if Yehia was to be at Ras el-Tin by 5.30. As for the reasons behind sending the Englishwoman to the King, well, it was known that his one hope of salvation was intervention by the British, and General Naguib had decided they should be given not the slightest excuse for it; not even the lawful restraint of an Englishwoman who, it was well known, was a secret agent.

Yehia shouted in anger. They were halfway between the ablution hut and his room. He cracked his towel like a whip. "The woman is nothing, nothing! She is not a secret agent. It is a lie!"

Gamal took him by the arm and spoke gently, striving against his stutter: "Dear Mahmoud! We are old friends and we have shared danger. As soon as I heard of your situation I decided to intervene. Who is Mahmoud Yehia to be shot by a lot of peasants? We are comrades, precious to one another. Go now! Do not lose your temper with me. Much work lies before both of us."

Yehia was aware that his voice was tremulous with rage and that he was making a fool of himself. But the excitement which had been growing since Gamal arrived was overpowering him.

"Gamal," he cried, stalking off towards his room, "when this is all over I shall demand a court of inquiry."

Once dressed, Yehia hastened over to Emad el-Dine's room, where he found not only Gamal Attallah but a number of other senior officers, most of whom Yehia knew, looking grey-faced from lack of sleep. Gamal presented him with his own revolver (there was no time to visit the armoury, and Yehia's revolver had been taken from him at the time of his arrest), and Yehia apologized for losing his temper, saying it was not a time for anger.

"Remember," said a cavalry colonel, "your object is to take Ras el-Tin without bloodshed. You're quite sure, Attallah, that this is the man for the job?"

"I know Yehia's qualities."

"Well," said the cavalry colonel, "the rest of us will be there in time for breakfast, and I'll have eggs. Four boiled eggs and coffee off His Majesty's own table."

Yehia left amidst laughter.

He was ready to sing with happiness. The jeep, in which he was sole passenger, hurled itself along a yellow tunnel of light which faded moment by moment as the sun crept up behind them. Yehia gripped his knees and leaned forward. The speed screwed up exhilaration to a point almost beyond bearing. He *had* to sing! The sound burst from his throat, not in any recognizable song, following no tune, observing no rhythm; he roared as the jeep roared, a solo cheering, a loud croon of delight that meant life had come right for him. The confused ambition which had sustained him through the past few days, an ambition concerning the Englishwoman as well as his country, found perfect expression: the same blow would destroy the King and release Elaine. She had not gone to the palace of choice; given the opportunity, she would have declared for the New Egypt, repudiated colonialism, and turned from the King with horror. Yehia was certain of it. At last the man and the patriot could act in harmony. The jeep shot into Mohamed Ali Square, and Yehia looked up at the equestrian statue thinking that the time would come, perhaps, when statues were put up to him. The man who caught the King!

The driver brought up his left arm, and the jeep bore down on the Eastern Harbour. The colourless sheen expanded before them, vast as space, infinite, a gap in the universe! Yehia thought he would never again be so happy. This moment had brought fulfilment. If he now drew Gamal's revolver and shot himself through the head, he would have experienced all. He now knew why men lived. It was to train as a soldier, attack palaces, release beautiful women, and to destroy kings. He was a lover and a republican! Yehia saw the meaning of his life. It was more glorious than he had suspected. As the jeep passed the truckloads of troops, the armoured cars, and the occasional decrepit tank, Yehia stood up and waved. Everyone should be cheering, he thought.

Even the coolness with which he was received by the officer in charge of the detachment did not check him. He was a cavalry major, a dark-faced little man, grimy from the night drive through the desert; he struck about with a fly-whisk, saying that a single armoured car, a corporal and six men, had been assigned for the seven-o'clock attack. Only when they had sustained casualties would the major himself take action against the Royal Guards.

"But there's no need for casualties," he said. "The whole thing's farcical. We could walk in now if we liked. What the Council sent you for I can't imagine."

By half past six the sun was high enough for the flanks of the armoured car to be hot to the touch. To kill time Yehia inspected it thoroughly, thinking all the time of the afternoon vigil with an armoured car at Sidi Bishr when he had spotted a motor boat nosing in from the sea. He asked the crew their names, where they came from, whether they were married and had children. The corporal, he discovered, came from Tanta, and they talked of the place.

"Do you know what we're here for?" he asked.

"To capture the King's treasure," said a peasant, his face round as a melon, "and give it to the people."

"If any man starts looting, I shall shoot him," said Yehia. "Do you understand? You, corporal, and you six men and I, we're to attack this palace and force its surrender. Remember, they are Egyptians like ourselves, these Royal Guards. Perhaps they will not kill us and perhaps we shall not kill them."

"*Inshallah!*" said the men in chorus.

"It's too late for the British to move now," said the major at his elbow. "Everything now is between the King and ourselves."

Yehia looked back down the hill. A camp kitchen was

poking a black finger of smoke into the clarity of the morning. Men were breakfasting in the sun. He was struck by their gaiety; they were, most of them, still filthy from the desert, but excitement made them merry, gave a shine to their faces. Yehia could neither eat nor drink.

If I die now, he thought, that will have been enough.

He turned from watching the fishing boats edge with single sail past Kait Bey after a night's fishing; the time was 6.45, and a loudspeaker on a green van began addressing the palace, stating that at seven a.m. precisely a detachment would advance to take possession of the palace, inviting the Royal Guards to lay down their arms. The voice promised that no harm would befall them. Yehia put on his steel helmet and spoke to the crew of the armoured car. He said that at his signal they were to advance very slowly on the main gates; at a distance of twenty yards from the gates they were to halt and wait.

"You may have to knock a hole in those gates," he said.

Everyone waited. It seemed that the only sound came from a couple of jets making long, snoring sweeps over the lake to the south of the city. In the Western Harbour the many ships bore no sign of life. The morning stank of salt and petrol. Yehia, scratching the side of his face, startled himself with the rasp of nail on bristle. He wondered what the King was doing. He wondered what Elaine was doing.

The major looked up from his watch and nodded. Surprisingly, a siren sounded. A church bell rang in the city. A chain rattled, metal scraped on metal across the water, a steam locomotive whistled. The morning was full of sound. In a panic, Yehia looked at his watch, supposedly synchronized with the major's, and saw the time was already a minute past the hour. For a moment he could stir neither tongue nor limb.

"All right, corporal," he said at last to the armoured car. It lurched forward, and Yehia, with his six men and an N.C.O., marched in attendance.

More to avoid the exhaust than from overeagerness, Yehia swung his men away from the armoured car and he himself began to trot. He told them not to bunch together. The usual guard was posted: a couple of men in sentry-boxes on either side of the gates. Resistance would not, in all probability, come from them. Yehia held his revolver forward. He had never been a good shot with a revolver, and he knew he would almost certainly miss anyone who suddenly popped up and fired at him. On a tower to the right of the gate a shutter flapped open; he saw the blue glitter of some kind of weapon and decided that the time for gesture was now rather than later. He rested the barrel on his left wrist and fired. He ought to have dodged back behind the armoured car, but instinct drove him forward. He shouted at his own men as he ran. He told them to shelter behind the car, but his words were masked by the gun; the corporal had fired one burst at the tower, ripping the shutter like a flag and scoring the stonework.

Yehia raced for the gate. He saw the sentries come out of their boxes and make for a side gate. He would have fired as he ran had he thought there was the remotest chance of hitting one of them. The side gate was important. If he could only reach it before it closed, he could force his way into the palace grounds and *talk* to the Royal Guards. That was the objective—to persuade them that they were Egyptians too. He shouted the first words that came into his head: "Remember Palestine!" Behind him he could hear the armoured car firing another burst. Yes, it was right, in spite of orders, to kill some of the Royal Guards. They were not real soldiers. They hadn't been to Palestine. It was blasphemous to shout "Remember Palestine!" to such men.

"Throw down your arms!" he shouted.

He was so close to one of the guards that he could hear the gurgle of terror as the fellow slipped through the gate and disappeared to the right. Anyone who defied the Council of Officers at such a moment deserved to die, and Yehia was prepared to shoot down any man attempting to close this side gate. But no one did. He was the first officer of the Liberation to set foot within the precincts of Ras el-Tin, and he pushed over the greased bolt of the main gate to admit the armoured car, the corporal, and the six men with the extravagance of a man knowing he is committing historic act. The armoured car made such a noise that he did not realize they were under fire once more until he saw blue scratches appear on its flank.

They were breaking into a courtyard, quite orange in the morning light; green shutters were closed over the windows of the façade opposite; the firing had stopped, and it became impossible to know just where the gunmen were lurking. A group of men in what Yehia recognized as the uniform of officers of the Royal Guards stood under an archway. Yehia, ahead of the armoured car, trotted steadily in their direction, calling on them to surrender in the name of General Naguib; but they made no move, they stood like dummies, and Yehia began to wonder what he would do if they refused to speak to him.

He realized subsequently that this was the moment when the attack developed its flaw. He should have thrust his revolver back into his holster and approached the officers unarmed. Orders had been explicit: take the palace without bloodshed. At the risk of his own life he should have approached these officers with open palms; but he was trotting towards them with the revolver at the ready, daring them to resist. God knows, he might have wanted them to resist!

One man moving his right hand caused Yehia to fire. Naturally, he missed, but his one shot was the signal for a fusillade from somewhere unexpected—somewhere away to the right, somewhere high up, somewhere in the shadow. Yehia could not possibly know. His revolver hit the orange sand first. It jerked forward on the bounce so that it was out of his range of vision when he lay down, fighting to keep his face off the ground and all the time reaching forward in search of his weapon. The rim of his helmet struck the ground with violence. The flat-faced buildings threw back the machine-gun bursts in remote, mournful echoing, and Yehia stared along the surface of the sand.

"Stop that shooting," he heard the major say.

Yehia realized that these were the words he himself should be delivering. Why couldn't he? Why had he failed? Why had he been so inefficient? Before carrying him into the shade the men turned him on to his back, and Yehia blamed the sun for forcing the tears from his eyes. He closed them for shame. When the sun was withdrawn he opened his eyes cautiously once more and saw—very near, dreamlike, pale, and painfully beautiful—the face of Elaine herself.

On the right side of her nose was a freckle. He studied it for a moment and then looked into the blue eyes. Having assured himself that this was no illusion, that Elaine was really there, he lifted his head slightly and spat in her face.

Unlike Tim, to whom the sight of pen and paper had been a stimulus, Elaine found that the expectation of a written "statement" for His Excellency brought on the final touch of fatigue. A statement about what? Did they want her to substantiate her claim to be the woman who had made it possible for the King to escape from Montazah? The officers had not been specific. Before closing the door of the cell they placed writing material on the table and said they would return in two hours' time, when they hoped to find her statement complete. The examination-room atmosphere added its special melancholy. Finding a paillasse in one corner, Elaine switched out the light and listened for some moments in case anyone guessed what she was up to; but no one stirred. She extended herself gently on the paillasse and plunged into sleep with all the deliberation of one seeking refuge.

Sleep had such a hold on her that when the light snapped on once more and her name was spoken in her ear she responded only to the extent of deciding she would *not* wake up. If the punishment for not writing the "statement" was death, then let them carry her to the scaffold. She would not leave the sanctuary of slumber, even for death.

"Elaine!" said the voice. "It's Tim."

"I'm asleep."

"But, Elaine—"

"For God's sake, go away."

And that is just what he must have done, because when she woke again there was a pink cloud beyond the barred window, enough diffused dawn light in the room to make out the chair and table; but no Tim, no one but herself, not even the two officers waiting for her statement. She struggled to her feet and yawned her way to the table. Perhaps Tim's visit had been a dream. She produced a mirror from the handbag that had mercifully been spared her and looked at her face unsympathetically. That puffiness under the eyes! Those lines from nostril to mouth! She had become old and sour. In a few years' time they would be calling her Old Brent in the office, if she ever got back to it. She combed her hair, and, as she did so, recollections of the past night trickled into her consciousness. She was still so drugged by sleep that she was only half aware of where she was. The insistent, cool rustle at last, however, identified itself as the sea, and Elaine remembered the nightmare walk across the moonlit square with Mrs. Dragoumis. She rushed to the door in a spasm of terror, tugged it open, and (without wondering why the officers had not bothered to lock her in) stepped into the corridor. Immediately opposite was another door, half open. Through it she saw Tim fast asleep on a paillasse identical with her own, and she rushed upon him, crying: "Wake up, Tim. For heaven's sake, get up. There's nobody about. We can escape. They're going to attack the palace."

It was Tim's turn to be helpless with sleep, and his only response was to snore.

Elaine seized him by the nose. "Tim! There's nobody here. Wake up, you beast."

He sat up, rubbing his cheeks vigorously. "Oh, hullo, Elaine."

"For heaven's sake, get dressed and let's get out of this awful place."

Tim was sufficiently awake by this time to ask whether she would mind stepping into the corridor while he put on his trousers. When she refused he stood facing into a corner and pulled them up, still damp from the sea, over his shirt and underpants. Once he had borrowed Elaine's comb and mirror to attend to his hair, he was almost his normal self once more. The guard had unlocked his door in the small hours and made a noise—boom! boom!—throwing his hands about, as though to explain there was going to be an explosion; and he was, Tim explained, just finishing some notes on his impressions of Alexandria when he had heard Elaine being installed in the room opposite. He had recognized her voice. And, anyway, her presence was not unexpected because he knew, after their adventure in the boat, that she would be bound to try and get in touch with him.

"I thought you and Eric were extraordinarily brave to come back in the gondola," he said.

"My presence here has absolutely nothing to do with you," said Elaine.

"Oh!"

"They're going to bomb the palace, that's what they're going to do. Why did they unlock these doors and clear off?"

"Who are going to bomb the palace?"

"The Egyptians, of course, the revolutionary ones."

"I wish I weren't so hungry," Tim complained. Casting about in the hope of spying food, his eye fell on the notes he had compiled during the previous evening. "Elaine, do let me read out to you what I've written about Alexandria. I know I shouldn't say it, but it's really good. Before last night I really wasn't a writer. And then something happened. I've crossed a bridge. Take this, for example—"

"Good heavens!" said Elaine. "I've just remembered. Mrs. Dragoumis!"

"What about her?"

"She's here. She had a fit or a stroke or something. I *must* find her."

"But—"

"Are you coming or aren't you?"

Pausing only to give him time to put on his wet socks

and shoes, Elaine led the way into the corridor and so into
a gravelled courtyard where a palm tree grew in a tub. Still
there was no sign of life. High clouds caught the rising sun
in a remote blue sky. Down here in the shadow of walls
and buildings the air was grey. The sound of running feet
made them pause in a doorway, but when the man arrived, a Negro soldier holding his tarboosh on with one
hand, he ignored them; he disappeared round a corner, gasp-
ing agonizingly. To Elaine it seemed that the palace had
been abandoned during the night and this one man sent
back to pick up some forgotten item. But now there were
other sounds of human occupation. Boots tramped on a
wooden floor, rifle bolts clicked, words of command rang
out. The worst happened almost immediately. Elaine and
Tim walked into a cobbled yard surrounded by empty stables, and here a group of officers—the two who had seen
Elaine to her cell might even have been among them—
were listening to a speech by a swarthy man in civilian
clothes who stood on a mounting-block, revealing a green
cummerbund every time he threw his arms back. The flow
of words was not checked by the sight of the newcomers;
he eyed them thoughtfully, but continued to breast invisible waves. Some of the officers turned, but they had
worried expressions on their faces; they looked at the orator
once more. The presence of a couple of Europeans was
plainly of little interest. Only the remote booming of a loudspeaker which now made itself heard could distract them
from the man in the cummerbund; some of the officers, indeed, began to walk in the direction the sound came from.

"Up here!" said Elaine. Climbing a flight of stone
steps, they entered what could only be an ante-chamber
to the royal apartments themselves. Enough pink light came

through the tall windows to reveal carpet reflecting the arabesques of the painted ceiling, chairs and divans in gilt and plush, mirrors, a marble cup big as a font on bronze claws; and the whole décor was poised, as it were, in relation to a huge candelabra which hung like the fragmentation of some fabulous diamond, pulsing and glittering in the growing light.

Before leaving his cell Tim had stuffed his papers into his hip pocket. They had become the most important factor in the present situation, so far as he was concerned, and he could allow no more time to pass without checking to see if they were complete.

"You see," he explained, "when you write about something you get it under control. Coming to Egypt is the most wonderful thing that could have happened. This time last week I hadn't anything worth controlling."

Elaine was agitated by the thought that at any moment they might come on the King. "As far as I'm concerned, I wish I'd never left that boat."

"But, Elaine—"

"We're not here to talk. We're supposed to be looking for Mrs. Dragoumis."

"And that's another thing! What's Mrs. Dragoumis doing here?"

Elaine was still trying to take her bearings. This ornate room would probably be as far away from Mrs. Dragoumis's present quarters as the precincts permitted. But in which direction? They ought to have followed the officers in the direction of the loudspeaker; it was almost certainly the one that had announced her approach the previous evening. Therefore, that way lay the main entrance. Once more the loudspeaker began to boom, and, walking to the far windows, Elaine lifted the gauze curtains, opened a glass door, and found herself on a marble balcony overlooking a sandy square. Over there to the left were the main gates. The sun was high enough to stamp shadows on the sand and set occasional windows flaring. The loudspeaker fell silent.

"What I can't understand is where everybody is." Tim had joined her on the balcony. "What's that?"

There was a crackle like fire among dry sticks. Soldiers scampered through a doorway at the side of the main gates and ran into one of the low buildings to the left. Elaine realized that must have been the place where Mrs. Dragoumis and she had been received the night before. The obvious approach to this building was across the forecourt of the palace, and Elaine was about to take a flight of steps which led down from the balcony when she realized that the main gates of the palace were being opened by a helmeted Egyptian officer. Firing broke out. It was impossible to say where the shots came from. The echoes chattered round the façades. No one appeared to be hurt. For this reason the firing merely added to the unreality of the scene. Elaine found it impossible to credit what she guessed to be the truth: this was the assault on the King's last position and she was probably the only journalist to be witnessing it.

"It's crazy to stay here." Tim took her by the arm. "They're as likely to take a shot at us as anybody else. You know, those chaps mean business, and it isn't really ours."

But she had recognized Yehia. She knew by his shoulders and his walk. The armoured car wheeled slowly into the palace yard, soldiers trotted at its side, and the man Elaine took to be Yehia was running across the sand with a shadow twice as long as his body. The helmet threw his face into shadow, so she could not be certain. And yet, how was certainty conveyed? She wanted to call out to him. Her body told her it was Yehia by a kind of dizziness in the stomach, a tingling in the arms and legs.

Some moments before he went down she knew he was going to be hit. Once she saw him sit down on his haunches and pitch forward on to his face, the wave of emotion subsided. She was calm enough to order Tim to remain where he was. Her intention was to go down the steps and out into the yard and either drag Yehia into cover or remain with him until the fighting was over.

As it was, Tim and she reached the yard together. Yehia was being carried towards them out of the sun. Uniformed men seemed to be rushing to shake one another by the hand. The shooting had ceased, armoured cars and troops appeared to be pouring into the yard, there were shouts of laughter, cheering even; what danger there had been was now past, and Elaine, unable to express herself by sharing it with Yehia, waited under an archway until, helmetless and with a bloody right leg and breast, he was laid on one of the marble benches which were placed at intervals along the colonnade.

She pushed between the soldiers and bent over him. Until she saw the flicker of amazement in his eyes she could not have sworn that the man was Yehia. For Elaine as well as for Yehia it was the moment of recognition. She saw his lips trembling and the colour gather under his eyes. Until he spat, she thought these were signs of pain.

"I hope you're not badly hurt," she whispered and stood up. She wiped her cheek with the back of her hand. She was too frightened to cry. Never before had she felt so much anger directed upon her. It was like staring into a furnace. Egypt! she thought. Foreignness! Not England! Egypt!

Egypt! Foreignness! The shock of foreignness! Shocked! She was shocked by heat, sand, violence, the incomprehensible language which could be heard on all sides.

"It was Yehia," she said to Tim when she reached his side once more.

"What an extraordinary coincidence."

It was astonishing that Tim had not known it was Yehia until she told him. "He spat at me," she said. "He spat in my face! A nice thing, isn't it? He spat in my face!"

"He did *what*?"

"Let's go to the end of these columns. I recognize where we are now. That's where Mrs. Dragoumis was when I left her."

They walked steadily away from the Arabic. Elaine repeatedly touched her cheek, and Tim began sentences which he did not know how to finish. He even suggested that Elaine might have been mistaken. "Was he badly hurt?" he finished up.

Elaine shrugged. Not once did either of them look back.

"But this is absurd," said Tim. "He couldn't possibly have spat at you for the usual reasons. Not that I know what they are. It isn't something I've ever actually witnessed. I didn't know people still did it."

The room where the brown-headed sergeant had received them the night before was easily located, but Mrs. Dragoumis was no longer there. The guardroom, the small room beyond—indeed, the whole wing was deserted.

Elaine sat in the sergeant's chair. "You mustn't tell anyone what he did, Tim. I think he's dying."

"These things always look much worse than they really are."

"Anyway, you mustn't tell anyone. Promise."

"No, dammit," he said angrily. "To *spit* at you! The fellow's an absolute swine."

Mrs. Dragoumis was eventually found—quite fortuitously, it seemed, but in reality it would have been difficult for Tim and Elaine to go anywhere else. Troops were pouring through the main gate—impossible to escape that way. It was out of the question, too, to return to the State Apartments. This meant that, if they were not to stay in the guardroom, they would have to explore northwards. Never had Elaine been so conscious of compass bearings. Egypt lay to the south. She and Tim walked northwards, away from the shouting in the palace yard, away from soldiers, through archways and courtyards to a garden where palm trees spouted through flowering shrubs and a calculated tangle of creeping stems, tendrils, and blue trumpets. Here, overlooking the Mediterranean, was a stucco-faced villa with fly-netting at the windows and beds on a balcony—obviously a hospital of sorts.

"*Mademoiselle!*" they heard her calling. "*Mademoiselle! Monsieur!*"

Through an open window they saw her sitting up in bed to a tray of breakfast. "Ah! *Monsieur,*" she said, sucking butter from her fingers when they had made their way to her bedside, "they told me you were drowned in the harbour." Her hands made quick grabs at the food, fingers hanging. "People walk in and out of life. It seems unimportant. What does it mean, to be alive? It seems accidental to me, life. Very well, very well. I feel tired. They tell me the King has been deposed. He's got to be out of the country by six this evening. Everybody's carrying his baggage to the yacht. Everybody! Six o'clock this evening and they're all of them off to Naples, that's what the doctor told me."

"How big is this yacht?" asked Elaine.

Judging by her appetite, Mrs. Dragoumis seemed likely to recover from whatever had ailed her. Elaine supposed that the trouble was hysterical in origin, and thought there was some excuse for hysteria. She felt hysterical herself. The little hospital, run apparently for the benefit of senior palace servants and officials, had a staff of two Swiss nurses, who were ready to give Elaine as much sympathy as they had already bestowed on Mrs. Dragoumis. She was steadier after swallowing a calmative.

"Is it certain that the King is sailing for Naples?" she asked.

Waldo Grimbley, breakfasting with the others on the terrace of the Embassy, heard the news about Elaine as a trumpet call. He was less moved by the assurance that Mrs. Dragoumis was also safe. She was not a British subject. As Acting Vice-Consul it was his duty and privilege to go to Ras el-Tin at once, procure Miss Brent's release, and warn General Naguib, or whoever was in charge, that the bill for damages (unlawful detention, that sort of thing) would be presented later. Mr. Dragoumis, Eric, and Lydia wanted to go with him, but the Second Secretary said: "He's right, you know! It's his job, and he ought to do it alone. No, it's quite out of the question. I can't let you others go. We don't know that the trouble's over yet. It wouldn't be safe for you. Those are my instructions."

Grimbley had considerable difficulty in persuading Thompson to let him fly a Union Jack on his car. This was the prerogative of an Ambassador. Grimbley pointed out that his chances of getting through the cordon of troops would be slim without a show of importance, and Thompson compromised by forbidding the insignia and allowing

Grimbley to go off with it in his pocket to be set up as soon as he was out of sight.

Even so, Grimbley would never have entered the palace had an American Embassy car not been on the same mission at the same time. Grimbley's Daimler fell in behind the beflagged Cadillac as soon as they struck the Corniche Road. Troops were drawn across the road some half a mile from the palace gates, and the American Ambassador (Grimbley assumed it was no one of less consequence) was held up while the officer in charge went off to telephone. During the five minutes' wait half a dozen soldiers were kept busy driving off the boys who wished to sell sherbet and hard-boiled eggs to the representatives of Great Britain and the United States.

"Don't let anybody get between you and that car," said Waldo Grimbley to his chauffeur.

The two cars eventually moved off together. The Daimler might have been on a short tow rope. No one, however, attempted to interfere. Once inside the gates, Grimbley told his chauffeur to beat the Cadillac to the Reception Hall, but the American car accelerated fiercely across the yard and Grimbley had to content himself with following up the steps a youngish man in a grey suit whom he recognized as not the Ambassador after all but his First Secretary, he couldn't remember the name. At the top of the steps the American was still running, and Grimbley blew out his lips derisively. He knew what dignity meant to the impressionable Oriental mind.

A couple of soldiers with rifles were posted just inside the door. They looked at Grimbley doubtfully, and he was about to cross the hall to a table where half a dozen senior-looking officers were seated, drinking coffee, when he felt a hand on his shoulder.

"Mr. Simpson has gone through there. You are with Mr. Simpson?"

"No, dammit, I'm an Englishman," Waldo said to the little officer (bare-headed and breeched like a stable boy, he thought), "and I want to know who's in charge here." The little Egyptian appeared to find this amusing, and Grimbley went on: "I'm the Deputy Vice-Consul, if you want to know. You've got a couple of women here, one of them's a British subject, and if you want me to prove I'm a British subject too I'll go and get the Union Jack off the car and carry the bloody thing about with me."

"Miss Elaine Brent?"

"Yes, that's the name." Grimbley looked at the Egyptian in surprise. "How d'you know? Who are you, anyway?"

"Gamal Attallah."

Grimbley shrugged. "There's a boy here too. Name of Blainey."

Attallah asked Grimbley to accompany him. They left the hall, walked along a corridor, crossed a paved yard, and climbed some stone steps to a large room with a view of the sea. An open grate was filled with charred paper, drawers sagged like parched tongues from a huge desk which now bore nothing but a small bronze hand and a grey head resting on folded arms. Grimbley observed the general disorder coolly. Remarkably little blood, he thought.

"I must tell you frankly, Attallah, I'm quite neutral in this business. As far as I'm concerned, you're at liberty to murder the whole royal family, and I'd be equally delighted to see them put paid to you too. Now, who's this joker? *He's* not the king. Too old."

To Grimbley's surprise, the grey head was now lifted. "No, I am not His Majesty," said a weary voice. "Why do the English keep thinking I'm His Majesty?"

"Oh, you're not dead," said Grimbley, inspecting the sagging face. "Well, Attallah, what's the game, eh? If you've murdered this girl, you'd better out with it."

"She's on the *Mahroussa*."

"On the what?"

"On Farouk's yacht. It sails for Europe this afternoon."

Attallah made Grimbley sit down and smoke a cigarette while he explained. The grey-headed ex-Excellency behind the desk cheered up sufficiently to accept a cigarette also. He nodded when Attallah said that Miss Brent was on the *Mahroussa* entirely at her own request. His eyebrows were feathery, plucked from the breast of a goose, and they sailed gently upwards to signify: true, true, trivial but true, so un-important. He looked for the familiar ash tray, failed to find it, hesitated, and finally flicked the ash on the carpet. Pre-sumably it now belonged to Egypt. "She had no interest in the antiquities," he said, "none whatsoever. Well, nobody cares any more, I suppose. A journalist. No interest in the past. Think of the Tomb of Ti, for example."

"It seemed only right," said Attallah, "that a woman who had helped the King escape from Montazah should accompany him into exile. Frankly, there are a number of reasons why the Council of Officers are glad to have her quickly out of the country."

"Ah, so there was something in it, after all." Grimbley had abandoned his cigarette in favour of his pipe. "I must see her at once."

"This gentleman is Medani Pasha. He represents the palace. I represent the new government. We both agreed that Miss Brent should sail on the *Mahroussa*, but we must both insist that Miss Brent herself demanded this course. She was rude about it."

"I reserve all opinion in this matter," said Grimbley.

"It seems quite improbable. I can't understand what she's doing in the palace, anyway. I must tell you, it was most unsatisfactory from our point of view. If Naguib had hung on to her only a little bit longer, we'd have had Slim in the Citadel. And now she's on a yacht!"

"When you see her," said Attallah gently, "please be kind enough to say that Lieutenant Yehia is not considered to be in any real danger."

"Better write it on a bit of paper. I *can* see her, then?"

"You're an Important British Official, aren't you?"

"Yes, yes, I suppose I am." Grimbley blew fragments of flaming tobacco from his pipe. "But you've both been very charming. I hoped I should not have to stand on my official dignity, and I'm glad to say I haven't.

"Of course," he was barking at Gamal Attallah some ten minutes later when they were standing on the jetty waiting for a launch to take them out to the yacht, "there's a great deal more in this than meets the eye. I'm not a fool, you know. I don't trust you bastards, to speak frankly. However, if the girl shows willing, there's precious little I can do about it. Who did you say was not in danger?"

The *Mahroussa*, with a curl of vapour at its funnel, was anchored in the roadstead over a fluttering reflection, an extraordinarily white craft, enamel white, with gold at the prow, almost effervescent with light. The officer deputed by Attallah to accompany Grimbley insisted on remaining in the launch while Miss Brent was interviewed. Altogether, thought Grimbley, it was the most extraordinary experience he had ever had. He could not be sure that the Egyptians (he thought of Royalists and Naguibites impartially) were not trying to pull the wool over his eyes, and when he had climbed the jacob's ladder he was mentally swinging a cutlass. He was not reassured to discover that not only was he expected but his mission known. A ship's officer with a lot

of gold braid on his white hat saluted and handed Grimbley
over to a uniformed nurse (Armenian by the look of her,
thought Grimbley, who prided himself on spotting nationalities), and she led the way down to a cabin about the size
of a sleeping berth. Grimbley stood in the corridor out of
a sense of delicacy. Even so, he could have touched Elaine
with the stem of his pipe.

"Assuming you are who I think you are," he said with
an attempt at swagger, "you've only to say the word and I'll
have you off this boat like that!" Clicking his fingers.

Until the tap on the door Elaine had been lying on
the bunk staring up through the port at the cloudless sky,
dazing herself with staring. Expecting a steward, she had
been alarmed by the unheralded presence of an Englishman.
He had a hard, gouging voice, and in the confined space he
soon began to give off a reek of strong tobacco. Slowly, as
her eyes adjusted to the different light, Elaine saw the
narrow Anglo-Saxon face and beaked nose.

"If you want me off this boat, you'll have to drag me,"
she said. "And you haven't introduced yourself."

"Waldo Grimbley. I used to be Professor at Cairo until all British state employees were thrown out, and now I'm
in the Consulate here. That good enough for you? I only
want to be assured of your welfare, that you're here at your
own wish, et cetera."

"If I'd stayed ashore another hour, I should have died."

"Well, I daresay there are two sides to that story," he
remarked, beginning to dislike this hard young woman.
Now that he had seen her, he was quite prepared to credit
the rumours. "At least I can arrange to have your luggage
sent on board. I suspect you left rather quickly."

She nodded. "You could do that. It's at the Hotel Beau-
Soleil."

"But you don't much care if I don't."

"All I care about is getting out of this awful country."

"Awful? I wouldn't go so far as to say that." Grimbley was taken aback to discover someone who was even more unreasonable than he was himself.

"Do you mind?" Elaine sat up and closed the door gently in his face. She did not wish to be rude, but if this strange man remained any longer he might find reason for insisting on taking her ashore. She listened to him expostulating with the steward. When his footsteps had retired along the corridor and clicked up the stairs, she allowed her head to drop back on the pillow. Sticking out one foot, she bolted the door. If anyone wanted her before the ship sailed, they would have to break it down.

She was awakened by someone with apparently just that intention. When some moments later the day shook once more under the concussion, she realized it was gunfire. Through the port she could see nothing but sky, blue water, and a strip of lemon-coloured shore. Again the heavy thump. And again. She began counting the volleys. A shore battery was firing a salute. Laced into the measured booming were the strains of a military band; and finally, when guns and band were silent, a thin wailing was carried across the water. As a journalist Elaine thought that the time had come to put away personal feelings. She unbolted the door, made her way to the deck, and was immediately ordered down towards the stern, where her view was blocked by a lifeboat.

"The King and the royal family are coming on board," an officer was good enough to explain.

She was preparing to climb into the lifeboat when the officer checked her. Never mind, there would be plenty of time for an interview on the trip to Naples. Baggage was being swung on board by derrick, and Elaine, aware of the importance of detail, began to count the pieces. In this way hours seemingly passed.

The officer was resolved to make himself agreeable to her. He was young, smart, and possessed of the very slightest disdain for the work he was doing; nominally he was in charge of the loading party. Elaine found it a relief that he did not appear to be speculating why she was on board; so far as women were concerned, he was probably ready to accept life as he found it. Elaine had given up counting the pieces of baggage and was leaning over the rail to look shorewards when a cutter appeared, circling the *Mahroussa*, to the evident annoyance of one of its passengers, a thickly built figure who made gestures in the direction of the yacht. The cutter turned, and in the new angle of light it was possible to see that the half-dozen or so passengers were in khaki and wearing peaked caps.

"Naguib," said the baggage officer.

"Who?"

"General Naguib." The lilt of pride was unmistakable. "That man standing up. He is now the head of this country."

Elaine could neither see nor approach the point where General Naguib came aboard. The baggage sling remained in mid-air. The wailing from the shore had died out. A funereal silence, broken only by the lapping of water and the hum of wind in the stays, settled down on the ship. What could possibly be happening? Why was everyone so still?

She followed the direction of the baggage officer's eyes and saw that a man in white naval uniform had appeared on the bridge. He stood quietly looking about him, the sun flashing on his dark glasses. A second man, a soldier this time, came into view and saluted. They stood for some time, motionless but apparently talking, until Elaine could bear it no longer and turned away, her eyes filling with tears.

She walked aft. As she guessed, there was access here to the crew's quarters (all unoccupied), from where it was only a matter of walking along a corridor and opening a door to find her own miniature cabin. The bony Deputy Vice-Consul had taken her hint. The two suitcases from the Hotel Beau-Soleil were standing side by side on the floor. The cases were not, however, the first to catch her eye. Lying on her bunk was the huge bouquet of yellow roses. Petals fell as she watched. They were so delicate she wanted to hold her breath for fear of shattering them. She could not move. The browning petals, withering at the tips, opened over the amber stamens. The perfume was scarcely strong enough to carry through the salt air; just a hint, a dry hint of gardens.

On the table was an envelope addressed to her. It contained a card which said: "I quite forgot to mention but Lieutenant Someone (can't remember name) is not thought to be in danger. Hope you can make something of this. Trust your baggage is complete. I didn't see why the roses should be allowed to waste. Your hotel bill is paid but as soon as you return to London report to the Foreign Office. They'll want the money. Yours faithfully, J. Waldo Grimbley."

She noticed that there was a card, too, among the roses. Clearly it was the original card because it was so badly stained by the petals. Wondering why she had not seen it before, she stretched her fingers between the thorns and gently turned the card over.

"To Elaine," she read, "with love from Mahmoud."

Abbassia Military Academy,
Cairo, Egypt
Nov. 15th, 1952

MISS E. BRENT,
JOURNALIST AND FOREIGN CORRESPONDENT,
"THE SUN NEWSPAPER,"
LONDON, ENGLAND

Dear Miss,

I am very well who write this letter after some time in hospital. I do not walk easily but I am very well because living in my country now is wonderful. It is morning. All the people are waking up to the new life. They know there is one law for all, rich and poor, and there is hope to better himself by his own efforts now that the big estates have been divided. No man has more than two hundred acres. For the first time the poor fellah can become the owner of his land and so he is no more just a two-footed animal. Miss Brent, there have been times of crying with happiness to see the faces of poor fellaheen learning that they can own up to five acres of land in a government cooperative. It is not correct to think of this country as Ancient Egypt of the Pharaohs. This Egypt is new and younger than England. There is great work, reform. All look to the future.

Perhaps you will not remember me. That would be very good. Please write and say you have forgotten me. I suffer continually from the thought that you remember me with hatred. Much better to forget than remember me with hatred. I have been mad with this anxiety.

Mad with this thought and with other things but chiefly with this thought that you remember me with hatred. God is to be thanked that I have good friends or I should be mad altogether. Tell me it is a dream, I asked them. Over and over again I begged them to say I was ill and saw you when you were not there. You were there and I was there, they said, but what does it matter? I am Egyptian and you are English. It is right for me to curse you.

No, it is not right. The memory of it crushes with shame and despair. Please write and say you do not remember the writer of this letter. Who am I? Why do I concern myself? Is it perhaps a confidence trick? you might ask.

In truth, I write to ask your permission to come to England. If you do not know who I am it will be a small thing for you to write and say, "Yes, come to England, for I do not know who you are and it is no care of mine whether you are in Egypt or England."

But perhaps if you do remember, please also write and say yes or no to my coming in England. I cannot come without your permission. I could not breathe comfortably the

English air without permission. I do not ask to see you. That would be too much. I will keep away. But I must have your permission to land. I should feel that I had lost dignity as a human being if I came without your permission. To meet you accidentally and for you to say, "You, Mahmoud Yehia, here in England!" and be surprised and shocked! No I could not run that risk.

My government has offered me the post of Military Attaché in London. It is a great honour. Certainly I do not deserve it. I know this and my friends know it too but they pretend that it is a suitable reward. How can they pretend this when every soldier must know that I disgraced myself at Ras el-Tin? I disobeyed orders. I lost my head. I have never been like this before. My mind was in two. Partly I was thinking of the king and partly of you. The king and you. You became mixed. If I could have put you out of my mind I should have behaved well. If I could have put the king out of my mind I should have been a traitor but I should not have muddled. It was all no good. I cursed you. Really, I was cursing myself.

May I accept this post of Military Attaché in London? If you say yes I will come and there will be no bother to you. If you say no that also will be understood and I shall go to France, possibly, or the United States. I shall go somewhere in any case out of Egypt because here, in my native country, my feelings and ideas have become too much for me. The newness excites me too much. All the promise of happiness is not a promise of my happiness. I am a stranger in my own country. So I would like to go abroad and serve Egypt there.

You are a journalist, of course. If you hated me a great deal I could be injured if you printed this letter in your newspaper. All Egypt would cry out, "See, an Egyptian asks an Englishwoman if he can come to London in Egypt's service!" I should be held in contempt and derision. So please do not publish or talk of it. Answer me or burn it.

Yours sincerely,
MAHMOUD YEHIA (*Lieut.*)

14a Oxford Close,
London N.W.3
Nov. 20th, 1952

TIMOTHY BLAINEY, ESQ.
℅ DRAGOUMIS,
28, RUE SEGAR,
SIDI BISHR,
ALEXANDRIA, EGYPT

Dear Tim,

Don't tell Eric, but your mother and I are becoming friendly. Perhaps that is not the most accurate way of describing the relationship. She has been pleased to interest herself in my welfare. She is such a romantic. She is quite sure that a woman like myself getting on for middle-age and still unmarried must have a poignant background. A lover killed in the war at very least. She is quietly determined to get the whole story out of me and, of course, she's such a charmer that it's impossible to mind the tiniest bit and I know I shall finish up by inventing. Poor dear! She likes talking about your father, doesn't she? And then, when she's tried to convey one or other of his characteristics, she says, "Now, you've seen both the boys recently. Which of them is most like his father?" I know what she wants me to say: you, Tim. For her the great thing in life is to produce a son as much like his father as possible. She would never forgive me if I suggested that Eric is very like the man his

father must have been. That would imply too much credit
to *that woman!* Surely even Eric must see that this jealousy
is really rather appealing.

Oh, damn this fog! There's enough acid in it to eat the
flesh off your bones. I can see it coming under the door as
I write. Even the fog, though, doesn't reconcile me to the
thought of Egypt, no, not even when I have your eloquent
letters to paint the scene so attractively. Give me Hampstead
Heath. Your last letter was opened by the censor, I might
tell you; so don't say any rash things about the regime or
you'll find yourself out on your ear, almost as precipitately
as I was. Stick to the pyramids by moonlight for subject.
Of course, I recognize that my views on Egypt are not entirely rational. I was so terrified. It is humiliating at my
age to discover that one is a coward.

Do you remember that Egyptian officer, Mahmoud
Yehia, the one who got himself shot so stupidly? I expect
you've met so many Egyptians since then your memory of
this one may have become cloudy. But he was the only
one I seemed to have any real dealings with; he kept popping
up all over the place. Anyway, believe it or not, he's had
the effrontery to write to me. He wrote % the *Sun*. Of course
I'm not going to answer him, and I only mention it now
in case you should run into him somewhere. He might ask
you. As a matter of interest I'll send his letter along because,
as you'll see, it's something of a curiosity. Asking my permission to take up an appointment in London! I suppose
that's his idea of sarcasm. If you do see him, you might find
occasion to say it's a matter of indifference to me where he
is. He could even come to London with impunity. In the
unlikely event of our meeting I should not recognize
him.

Since my promotion it's been possible for me to run a

flat on my own for the first time, but being here by myself so much on my own was a bit wearing, so I've decided to let the spare bedroom and, Tim, I must warn you that I shall probably try to marry her off to you when you come back to England. (When will that be, by the way? Your mother says you can't possibly have any money left.) She's too delightful. A little doll's face. She took a first in something or other at Oxford and works in the Ministry of Fuel and Power. But, in spite of Marguerite, I don't really feel settled. I want a holiday.

By the way, *re* the foregoing. It isn't your mother who's delightful and has the doll's face. It's Marguerite. She's so intelligent. You know how it is with some people. They don't have to say anything or do anything. They have a glow of intelligence on them. Of course, she'd be much too good for you, but I feel that in my old age I'll be a real match-maker and I've got to start sometime.

Why in God's name do I write all this rubbish? Sorry! I must be getting soft in the head.

Perhaps I ought to take more exercise. I'll buy a dog and take it for walks. This is a very silly letter, but I wanted to send you and Eric and Lydia some sort of salutation. I'll write to Mr. Dragoumis about the publisher, but I hope you'll prepare the ground. There isn't a publisher in London who'd touch utopianism these days.

Love,
ELAINE

P.S. On second thoughts, I won't send Lieut. Yehia's letter. His address is Abbassia Military Academy, Cairo. In case you don't meet him, you might drop him a line and give him my views. I don't feel I want to get involved in a lot of letter writing.

28 *Rue Segar,*
Sidi Bishr
Nov. 24th, 1952

LIEUT. MAHMOUD YEHIA,

ABBASSIA MILITARY ACADEMY,

CAIRO

Dear Lieutenant Yehia,

      I'm giving a small party on Wednesday, December 10th, and it would give me a lot of pleasure if you could manage to come. It's by way of being a farewell party because I plan to be in England for Christmas. I wanted to say goodbye to everyone. Apart from my brother, you were just about the first person I met in Egypt. No doubt you will remember that morning as vividly as I do. Will 6 p.m. on the 10th be all right?

Yours Sincerely,
TIM BLAINEY

28 *Rue Segar,*
Sidi Bishr
Nov. 24th 56

MISS ELAINE BRENT,

14a OXFORD CLOSE,

LONDON, N.W.3

Dear Elaine,

      By this time Mother will probably have told you I shall be home for Christmas. I was horrified by your remarks about her. Not that they are necessarily untrue, very likely they are not, but it is disturbing to have one's mother, one's family situation, one's brother, spoken about as detachedly as you did. This jealousy you speak of—well, it is my matrix. Honestly, I was so taken aback that I was surprised into showing your letter to Eric. He laughed, which annoyed me even more. I won't have him laughing at Mother in this way. Of course, he denied he was laughing at her.

What is all this about Yehia? You didn't send his letter, so I've only the vaguest idea what he's up to. Anyway, I've invited him to a farewell party I'm giving on Dec. 10th and I daresay he'll tell me all about it then. I get the general drift, of course, that you don't want to write to him or have anything to do with him. After what happened I don't blame you. Perhaps you'll think me odd to invite him to the party. The fact is that no one I've met has made quite the impression he did during those days of the revolution. At the word Egypt I used to think of—oh, I don't know, a sphinx, Cleopatra, that sort of thing. Now I see Yehia, like a bear, spitting. Do bears spit? This incident still seems extraordinarily mysterious to me.

During the past month I've been writing. The more one sees of Alexandria, though, the more disappointing it becomes. I got into a most sordid quarrel yesterday with a Lebanese Jewess who said the French started the 1914 war. Just fancy a Jewess saying this, particularly one educated in France as she was. I daresay when I meet her tomorrow she'll be quite ready to argue it was the Germans after all. You will understand why I have the reputation of being *serieux*. Lydia is trying to marry me to one of her cousins, by the way. What is it about me that brings out the matchmaking qualities in women? You and your girl in the Ministry. There is only one girl for me, and that's you!

So what am I to say to Yehia if he comes?

Yours with love,

TIM

Abbassia Military Academy,
Cairo
Nov. 26, 1952

Dear Mr. Blainey,

It was very kind to invite me to your party.
I should like to come and shake your hand once more. I
am awaiting the announcement of my new appointment.
It is possible that I am leaving this country early under
orders. Only this can prevent me coming. In the meantime,
allow me to wish you, sir, good fortune and all success.

Yours sincerely,
MAHMOUD YEHIA (*Lieut.*)

14a Oxford Close,
N.W.3
Nov. 29th. 52

Dear Tim,

I forbid you to discuss my affairs with Lieutenant Yehia. I merely authorized you to write and say he
was quite free to come to England so far as I was concerned. If he asks you whether you know if I've received
his letter, you can say yes. But if he wants to know whether
I'm going to reply, say you don't know. Anyway, it's absurd
to pretend that an important military appointment should
depend on anything I say. He'll never be offered the job
of Military Attaché in London again. In haste,

Yours,
ELAINE

> 28 *Rue Segar,*
> *Sidi Bishr*
> *Dec. 3rd*

Dear Lieutenant Yehia,
> So glad you can come.

> *Yrs.,*
> TIM BLAINEY

For the rest of that summer and during the autumn Tim had been travelling. The country was under martial law, but there was no interference with one's freedom of movement, and Tim went first of all to Aswan, working his way north again through Luxor and Thebes to Assiut and Cairo, taking notes and photographs. Whenever he found himself on sufficiently friendly terms with an Egyptian he would ask him as tactfully as he could about native beliefs and customs; for example, did spitting have any special significance? At the back of his mind was the thought that in some countries quite gross gestures (by our standards) were thought polite: Tibetans sticking their tongues out, that sort of thing. But his informants said that Egyptians thought about spitting as everyone else did; and, as for spitting in somebody's face, it could only lead to bloodshed.

A business associate of Mr. Dragoumis's, a certain Mr. Asmy, invited Tim to his native province, the Fayoum, for a few days. They drove along dirt roads in a hired car, discussing whether or not the doctrine of the Trinity made Christians polytheistic (for Mr. Asmy said that he was a philosopher like Mr. Dragoumis, but on a higher level), and at one point inspected a contingent of policemen with some formality, their captain presenting Tim with a bunch of flowers afterwards and saying what an honour it was to be visited by an Englishman, particularly as the bad old days of Imperialism were over and all men were brothers. The police launch took them for a trip on Lake Karoun. In a Coptic monastery Mr. Asmy insisted on Tim's putting his hand through a screen and shaking hands with a holy man who had been dead two hundred years. Mr. Asmy said that, as a Moslem, he could only smile at such a crude custom—really, the Christians had made themselves absurd with their cult of relics, their holy bones, their pictures. Before Tim could think of a suitable reply they were in the car again, driving across the undulating countryside. As they passed through the villages, Mr. Asmy pronounced their names with great sonority: So-and-So of the lemons, of the grapes, of the guavas, or whatever the local crop happened to be. Enormous wooden irrigation wheels groaned with passion. Tim had to raise his voice to ask the necessary questions. He was drugged by heat and dust, but still he wanted to know. Did parents arrange their children's marriages? Was it true that each village had a professional murderer who could be hired for a few pounds? They climbed to the first floor of Mr. Asmy's house and ate a meal of fish with their heads on, green Moulakhieh soup, beans and rice, kebab, cold chicken, Yusif Effendi oranges, and sweet coffee. They sat before an open window looking out over a field of brilliant greenness, the colour shaking like a flame, and Mr. Asmy said that an Egyptian who spat in a woman's face would need extreme provocation and must be a low type into the bargain. Such things did not happen, except privately, perhaps, between husband and wife.

Tim liked the Egyptians.

The revolution had clearly been for the best. Shortly after the Fayoum trip he wrote a copious note warning himself against mistaking his own happiness for some general truth about Egypt itself. This was an error into which travellers frequently fell. Because he woke each morning with pleasurable expectancy for whatever the day might bring, it did not at all mean that the average Egyptian led a life of gaiety. Never had he seen human beings living in such squalor. At the same time, there *was* gaiety. Real gaiety! He had seen little donkey carts rattling across the Cairo tram-lines bearing an impossible number of rejoicing people, clapping their hands rhythmically, swinging their dangling legs, chanting the name of Naguib.

If only Elaine had been able to stay in Egypt and travel about as he had done, he felt sure she would never have written those articles in the *Sun*. They arrived in a fat envelope which the censor had providentially not opened. Probably Elaine had not intended to make a political judgement on the Egyptian revolution, but her account of the voyage of the *Mahroussa*, for example, was clearly favourable to ex-King Farouk and critical of the followers of General Naguib, whom she described as a set of fanatics. Tim supposed that some palace official's hope that she would write in this key was the reason for her finding a berth on the *Mahroussa*. He trusted that she had not in her eagerness stooped to the making of any kind of promise. Anyway, she was wrong to be a Royalist and she was doubly wrong to permit the *Sun* to publicize her as the woman who had been arrested for abetting Farouk's escape from Montazah.

It all served to increase the expectancy with which he looked forward to meeting Mahmoud Yehia once more, even though he did have the painful task of telling him that Elaine loathed every recollection of her Egyptian experience, Yehia included. And *particularly* Yehia! Tim smiled to himself. Elaine could not pull the wool over his eyes with a pretence of indifference. She would never for-give Yehia for spitting in her face, she hated him, and it was only fair to give the chap some sort of warning if he was going to London. Elaine was quite capable of taking her revenge in public, and if Yehia was a military attaché it would probably have international repercussions. Foreign Diplomat Assaulted at Royal Garden Party! Tim could al-most see the headline.

About Elaine herself Tim thought with indulgence. In spite of her foolish newspaper articles, he now saw that he loved her. Even when he developed the theory that she merely imagined Yehia had spat at her (like Adela Quested imagining things in the Marabar Caves) it merely served to diminish the nine years or so that separated their ages. Well, even if she had not imagined the incident it had probably been quite accidental. Wounded men simply did not spit into women's faces. Yehia might have been clearing his throat at the time. He might have been breathing out rather hard to avoid groaning. But no, on the whole, Tim tended to the theory that Elaine hysterically imagined the gesture, because that would mean she really did hate Yehia and he, Tim, could love her all the more because of it.

However, when Yehia came to the party everything turned out rather different from Tim's expectations.

In the first place, Yehia was late. Lydia's cousins ar-rived on the dot, three rather pretty girls in clattering high heels who were immediately rushed off by Lydia, all shriek-ing, to some private confabulation. Their parents—Mrs. Dra-goumis's brother, a severe-looking man with sunken cheeks, and his delicate-looking wife—entered the room with some gravity and in turn kissed Mrs. Dragoumis gently. Paler than ever, she sat in a capacious chair, a confection of a chair in white and gold with a curved back that enclosed her as in a shell; her feet, puffed out over painfully small shoes, rested on a stool. She suffered the embraces of her brother and sister-in-law, but made little immediate response beyond sighing. The doctor had declared there was nothing really the matter with her, but nevertheless Mrs. Dragoumis had become an invalid; mysteriously, a friendship with Mr. Klingopoulos had developed—he called her the heroine of Ras el-Tin—and this evening he had already taken up a position at her side, holding a cup of tea close to her chin while she dunked biscuits.

By six fifteen there were about a dozen guests. Mr. Dragoumis could be heard saying that Aristotelian logic was dependent on certain grammatical forms and until these grammatical forms were abolished (for they persisted in modern European languages) there would be no true thinking. The Hopi Indians, said Mr. Dragoumis, did not know what subjects and predicates were. Eric said this hadn't done the Hopis much good, and the pair of them argued about the location of Hopi reservations in the United States. Eric seemed to contradict his father-in-law a great deal these days.

They were all waiting for Yehia. Mrs. Dragoumis might have been expected to object to his presence. But no! She was as curious as anyone. What were his motives? she asked Klingopoulos. What advantage could he see in keeping up an acquaintanceship with the Dragoumises? The Englishwoman had gone. He had nothing to hope for in that direction. Perhaps he was excited by the thought of stepping once more over the threshold where he had carried a shoeless, fainting girl. Sexual excitement, that's all he came for.

"Who's that man?" she asked Klingopoulos. "That one **over** there. I'm sure he wasn't invited."

Klingopoulos could scarcely catch the words over the babble which marked the entry of Lydia and her cousins, but on seeing the stranger they at once fell silent—out of surprise, it seemed—and their silence served to point Mrs. Dragoumis's question. Everyone looked at the man. He wore a grey suit so padded that he appeared about four feet across the shoulders. Obviously it was a new suit. Possibly this was the first time it had been worn in public, and its owner held himself stiffly and self-consciously as though a little ashamed of the fact. In his right hand he held a walking-stick, in his left a small bouquet of half a dozen or so yellow roses, and when he moved to present them to Mrs. Dragoumis they saw he had a pronounced limp.

"Good evening," he said. "I am happy to see all my friends again."

He blushed at the stir he had caused.

"I did not realize I had changed so much. You did not recognize me. And I was late, too. That is inexcusable. I make my apologies."

Mrs. Dragoumis had given the roses to Klingopoulos with instructions to put them in water before Tim spoke.

"Your plain clothes!"

"No, it is not only me not being in uniform. I have changed. I have changed, yes? You see my hair. Grey! Yes, grey here and here. I am an old man. We grow old in Egypt quickly."

"Oh, no! Once we *know* it's you. He hasn't changed, has he, Eric? Everybody expected a uniform."

"Recognized you immediately," said Eric. "Can't imagine what all the fuss is about. What'll you have, anyway? Nothing alcoholic? Well, tea, then? Or coffee? There's lemonade. Of course, major, as one of the new ruling class you've got to get used to these solemn entries."

"I am not a major," said Yehia, smiling. "I am a lieutenant."

"Still? I can't imagine what Naguib is playing at."

"You did not recognize me," said Yehia, smiling and boring into the carpet with his walking-stick. "Why should you recognize me? It does not surprise me. I have lost twelve kilos."

Tim was so confused that he fetched Yehia whisky when coffee had been asked for. Yehia declined, and Tim stood in front of him with a puzzled frown on his face, sipping the neat spirit as though it were sherry, and thinking that he could never tell Yehia that Elaine hated him. It would be too much like hitting a man when he was down. The fellow was actually hollow-cheeked!

"No, I am perfectly well standing," said Yehia when Eric tried to persuade him to sit down.

"And I," said Mrs. Dragoumis suddenly in her atrocious French, "I am prevented from standing by my bad legs." She was becoming increasingly eccentric in her manner. It was a little frightening. "This is the first time for twenty-five years—twenty-five years, you hear that?—anyone brings me flowers. My favourite yellow roses. God bless you, lieutenant. You are not a Christian, but I ask God to bless you for bring me roses. I am very touched. The last time we met, now, that was in the barracks. All has changed since those times. Do you ever hear from Miss Brent, may I ask?"

"No, *Madame*."

"A pretty young woman, but an atheist."

"Now, now, Mama," said Lydia.

"Why should I not speak the truth? Well, we all know what has happened to Miss Brent."

"What did she mean?" Yehia said to Tim when there

was general conversation once more and they could speak without being overheard. "What has happened to Miss Brent?"

"Nothing, so far as I know."

"Then why did *Madame*—?"

"Ever since her experiences at Ras el-Tin, you know, she has been a bit odd."

"But there must be *something*."

"No, nothing at all. As a matter of fact, I've a letter from Elaine in my pocket at this very moment."

"Let me see it!"

"What?"

"I beg your pardon. I shouldn't have said that. But you have actually received a letter from her! Does she say anything about me? Oh, please let us go somewhere we can talk. Please! Please!"

"We can talk here, can't we?" A pause. "Hope your leg isn't too badly hurt."

Yehia waved a hand. "My car is outside. We could go for a drive. There is an important secret I must tell you. A state secret. Besides, I want to say good-bye to you. I can't with all these people."

"You know," said Tim, still sipping at his whisky, "there's one important piece of information I must give you. The last time you saw Elaine—it was in Ras el-Tin—she firmly believes you spat in her face. Now, that may seem incredible."

"Don't you believe it?"

"Of course not. It must have been a misunderstanding."

"No, it is true." Yehia spoke so loudly that once more he was the centre of interest. "You don't think Miss Brent would tell a lie? It is quite true. I did it! Can you imagine that? If you doubt me, why do you doubt Miss Brent?"

Tim was so upset that he walked over to Lydia's cousins,
who were eating jam in the Greek way with small silver
spoons. He had scarcely settled himself in the chair before
Eric arrived, saying kindly: "I should like to remind you,
young Tim, that all disasters from now on are your responsibility. It was against my advice that you invited him.
One last service I am prepared to render. Say the word
and I'll ask him to leave."

"Good God, no." Tim was beginning to sweat with
anger and alcohol. The monstrous insult had in fact been
committed. The fellow admitted it. He did not even seem
ashamed. If Tim had not already carried out a thorough
investigation into Egyptian attitudes to spitting, he might
have been deceived by Yehia's manner. The man was gross
beyond belief. But Tim did not want him turned away.
In the first place, he was an invited guest, and, in the second, Tim was gripped by a rage that demanded more and
more fuel. He wanted an explanation from the man. And
if there were no explanation forthcoming, Tim wanted to
hear Yehia making his claim or confession over and over
again. I did it! I did it! I did it! Tim wanted to watch
the man's face, listen to these words, and blow himself
up into the most tremendous mad rage. He yearned for
anger as a drunk yearns for alcohol. He could not bear to
be parted from Yehia for a moment.

"Bet you ten pounds," said Eric, "that, once Yehia ar-
rives in England, he and Elaine will get on splendidly."

"Are you crazy?"

"They'll be married within a year."

"Ten pounds it is."

Mr. Dragoumis was making himself agreeable to Yehia.
He offered snuff, which was refused, and said he regretted
the disappearance of the old empires, the Ottoman Empire

and the Austro-Hungarian Empire, which had much more
to recommend them than people nowadays were ready to
admit. He spoke of his childhood in Alexandria, a time
when his father used to travel in Syria, Turkey, Greece,
even Italy and Austria—all without a passport. But, certainly, they were days before science and technology; and,
talking of science and technology, perhaps Lieutenant Yehia
would like to meet Dr. Zervos, who had made an ascent
with Professor Piccard in his celebrated balloon.

"What did you mean?" Tim asked Yehia as soon as a
few polite words had been exchanged with Mr. Dragoumis's
scientific friend, a middle-aged, clown-faced man who
seemed more interested in Lydia's pretty cousins than in
technology. "What did you mean by saying you had a secret
to tell me?"

"We cannot talk here, you understand me?"

"Let's go and sit in your car for a bit."

Tim knew he was on the threshold of the crucial. He
thought of an evening in Marseilles when he had spoken
to some girls in a little street off the Cannebière. He had
been dizzy with excitement. And there was anger too! He
thought of the way they had laughed at him. Excitement,
rage, and—oh, yes, over and above all, fear! He remembered
going back to his hotel and getting drunk on Pernod. Well,
that was not the kind of defence he could have used at this
moment, even if he had wanted to.

Rain was falling, the first rain Tim had seen since
landing in Egypt. Yehia put the windscreen-wipers to work,
and they sat looking westwards at the rain bouncing on
the bonnet and gleaming in the last yellow light. Straight
ahead was a lemon-coloured flaw in the clouds to mark the
direction the sun had taken.

"I've been asked to go as military attaché to London.

You will understand how confidential this is. But Miss Brent does not write and give her permission."

"Permission?"

"I could not go to London without her permission. This is my own pride. I must do what pleases her. Think of this situation, please. You are injured. You are in great pain and disappointment. You feel that you have betrayed all you believe in. You are not yourself, you admit that? You are another person. So you insult very badly a woman."

"No, I don't think there's an excuse. It was filthy behaviour. After that, why can't you leave Elaine alone? Is it any wonder she hates the very thought of you?"

"You have a message for me?"

"I have no message."

"You can at least tell me whether she received my letter."

"Yes, but, as you see, she doesn't want to write to you."

"Then I am answered," said Yehia simply. "I shall not take up my appointment."

Tim turned slightly to look at Yehia's face, but it revealed nothing. It was impassive. There was no doubt that Yehia meant exactly what he said. So the moment was crucial for him too.

"London is a big place."

"I will not go."

Rain drummed on the roof of the car. In the distance a street-light winked through the sheets of water. The air was cold. The evening had become European, and Tim felt his anger being drugged out of him by the new sweetness of the air. He was stirring from a six-month dream. It was Egypt, now, that threatened to become unreal.

Yehia lit a cigarette and wound down his window to flick the match into the murk. "She is quite right, Miss

Brent. I get what I deserve. If I was Miss Brent, I would not answer. She acts with right spirit."

"I daresay there are other good jobs."

Yehia did not answer for a while. "Can't you let me read Miss Brent's letter? As I shall not see her, how will it matter?

"You are in love with Miss Brent yourself?" asked Yehia when Tim made no reply.

Tim flushed. "That's my own business."

"Yes, you do love her. But she is too old for you. She doesn't love you."

Tim made to get out of the car, but Yehia put a restraining hand on his arm. "Let me at least see her handwriting. Give me a fragment of her notepaper, even if it has no writing on it."

"She wants to have nothing to do with you. Don't you understand?"

"Please! A fragment of paper she had touched. She would never know."

Tim hesitated and then pulled the letter out of an inside pocket. It had arrived by the afternoon post and he had had time to read it only cursorily; the substance of the letter was clear enough in his mind, and in Tim's view it would answer Yehia more eloquently than anything he could say. Tim decided that he would not hand the letter over—that would be a real breach of faith; he would read it aloud and silently censor any passages Elaine might not wish Yehia to hear. Yehia switched on an overhead light. Tim smoothed out the folded sheets and began to read. After he had been reading some moments he began to feel that Elaine's sentences might bear an interpretation slightly different from the one he had originally placed upon them.

" 'Dear Tim,' " he read. " 'With a bit of luck this letter should arrive before your farewell party, and if Lieutenant Yehia does in fact come, I think I ought to tell you a bit more than I have done so far. You should be forewarned. I ought to have been more explicit in the first place. Let me make it quite clear that I do not wish to get involved in correspondence with him. That is why I write to you. You can tell him that his movements are a matter of complete indifference to me. He can go to Patagonia for all I care.' "

"Then there *was* a message for me," said Yehia in surprise.

"I don't call that a message really," said Tim.

He continued: " 'On rereading his first letter I have come to the conclusion that he was not being sarcastic when he asked my permission to take up an appointment in London. I think he wrote out of pure ignorance. He simply did not know it was effrontery of a different order. If I wrote back and said, "What does it matter to me where you are?" he would only reply and I should end up by saying, "All right, come to London, but please don't expect to see me." Since coming back to England I have read a great deal about Egyptians and the status of women under Islam, and I can quite see that a Moslem might grow very presumptuous on a letter from a woman which said, "Please do not rely on my having anything to do with you." ' "

"This is dreadful," said Yehia. "I am not that kind of man. What does she know of Islam? A lot of books! Are there not gentlemen in Egypt, as there are in England?"

"The position of women in the two countries is quite different," said Tim.

He went on reading Elaine's letter: " 'However, the main point of this note, Tim, is to apologize for putting

you in a difficult position, and I could perfectly well understand it if you were angry with me. Why should you have
to act as an intermediary in this way?' "

"This is a long note," said Yehia. "Good! Good!"

"I don't see what's good about it."

"She goes into a lot of reasons. Forgive me, I must
not interrupt."

"She goes on to say (I'm missing a lot of stuff out
here)—and this is why I'm reading her letter to you. She
says: 'I really think that the last morning I spent in Egypt
was the most frightful experience I have ever had in my
life, and I am sure it has left a mark on me. First of all,
being handed over in the middle of the night, not knowing
whether we were to be shot down; then the atmosphere of
siege and departure, the sense of a dynasty coming to an
end, because I don't for one moment believe Naguib will
be satisfied until he has set up a republic. That little boy
being king is absurd. And then, with all these thoughts in
one's mind, to be insulted by a man who, although he was
a foreigner, one had come to like and respect in many ways.

" 'My mind is quite made up. I shall not give Lieutenant Yehia the satisfaction of saying no to his request for
permission to come to England. That could only imply
that I took him much more seriously than I know (or he
knows) he deserves. I have quite made up my mind to take
this extraordinarily silly man as seriously as I can. So I am
not even going to say it is a matter of indifference to me
whether he comes or not. If he has so tortuous a mind,
what might he not read into that? No, I am quite prepared
to deal with the situation rationally. He will never be able
to say that I was guilty of any kind of pettiness.

" 'So, Tim, tell Lieutenant Yehia that he *has* my permission to come to England to take up his post, and if this

contradicts what I said at the beginning of this letter, it nevertheless represents my true state of mind. I haven't time to write it all out again in a more sensible form. Yours, in haste, Elaine.' "

When Tim had finished reading this letter he folded it carefully and replaced it in his pocket, half expecting that Yehia would try to take it from him. But Yehia sat quite still, his hands resting on the steering-wheel, his ciga-rette—the merest stub—glowing between his lips. The wind-screen-wipers creaked like leather pinions, and Yehia looked ahead into the evening through the cleared half-circle of glass where raindrops perpetually flawed the surface and were gone.

"Why did you say you had no message for me?" he asked at last.

"Well, I don't really call that a message," said Tim uncomfortably. He had, in fact, been caught out. His im-pression on reading the letter that afternoon had been of a diatribe. "The unfortunate fact is that Elaine has taken a very strong dislike to you and doesn't want to be bothered with you any more. That's the hard truth. Well, that was a poor sort of message to give anybody, and I suppose I toned it down a bit."

"You said there was no message," Yehia insisted.

"Oh, well, dammit, I was wrong," said Tim passion-ately. And this time he did jerk open the door of the car and step out into the rain. Yes, he was wrong, and the rain fell on his upturned face, on his closed eyelids. Of course he was wrong, and he had known it ever since Elaine had cast him in the role of go-between. He entered the house wiping the rain from his face.

Two days later he sailed for England, convinced that he had a duty to perform. "Elaine," he would say, "the time has come for you to recognize reality. You say you hate Mahmoud Yehia, but you are deceiving yourself. In fact you love him."

Early in the New Year she telephoned to say that she had the impression he was avoiding her. Only once had they met since Tim's return, and that was when he had come round with a piece of Coptic tapestry, a camel saddle to be used as a stool, and a box of real Oriental Turkish delight stuffed with nuts. They were Christmas presents. He had handed them over, been very merry, and departed all within the space of half an hour. There was no mention of Yehia; indeed, there was a fairly obvious avoidance of the subject. Seeing each other for the first time in English surroundings, they were surprised. It seemed impossible that they were the same people who had travelled on the *Tewfikieh* and then had those extraordinary few days together in Alexandria. Elaine wore a smart knitted suit in smoky red which made her look so self-assured Tim could only marvel that her manner concealed such a lack of self-knowledge.

"Avoiding you! Why should I do that? As a matter of fact, I've been busy writing up my notes. I showed my photographs to a publisher. He said there might be a book in it, but I've got to write a sample chapter. Travel books are *the* thing nowadays, Elaine." He chattered on because her tone alarmed him. And it was quite true that he had been avoiding her. The plan, as suggested by Eric while waiting for the *Tewfikieh* to sail, was to confront Elaine with Yehia in a totally unexpected way. So far as Tim could discover, Yehia had not yet taken up his appointment at the Embassy. Until the meeting was arranged Tim thought he had better keep out of Elaine's way. The state of his own feelings was too delicate to expose them to unnecessary hazards. He was quite set on being noble and had addressed a letter to Lieutenant Mahmoud Yehia at the Egyptian Embassy, marked *To Await Arrival.*

"Well, would you be free for supper tomorrow night?" Elaine asked. "You haven't met Marguerite yet."

Having pondered Eric's advice, Tim had come to the conclusion that the only way to make Elaine face the truth about herself was as a result of shock: Yehia appearing out of a cupboard, for example, and advancing with the aid of his stick. Once she realized she was in love with the man, what then? Sometimes Tim thought that his motives were entirely therapeutic. If the letters he had received from her in Egypt were any guide to her state of mind, she must be nearly demented. "Look, Elaine," he could imagine himself saying, like an analyst in a Hollywood movie, "you've got to understand this truth about yourself, and then you can put it behind you." If Tim was going to achieve the ascendancy over Elaine that would allow him to deliver this kind of counsel without rebuke, the situation would require the most careful contriving. Elaine sitting at tea in his mother's drawing-room! Enter Yehia from the hall, dressed exactly as she had last seen him—in uniform, that is to say, and wearing a helmet for preference! That sort of thing! Anyway, Tim wanted to avoid meeting Elaine too frequently before Yehia arrived in London. A conversation about Yehia, without the preliminary shock treatment, would almost certainly result in a further hardening of Elaine's present attitude towards the fellow.

"You mean that Marguerite will be there?" he asked.

"That would be part of the plan," she replied.

In that case the conversation could scarcely turn to

Yehia, except perfunctorily, and Tim would have an opportunity to study his patient. Truth to tell, he was yearning to see Elaine on his own account. Damn it! he thought, making up his mind to go, if she's particularly nice I can always drop the psychological subtlety anyway and allow Yehia to pass out of our lives.

"I'll bring some claret unless you've an objection," he said.

"There'll be a fourth," said Elaine. "A man, so you won't have to do the washing up *all* by yourself afterwards."

Oh, Eric, Eric! he thought as he replaced the receiver. If only his brother were there to advise whether he had been right to accept this supper invitation! During the last week or so of Tim's stay in Alexandria the two brothers had drawn together. Eric had insisted on buying Tim's steamer ticket, for example. He told some stories about their father, whom Tim remembered only indistinctly; a bright, cheerful man he sounded, though Eric said he had a sarcastic tongue when he liked, and he talked loudly in railway carriages about private matters, scandalizing everybody and particularly Eric, who (Eric said) was an absurdly sensitive child. Sensitive? Tim wished he could be sure he knew when his brother was joking. Even now he could not be sure that the advice to produce Yehia suddenly ("through a trapdoor," Eric had said) was entirely serious.

"I want you to remember," Eric said as they walked up and down the quay while the baggage went aboard, "that I have decided to make you my heir. No, wait! Don't thank me! If things go as I imagine they will, nothing could be more inconvenient or dangerous for you. Naguib is bound to let a mob or two loose on the foreigners. When the Dragoumises and I have been massacred you'll be able to sail into Alexandria with the British Navy and take over the coffee-importing business where we left off. Frankly, I think you'll make a frightful mess of it."

"Why don't you bring Lydia and live in England?"

"You don't believe a word I'm saying."

"Of course not."

"Cynicism! One thing you can say about Mr. Dragoumis. He's not a cynic. Neither am I. I'm a realist. He and I ought to cancel each other out in a few years' time.

"As a matter of fact," said Eric in the pause that followed, "I think you can reckon on Lydia and me being in England for a holiday next summer."

And Tim had laughed with pleasure, saying: "I'll start planning the details right away. Mother'll be delighted. This really is the best possible news I could take back to her."

"Frankly, I doubt it."

"Eric, we'll never quarrel, will we?" he had said. "That's a silly question. I don't know what I'm saying. But we're brothers, aren't we?"

How clearly he remembered the expression of astonishment on Eric's face.

"What I mean to say," Tim went on hurriedly, "is that I'm quite delighted that there's a chance of your coming to England next year. It'll be wonderful. I'll take you and Lydia about. I know! We'll go to Scotland. I don't know why we should go to Scotland, but let's go to Scotland! Eric," he had said, "thank you for putting up with me these last few months. I don't take it for granted. We *have* had a good time, haven't we?"

"I think you were very lucky not to get gyppy tummy."

"It looks as though I'd better be going on board."

"Scotland," Eric said, as they walked up the gangway

together. "Why on earth should we go to Scotland? Mind you, if you insist! But Scotland? Why Scotland?"

And it was at this point, just when Tim was on the verge of saying something quite silly about brotherly feeling, that Eric began talking of Yehia popping up unexpectedly out of trapdoors to startle Elaine. It would only be justice. To ensure that the encounter developed its full dramatic potential, Yehia ought first of all to be provided with the opportunity to study the many anti-Naguib articles which Elaine must have published.

"The time has come," said Eric, "for complete frankness."

After Eric had gone ashore, Tim walked about the decks thinking a great deal about this last remark. For the first time he saw what a merit frankness was. In the past he had valued the goodwill of all and sundry to an absurd degree; his instinct had been to agree and placate. What it came down to was that he lacked guts. Well, Elaine would not think that by the time he had finished with her. He was going to be as frank as a psychoanalyst, no matter how disagreeable she thought him. Too much was at stake for blandness.

As these reflections passed through his mind he suddenly saw Mr. Dragoumis gliding across the harbour in the launch. Sa'ad, wearing an old Army greatcoat, drove. Mr. Dragoumis sat near the bows of the launch, reading a book. The breeze flattened the brim of his straw hat and rustled the pages of his book, but Mr. Dragoumis's attention was not distracted. Tim waved and shouted, and after a while Mr. Dragoumis, roused by Sa'ad, looked up and waved absent-mindedly. If he had known Tim was on the *Tewfikieh* he had by this time plainly forgotten, and the launch bore him on to the Outer Harbour, where from the departing *Tewfikieh* some half an hour later Tim saw him seated on the deck of a Brazilian cargo ship, still reading. Mr. Dragoumis represented another failure to be frank. Tim realized that he should have defended Aristotle more vigorously.

The morning of Elaine's supper party Tim telephoned the Egyptian Embassy to ask whether Lieutenant Yehia, the new military attaché, had arrived from Egypt. No clear answer was forthcoming. The question seemed to be regarded as a fishing after military secrets, and Tim had his name and address taken. Useless to protest that he was a friend of Yehia's. Eventually he was advised to write to Yehia, care of the Embassy, and before Tim could protest he was cut off. From this exchange Tim derived the certainty that Yehia had not arrived. If there were too much delay in his taking up his appointment, Tim foresaw the possibility of having to avoid private encounters with Elaine. He might even have to go abroad for a while.

Elaine's flat was on the ground floor of a house adjoining a Nonconformist chapel, and when Tim arrived with his bottles of claret in a straw bag, organ practice was in full swing. Even when Elaine had closed the door behind him and they stood in her prettily papered hall—pink and grey stripes—their ears throbbed under the diapason.

"Wednesday evening is choir practice," she said. "I'd quite forgotten. In you go." She took the straw bag and pushed him through an open door. "I'm so glad you've been able to come because we've an old friend."

"So I see," said Tim; for there, struggling out of one of Elaine's deep armchairs and grinning with mingled discomfort and happiness, was Yehia. Once erect, he was able to put his straight leg to the ground. He looked very smart. He was in uniform, with a British Sam Browne and green

crescents on his lapels. Even in the short time since Tim
had last seen him there had been a considerable improve-
ment in his appearance; he looked fuller in the face. His
front hair stood up in a stiff brush. Once Tim had recovered
from the shock, he noticed that Yehia had been drinking
sherry. Either he was changing his way of life or did not
know it was alcoholic.

They shook hands.

"I flew," Yehia said. Seeing the expression on Tim's
face, he lifted his head and shouted with laughter. The
man was almost insanely happy. "At last I am here."

After that Tim ignored him for quite a while. He discovered a young woman with cropped black hair, assumed
this must be Marguerite, and carefully invented a long conversation about whether or not Celtic blood was responsible for the vein of poetry in the English character.
The subject sprang from the circumstance that Marguerite's
home was in Cornwall. But all the time Tim was working
up a great rage against Elaine and Yehia. As the shock
induced by the unexpected presence of Yehia wore off, so
Tim's rage grew. And the more fiercely he stared into Marguerite's eyes, the louder the organ roared in the chapel.
The house buzzed with the vibration. Yehia had clearly
been able to interpret Elaine's letter as well as he. And
Elaine looked too beautiful—a flushed, rosy beauty—to be
under any kind of illusion about herself. Tim felt that she
had once more practised a deliberate deceit.

"Well, boys and girl," Elaine said, with an assumed
girlishness that Tim found nauseating, "let's go and eat."

"How you can live in a house with that row going on
next door," he said, "I can't imagine. It's like being in a
loft with five hundred snoring donkeys."

"It's only Wednesday evenings. And Sundays, of course,

and the caretaker does our charring. Mahmoud, you sit there, on my right. Marguerite! Tim! There now! I made this soup out of a packet, so it's probably atrocious."

Tim knew he was going to make a scene. It was all very well for Elaine to put on this act of fluttering, blushing, and seductive domesticity. For the first time he noticed her dress; it was black, shining, and clinging, with a yellow rose—a yellow rose!—at her bosom. Tim was tempted to produce her letters there and then (he carried them in his wallet), smack them on the table, and begin to read them out aloud. How do you explain that? he would shout. Have you ever heard such bloody hypocrisy? Don't words mean anything to you? Are you utterly corrupted by journalism?

Instead, he heard himself saying: "The soup's all right."

He was appalled by his weakness. His head began to throb with emotion and he noticed that his hand, as it lifted the soup to his lips, was trembling.

For the first time he addressed Yehia. "I'm very sorry to see that you've set up a military dictatorship in your country and suppressed all the political parties."

"But you do not understand." Yehia laid down his spoon.

"I understand very well what it means when a democratic constitution is overthrown."

"It is Egypt you do not understand. You talk of suppressing political parties. Egypt never has had any political parties. Just groups of men working in their own interests. All false and wicked. But let us talk of this some other time."

"Let us talk of it now!" Tim cried and began hammering the table with his spoon. "Is there or is there not a dictatorship? Answer me that."

"Of course there is dictatorship! And what better kind

of government could my country ask for at a time like this?
It is dictatorship *by* Egyptians!"

"Some other time," said Elaine. "Mahmoud is right.
We don't want politics for supper. For heaven's *sake*, Tim—"

Tim thought of his brother's parting words. "No, we
must be frank with one another. This is a time for complete
frankness. Elaine's been attacking Naguib like mad—"

"Tim!"

"Why don't you show Mahmoud your precious articles?"

"Now you're being offensive."

"Isn't it rather naïve," said Marguerite unexpectedly,
"to imagine that a country like Egypt could become a
true parliamentary democracy overnight?"

Her intervention was much resented by Tim—his sense
of proportion had persuaded him that she, at least, might
be on his side—and he could not be stopped from making
a long statement on the success with which India, in a
state of development comparable to Egypt's, had adapted
British institutions to her own needs. Nonsense to talk of
needing an interlude of military dictatorship. The country
had been better off before the revolution when they could
at least vote for the party of their choice. Tim spoke until
the soup plates were removed. He scarcely knew where this
flow of ideas came from. They had certainly not been in
his head when he arrived.

He turned on Yehia. "You wouldn't deny that the British have done a great deal for Egypt?"

"I would not blame Britain for *all* the bad things in
my country."

"Not all! That's generous of you!"

"Such conditions are not to be blamed on the British.
The only thing that matters is that these conditions exist,

and the Egyptians are the only people who can improve them."

The rumble of the organ, the heat, the pressure of emotion in the room made every word and gesture of peculiar moment. They were not merely four people sitting down to supper. They were Attitudes Proper to the Occasion: a patriotic attitude with a touch of dignity for Yehia, a refusal-to-be-anything-but-interested attitude for Marguerite, an impatient-hostess attitude for Elaine, and for Tim —well, he spoke as an Englishman! As this was the first time he had ever played the role, it was a bit overwhelming.

Elaine cooked steak in an infra-red grill, Marguerite brought in a tureen of spaghetti, Tim was given his two bottles of claret to open, and still no actual blows had been struck. Elaine enjoyed manipulating her grill. She flipped the sizzling steaks on top of the spaghetti and almost visibly transformed herself from impatient hostess into the competed-for, gay, unrepentant, and almost scarlet woman! Yehia accidentally touched one of her hands and immediately became a swain. Marguerite ate heartily. Tim leaned back in his chair, drinking wine and listening to the organ, a bitter young man who knew he had been a dupe. Played for a sucker!

"I think you're very lucky to have been to Egypt," said Marguerite. "I've always dreamed of going there."

Tim discovered that she was addressing him. She had blue eyes, he noticed. What was more, she had a smooth duskiness in the skin as though she were a Latin. The combination of blue eyes and this faintest dark bloom of the skin was unusual. What was it Elaine had said about this girl in one of those letters?

"I was just a tourist, I suppose. You want to live in the country really to know it."

"What's wrong with being a tourist?"

Yes, what's wrong? Tim thought. He had been to Egypt for six months. Now he was home. He was sitting in a room with two people he had met on his trip. They were eating, listening to the organ from next door, and talking about a foreign country. His brother happened to live there. Had it not been for that accident, he might have gone somewhere else. He had been on a long trip in a foreign country, and now it was over. He could forget all about it. He could forget Yehia. He could forget Elaine. For six months he had been a tourist, and now he was a tourist no longer.

He cheered up until he remembered his book. Well, he didn't have to write it. He could destroy his notes, scrap his photographs.

"The next thing that will happen in Egypt," he said to Yehia, "is squabbling among the Council of Officers. It always happens. And then what? Civil war, I shouldn't be surprised."

Yehia was so moved that he tried to rise to his feet. "What you are saying is not possible."

"Oh, stop it, you two, for heaven's sake!" Elaine was dealing out cheese soufflé, and she paused to wave the spoon threateningly. "Politics! Politics! We've had quite enough. Marguerite, lead the conversation into something cosier."

"Cosier! I like that!" Tim helped himself to the claret and took a cool draught to give himself strength.

"Politics are not very interesting." Elaine spoke with deliberate fatuousness. "People are interesting."

Tim pointed a finger at Yehia. "Do you believe that?"

Yehia, being too honest to agree, looked at Elaine with the seriousness of a vizier daring to speak his mind in the presence of the caliph. "Politics are naturally more interesting to men than to women."

"Women are interested in a different *sort* of politics," said Elaine. "They judge things differently. Until Mahmoud came I was rather critical of happenings in Egypt."

"And now?" Tim was attempting to pour wine into Yehia's glass of water. Yehia held his hand firmly over the brim.

"Well, I certainly think you're wrong about a civil war."

Tim ate his soufflé gloomily. "You think the revolution was a good thing?"

"Yes."

"All those articles you wrote—you disavow them?"

"In the main, they were descriptive articles. If they did contain any opinions, well, I'm always free to change my mind, aren't I? Don't tell me you've never changed your mind."

Tim hesitated. He could counter Elaine's challenge by revealing that until he had walked into the room and clapped eyes on Yehia he too had believed there was much to be said in favour of the new regime in Egypt. Certainly he had changed his mind. It could almost be said that he and Elaine had exchanged minds.

"I don't really think, Elaine, that Egypt is a subject on which you are entitled to an opinion. You saw nothing of the country."

"You're perfectly right, Tim."

"What?"

"I mean I haven't any opinions about Egypt. I'm open to persuasion one way or the other."

"Oh!" This was a strange invitation when one considered that she had just tried to stop them talking politics. Tim looked at Yehia, and the Egyptian appeared to brace himself for a lengthy statement of his government's policy. Hours of debate stretched before them. Elaine would listen to him, nodding from time to time and possibly making notes for one of her articles. Then it would be Tim's turn. He would have to attack military dictatorships and say why a Kemal Atatürk might suit Turkey's needs but be a misfit in Egypt. This was an argument he was prepared to develop.

How extraordinary that an hour or so ago, when he had walked up to Elaine's front door with the bottles of claret clinking in the straw bag, these views had been quite unformulated. The evening had brought him a political revelation.

"You've got to begin," said Tim, "with the realization that the Egyptians have never had any real independence since they were conquered by the Persians in 525 B.C. With that you've got to couple the thought that they're placed in a very curious geographical position."

But at this point Elaine broke in. She was without domestic help in the evenings. Within a matter of minutes Tim and Yehia were wearing frilly aprons and busy in the kitchen with the washing-up.

"Not one word of appreciation," she said, "do I get for my cooking."

Marguerite was in her room collecting some gramophone records for the concert which Elaine now said they were to have. She herself walked back into the dining-room and looked at her small reflection in the glossy blackness of the window-pane.

"My God," she said, and the reflection stretched its arms wide, "I'm happy!"

A NOTE ON THE AUTHOR

P(ERCY) H(OWARD) NEWBY was born of working-class parents in Sussex on June 25, 1918. The Second World War broke into his college career, and he served in France and in the Middle East. In 1942 Newby was released by the Army to teach English literature at Cairo's Fouad Ist University. When his first novel was published in 1946, he returned to England and settled in Buckinghamshire to write. In that year he received an Atlantic Award in Literature; two years later he received the Somerset Maugham Prize. He has contributed to most of the leading British literary journals; has traveled through the United States; is married and has a daughter; and works for the BBC's Third Programme. In addition to *Revolution and Roses* and *The Picnic at Sakkara*, his published books include *The Young May Moon* (1951), *A Season in England* (1952), and *The Retreat* (1953).

A NOTE ON THE TYPE

The text of this book was set on the Linotype in a face called Electra, designed by W. A. Dwiggins. This type is not based on any historical model, nor does it echo any particular period or style. It avoids the extreme contrast between thick and thin elements that mark most modern faces, and attempts to give a feeling of fluidity, power, and speed.

Composed, printed, and bound by Kingsport Press, Inc., Kingsport, Tennessee. Paper manufactured by S. D. Warren Company, Boston, Massachusetts. Designed by Harry Ford.